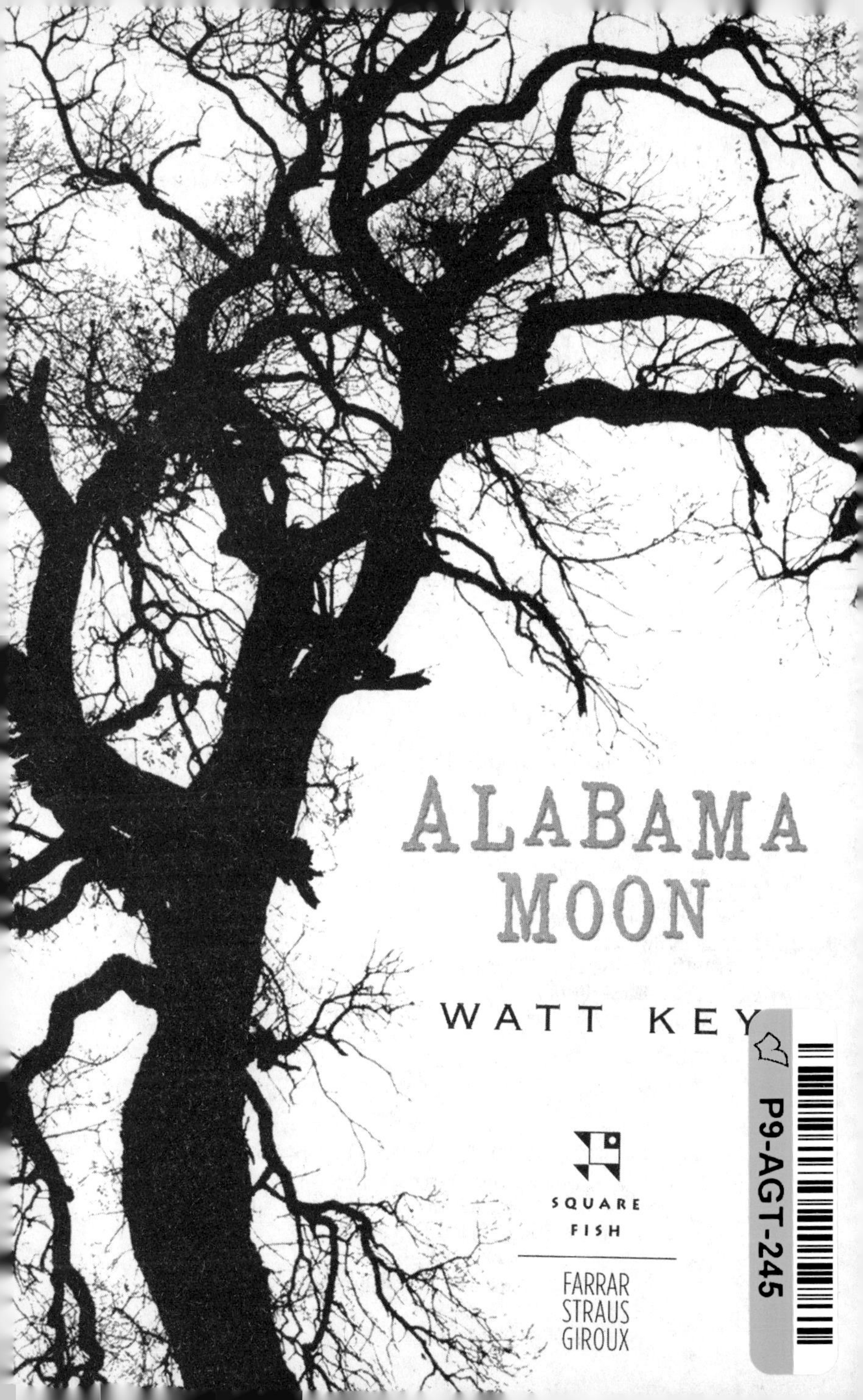
ALABAMA
MOON
WATT KEY
SQUARE
FISH
FARRAR
STRAUS
GIROUX
P9-AGT-245

Special thanks to Mom and Dad for all they have done and continue to do for their children, Virginia Stallings for convincing me that I could write books, the late Doc Watson for his encouragement and turning me on to great literature, Jeff Makemson for our adventures in the Talladega National Forest, my friend Dr. Andy Smith for his medical research and general support, my wonderful agent Marianne Merola, and my diligent editors Robbie Mayes and Margaret Ferguson for making the publication process so enjoyable.

An Imprint of Macmillan


Printed in August 2008 in the United States of America
by R. R. Donnelley & Sons Company, Harrisonburg, Virginia.
For information, address Square Fish, 175 Fifth Avenue, New York, NY 10010.



Library of Congress Cataloging-in-Publication Data

Key, Watt.
Alabama Moon / Watt, Key.
p. cm.
Summary: After the death of his father, ten-year-old Moon leaves their forest shelter home and is sent to an Alabama institution, becoming entangled in the outside world he has never known and making good friends, a relentless enemy, and finally a new life.
ISBN: 978-0-312-38428-9
[1. Orphans—Fiction. 2. Wilderness survival—Fiction. 3. Bullies—Fiction. 4. Government, Resistance to—Fiction. 5. Alabama—Fiction.] I. Title.

PZ7.K516 Ala 2006
[Fic]—dc22

2005040165

Originally published in the United States by Farrar, Straus and Giroux
Square Fish logo designed by Filomena Tuosto
Book design by Symon Chow
First Square Fish Edition: 2008
10 9 8 7 6 5
www.squarefishbooks.com

For my wife, Katie

# ALABAMA MOON

# 1

Just before Pap died, he told me that I'd be fine as long as I never depended on anybody but myself. He said I might feel lonely for a while, but that would go away. I was ten years old and he'd taught me everything I needed to know about living out in the forest. I could trap my own food and make my own clothes. I could find my way by the stars and make fire in the rain. Pap said he even figured I could whip somebody three times my size. He wasn't worried about me.

It took me most of a morning to get him into the wheelbarrow and haul him to the cedar grove on the bluff. I buried him next to Momma where you could see the Noxubee River flowing coffee-colored down below. It was mid-January and the wind pulled at my hair and gray clouds slid through the trees and left the forest dripping. I felt the loneliness he'd told me about crawling up from my stomach and into my throat.

I didn't put a cross on the grave. I never knew Pap to believe in things like that. The only way you could make out Momma's grave was the ground that was sunk in over her and 1972 scratched on a limestone rock nearby. I don't remember her face, but I remember somebody else in the bed at night, keeping me warm from the other side. Pap said she reminded him of a yellow finch, which is how she stays in my mind.

I found a rock for Pap and scratched 1980 on it with a nail. After placing it beside the dirt mound, I put the shovel in the wheelbarrow and started back for the shelter. The cedar grove trail was the only one we used enough to wear our tracks into it. It was worn like a cow path from years of walking it with Pap. Not only did he like to come see Momma up on the bluff, but we used it as a main trail to check the northeast trap lines. It had been almost a week since I'd run any of them because I hadn't wanted to leave Pap's side. I was sure the traps were tangled in the creeks, and it only made the sickness in my stomach worse to think that whatever was in them was most likely dead.

Pap had tried to explain death to me, but I couldn't make sense of it. Pap said you passed on and came back as something else. It could be a squirrel or a coon. It could be a fish or an Eskimo. There was no way to tell. The most confusing part of what he told me was that even though he would come back as something else, there would still be a part of the old him that floated around like smoke. This part of him would watch out for me. I couldn't talk to this thing or touch it, but I could write to it. I could make my letters and then burn them, and the smoke would carry my message to him.

When I got back to the shelter, I put the wheelbarrow and the shovel away and went inside. I took off my deerskin jacket and hat, lay down on the pile of hides that we hadn't been able to sell, and stared at the roots in the ceiling. There was always a lot of work to do and no time to rest. But now Pap was dead and things were not the same.

I thought about death again. Most things he told me made sense real quick. You boil steel traps to get the scent off. You overlap palmetto roofing so the rain slides down it. You soak a deerskin for two days and it comes out with two days of softness to it. I could understand these things. But what he said about dying and the smoky messages and his hate for government—they were the hardest ideas for me to understand.

He'd said the government was after us ever since I could remember. The shelter we lived in was set miles into a forest owned by a paper company and was a place no person besides us had any cause to be. Even had someone come by, he would have to just about run into our shelter before he noticed anything unusual. It was one small room built halfway into the ground with low ceilings so that Pap had to stoop to walk inside. The roof was covered with dirt, and bushes and trees grew from the top. Over time tree roots had come down into the shelter and twisted through the logs and made their way into the ground at the edges. Everything that showed above ground was from nature. Even the stovepipe sticking up through the ceiling was encased in limestone.

We practiced with our rifles three times a week. Our windows were narrow slits for shooting through and the trees that you saw out of these windows were pocked and chipped from years of Pap and me practicing a stage-one defense. In stage two we moved into the hole at the back side of the shelter where a muddy tunnel led to the box. The box was about a quarter the size of our shelter and made of steel sheets that Pap took from an old barn. An air pipe went up through the ground and was hidden inside a tree stump. Pap said if we ever moved to stage two, we'd cave the tunnel in behind us. We had dried food and water in the box that would last for a week or more. Pap said a stage two would be hard, but the box was made to keep people alive when things got really bad.

"It would be a while before they'd find us," he'd said.

There were no power lines or roads nearby. Except for the path to the cedar grove, we switched our trails every week so we wouldn't wear our tracks into the ground. We made most of our fires in the woodstove to hide the flame. If we had to make a fire outside, we used the driest wood we could find to cut down on the smoke. We couldn't carry anything shiny in the bright sun in case a plane caught the reflection. Our knife blades kept a thin coat of rust on them for that very purpose. Pap even went so far as to sneak up on his game from the south so that the sound from the rifle shot would be aimed down into the river bottom.

From my place on the hide pile I could hear the birds through the small window slit as the forest grew dark outside. I was used to paying extra attention to the late-afternoon and night sounds. Pap said if the government was coming for us, that's when they'd come. He got nervous and quiet when the sun started dropping. He liked to sit inside the shelter and work on chores that didn't make noise. The two of us sewed, whittled, scraped hides, and repaired traps while we studied the forest sounds. But I didn't do any of these things the afternoon after Pap died. I couldn't. I just balled up like a squirrel and cried.

# 2

It seemed like everything started going wrong the summer before Pap's accident. We heard through Mr. Abroscotto, who owned the general store in Gainesville, that International Paper Company had run into hard times and was selling off some of its land. Pap said that the paper company had owned the forest as long as we'd been there and that they were too big to know about us. If they sold out to smaller landowners, we'd likely be found.

I could tell that Pap was worried. He told me that the swimming hole was off limits and that I was to stay close to the shelter unless I was checking traps or getting drinking water. Without the creek to swim in, the days were hotter than any I can remember. We spent afternoons sitting in the shelter, covered with the tannic acid from boiled acorns to keep off the ticks and mosquitoes. Pap had me practice my reading while he carved fish hooks from briars and bound sticks to make catfish traps.

It wasn't two weeks after our visit to Mr. Abroscotto's store that surveyors found our shelter while we were out checking the traps. When Pap and I returned, we saw their orange vests through the trees and we ducked into the bushes and watched them as they walked around the shelter. They stayed there for about an hour, poking at our things. I asked Pap if they were the government, and he said no, but they weren't much better.

"Should we shoot at 'em?"

"No."

"If they're not any better than—"

"When the war comes, you'll know."

"How?"

"I'll tell you."

The next morning, Pap woke me at daybreak. "Get up," he said. "We need to go into town and find out what's happenin'."

I got excited about going to Mr. Abroscotto's. It was the only time I saw any of the outside world. But I was careful not to let Pap know how I felt. He said showing ourselves to outsiders was the most dangerous part of how we lived. One slipup and the law would be all over us. A trip to the store wasn't anything he wanted to see me excited over.

"We gonna take somethin' to sell, Pap?"

"Ain't got time. Get your britches on."

As the sun slipped over the trees, we made the six-mile trip to Mr. Abroscotto's. We used to sell our furs to him, but it had been more than three years since we'd sold any. He said the prices were so low that he lost money just paying for gasoline to get them to Birmingham, where he sold them to companies that made clothes and things out of them. Since then, we had sold him the meat instead, along with vegetables we grew in the garden, and we bought what we wanted of the outside world with the money he gave us.

Most of the journey was through the forest, but the last half mile was on the road to avoid the big swamp. Pap said this was okay because the road was straight and long and we could hear cars coming in either direction before they saw us. We had time to slip down into the ditch and lie still until they passed.

The store was on the outskirts of town, and the only building nearby was a small brick one that Pap said was owned by the power company. We could see a traffic light another half mile up the road which Pap said was the only one in Gainesville. I liked to watch the light as long as I could before Pap hurried me past the gas pumps and into the store. I'd seen a tractor go under the light once and even a yellow school bus.

Mr. Abroscotto was a strong man for somebody his age, like he used to be a logger or a policeman. His skin was dark as leather and his snow-white hair stood out against it. This time he told us that a lawyer named Mr. Wellington had purchased eleven thousand acres from the paper company. The property went from the Noxubee River to the big swamp and from the highway to Major's Creek on the east and west sides. By Mr. Abroscotto's landmarks, I figured our shelter was just about in the middle of Mr. Wellington's property. Pap must have been thinking the same thing. He walked out of the store without even saying goodbye. I hurried after him and had to walk fast to keep up.

"Slow down, Pap."

He didn't answer me.

"Pap?"

He turned quickly and grabbed my arm and jerked me along beside him. "You keep up this time," he said. "Run if you have to."

———

A couple of weeks passed before heavy equipment started making a road and a clearing three miles away. Pap was nervous all the time and snapped at me when I made the smallest mistake. He got particular about me stepping on sticks and making noise when we walked through the forest. He kept stopping and touching my shoulder, which meant for me to be still and listen. I could tell by the way he acted that all those workers and equipment meant trouble.

We began to check our catfish traps at night, slipping down the banks of the Noxubee River by moonlight. In the mornings we remained close to the shelter unless we had something special to do. We worked the garden, tending our cucumbers, eggplant, and beets. All of those vegetables, when spaced the right way, grew hidden among the natural forest plants and wouldn't give us away if someone was to come across them. In the heat of the day, we'd get back into the shelter again and stay there until late afternoon. Pap began to watch and listen out the window slits as much as he worked on things. Even my reading began to make him nervous.

"Read to yourself, boy. You're too old to read out loud anymore."

A month later, Pap and I were traveling a trail to the southeast of the shelter to get some red clay for pot making. We were less than a mile from the new clearing when Pap suddenly held his hand up in the air. I knew the signal and stopped. We stood there for several seconds and then, through the whine of mosquitoes, I heard hammering.

"Somebody's makin' somethin', Pap?"

I saw him clench his teeth and narrow his eyes. "Shhh!" he said.

After a few more seconds, Pap continued down the trail.

"What is it, Pap?"

"House."

"Somebody gonna live there?"

"Yeah."

I could tell Pap didn't want to talk about it, so I followed behind him and didn't ask any more questions.

After we heard the hammering, Pap couldn't keep his mind on his chores. He'd get me to working on something at the shelter and he'd say he had to walk off in the woods and tend to things. He was usually gone for a couple of hours. He didn't want me to know where he went, but I knew it was to watch the hammering.

One day he said, "You finish scalin' those fish. I got to go look for somethin' I left down the trail."

"I wanna go, Pap."

"Just a one-man job."

"I've only got two fish left."

Pap stared off at the treetops and bit his bottom lip. "All right," he finally said. "Come on, then."

Pap never meant to look for anything. We slipped through the forest using gallberry and cane for cover until we got to where the house was being built. They had cemented concrete blocks together and run timbers across them for the floor supports. The yard was stacked with lumber for the rest of the framing. I turned to Pap, waiting for him to tell me what it meant. His face was worried pale.

"Gonna be a big house, Pap?" I finally asked.

"Big huntin' lodge," he mumbled.

"I've never seen somethin' built that big."

He nodded his head and motioned for us to head back to the shelter.

We didn't go to the lodge together again. The days began to grow cooler and the breezes told us that fall was arriving. Things had changed between Pap and me. Even though I was with him just about every minute of the day, I didn't feel like he knew I was there. He was far away in thought most of the time, and even though I watched his face, I couldn't get clues to what he was thinking.

We got the steel traps out of storage and oiled them and wired the parts that were broken. The maple leaves had just started to turn and I knew we were over a month away from trapping season. But Pap didn't seem to be doing things in the right order anymore. One day he told me to go gather mulberries. It had been five months since the last mulberry dropped.

"Pap, there's not any mulberries."

"Just do what I tell you," he said.

I waited for a few seconds to see if he would realize his mistake, but he went back to sharpening his knife. I didn't know what to do, so I stepped into the forest and started walking, thinking that if I stayed gone long enough it would convince him that I'd tried my best.

Once I got away from the shelter, it felt good to be on my own again after such a long time staying close to Pap and feeling his worries. I looked up into the trees and studied the yellows and reds of the changing leaves. The birds flitted about and made shrill cries from deep in the bush. It felt like I could breathe easier, and the smells of cedar and stinkbugs flowed into my nose.

Without meaning to, I wandered within hearing distance of the lodge. Once the sound of power tools and hammers reached my ears, I was too curious not to slip closer for a better look.

The workmen had moved a house trailer onto the site, and they seemed to be living in it. More lumber was stacked in the yard, along with roofing material and bricks. The lodge was already framed two stories high. I wanted to stay and watch the men working, but Pap's warnings about contact with outsiders started to play in my head. I crept back into the forest and took a different trail to the shelter.

Pap was sitting outside, weaving a basket from muscadine vine when I walked up. I stood in front of him, ready to tell him why I didn't have any mulberries, but he didn't ask about them or anything else.

Finally I said, "They're puttin' walls on that lodge, Pap."

His fingers stopped and he looked up at me. "I don't ever want you goin' near it again."

"But it's not even finished."

"I don't care. You heard what I said."

"You think maybe when the lawyer moves in we could talk to him and he'd let us stay on?"

Pap looked at me again. "I don't know, son! Why don't you get back to work and forget about that lawyer and his business."

———

As fall passed, the leaves began dropping from the trees and the forest canopy became a solid green fan of pine needles. We pulled our deerskin jackets from between the cedar boards and waterproofed them with mink oil for the season. The carrots would stay in the ground for a while longer, but the other garden vegetables needed to come out before the first frost. I was always excited about the last harvest of the year because I knew it meant we'd go to Mr. Abroscotto's store to sell whatever we had.

I was afraid that Pap might tell me to stay behind, but he didn't. He shouldered the sack of vegetables one morning and told me to get my jacket and come with him. Pap would usually be walking slow and studying the forest. He'd look for deer scrapes and hog rootings and any other signs that might help us find game once the weather turned cold. But that day his mind was on other things and he stared straight ahead and didn't slow down.

Mr. Abroscotto was sitting behind the counter reading a newspaper when we walked in.

"Mornin', George," Pap said.

Mr. Abroscotto set down his paper and stood up. "Mornin', Oli. How you, Moon?"

"I'm fine," I said.

"What do you two have for me?"

Pap showed Mr. Abroscotto the sack of vegetables. "Cucumbers, eggplant, and beets," he said.

Mr. Abroscotto took the sack to the scales. He weighed the vegetables separately and then put them all in a brown box on the floor.

"How does twenty bucks sound?" he said.

"If that's what you can do, I don't guess we've got much choice."

Mr. Abroscotto nodded and paid him from the register. Pap fidgeted the money into his pocket, and I knew he was in a better mood.

"What more have you heard about that lawyer?" Pap asked.

Mr. Abroscotto shook his head. "Haven't heard much. See his workmen in here all the time."

"You know when they're gonna be done?"

"They're tellin' me December. Gonna be moved in for Christmas."

I stood behind Pap and looked around the store at the shelves of candy and canned food. I was careful not to let Pap see me, because I knew it would make him snap at me. Sometimes he made me wait outside while he went in and traded. He said it was too tempting for a boy inside the store.

"What's he gonna do with that big place?" Pap asked.

"I hear he likes to squirrel hunt."

Pap shook his head and looked mad. "All that to hunt squirrels?"

"Guess some people got more money than they know what to do with."

"Guess so," Pap grumbled. "Let me have some salt, some .22 bullets, vinegar, box of nails, and matches."

Mr. Abroscotto left to collect our supplies.

"How about some sugar this time, Pap?"

"Don't need sugar."

"How about some canned peas like we had that one time?"

"We've got a pile of toasted acorns you haven't touched yet."

I figured he wasn't in the mood to buy extras. "We've got everything we need already, don't we, Pap?"

Pap nodded. "Got everything we need," he repeated.

We walked back up the road and into the forest, where we took a trail that I liked through a grove of cedars and tall field grass. That was the last time Pap left the forest.

## 3

Winter had been on us for two months, and the forest creatures were fat and fluffy in their new coats. It had started to snow once, but the ground didn't hold it, which always disappointed me. I only remembered a few times when there was enough snow to make tracks in. One of those times Pap and I made pine-bark sleds and had races down the riverbank. I'd always wanted to do it again.

On the morning Pap broke his leg, the north wind was tossing the tops of the trees and gray clouds raced over our heads. Pap was always alert when the wind stirred the forest floor and cartwheeled the leaves. It was hard to tell which sounds were natural and which weren't.

We were checking traps along a beaver dam only a mile from the lodge. With the wind blowing like it was and us being so close to Mr. Wellington's place, Pap must have been extra nervous. I think he was too busy looking around for signs of people to pay attention to where he was going. He slipped on the dam and got his shin caught between two branches. He had just enough time to turn and look at me before he fell into the beaver pond on his back. The water was so clear I saw his face staring up at me and wincing in pain. I jumped down after him and jerked at the branches until his leg came loose. The rest of Pap splashed into the water, and then he dragged himself out of the pond. After he was propped against a cypress knee, I went and found some sticks to use for a splint, and we bound his leg with the leather shoelaces from my moccasins.

That afternoon, I got Pap back to the shelter in the wheelbarrow. He pulled himself inside, and I saw how much his leg hurt by the sweat that soaked his face and clothes. I helped him up on the hide pile and stayed next to him to give him water as he needed it. Pap didn't like doctors, and he didn't like medicine that you couldn't find in the forest, so there wasn't much else for me to do.

Sometime that night Pap told me to take his boot off. I watched his hands white-knuckle the roots above his head while I pulled slowly on the heel. He didn't make any noise because it was nighttime.

When I got the boot off, bloody water and sand poured out of it. I cut the sock away with my knife and placed it to the side. We saved everything. Even a bloody sock could make a rag to patch clothes.

In the dim light of the grease lamp, I saw parts of Pap's bone coming through his shin. Seeing bone and blood and wounds was nothing to me. I dealt with them almost every day killing, skinning, and butchering animals. I only hesitated so that Pap would tell me what to do.

"Get a rag and wipe it off," he said. "Boil some water and put the rag in the water before you do."

"So the wound won't get infected?"

"That's right."

I went to the wood stove and did as he said. When I returned and began to gently wipe his leg, I watched his face. I saw his expression change when the rag went over the jagged portion of bone.

"Does it hurt?"

"Just keep wipin'."

"You want me to go get Mr. Abroscotto?"

"Nothin' he can do you can't do yourself, boy."

I nodded and kept wiping. I stayed up with him that night after the wound was cleaned. After a while, Pap didn't seem to be concerned that we stay quiet anymore. He lay there and talked to me and told me most of what he was thinking.

"Tell me again why we live out here," he asked me.

"Because we never asked for anything and nobody ever gave us anything. Because of that, we don't owe anything to anybody."

"Who is it that thinks we owe them somethin'?"

"The government."

"That's right."

After a moment: "And what's gonna happen to everybody that relies on the government?"

"When the war comes, they're not gonna be able to take care of themselves," I said.

"They'll have forgotten how to grow food and trap game, how to make their own clothes and shelter," he said.

"How to find their own medicine in the forest," I said.

"That's right."

"How to shoot rifles."

"That's right," Pap said. "All of those things."

"And I know how to do it all."

He nodded. I stood, walked over to the stove, and put some more wood into it. Even when Pap let us burn it all night, the heat was rarely enough to keep our breath from streaming in front of our faces.

I returned to the hide pile. "I'm not gonna get better," he said.

"What?"

"I'm not gonna get better."

"You're gonna die?"

He nodded.

I felt my stomach twist. "Tonight?"

"No, but soon. Somethin' like this leg won't heal."

"How soon?"

"I don't know."

"But I don't understand."

"Think about it. Think about a deer that breaks its leg. What happens?"

"But you're not a deer!" I yelled.

"There's no difference. We're all animals."

I felt like I would get sick on the floor. "What will I do?"

"That's what I'm gonna tell you."

Pap said that it might not be long before Mr. Wellington ran me off the property. I would have to find someone else to live with. Pap said there were many other people like us all over the country. He said there were more now than ever. Most of them were out west, in Montana, Colorado, Utah, and Wyoming. Alaska was even better. A man could still homestead in Alaska. He could get to places where no one would find him. People could still make a living off trapping up there. Hides were worth something in Alaska. I'd have to find my way there.

"But how?"

"You'll figure it out. You can't rely on me anymore. Just remember the things I taught you. Take cover durin' the day and move at night. Use the stars. Don't trust anybody. Write me smoke letters if you get lonely."

"Do you talk to Momma with smoke letters?"

"Sometimes I do," he said.

"Does she say anything back?"

"She does, but not in the way you'd think."

"How will I get answers from the smoke?"

Pap didn't say anything for a few seconds. "You just do what I tell you," he finally said.

For the first couple of days I tried to keep our regular routine each morning while Pap was sick. I rose before daylight and checked the traps. I brought back what I caught, skinned it, butchered it, and prepped the hide. I hauled water from the creek and cut needles for tea. In the late afternoon, I did my reading lessons.

But it was hard to keep my mind on these things with Pap lying in the shelter getting worse. Suddenly it seemed like there wasn't a reason for doing anything. Mr. Abroscotto hadn't bought our hides in years. We had plenty of water stored up already, and if Pap was going to die soon, why did we need more? And how would I find a place like Alaska on my own?

I couldn't clean Pap's wound without him twisting about in pain. Finally, he told me to stop worrying over it and leave it alone. "It won't do it any good," he said. "It's too far gone to trouble over."

"It's not too much trouble, Pap. I don't mind."

"Leave it be. Put that rag away."

"What if we cut it off?"

"Too late. Infection's up my whole leg."

I started crying. "I can't live by myself, Pap!"

He shook his head. "Shut up, boy. You don't cry, you hear me?"

I wiped my eyes and nodded at the floor. I put my arms around his neck. "I can't do it, Pap. I can't make it to Alaska. I can't fight the government. I like it here. I don't see why I can't get Mr. Abroscotto to come help you."

"He'll just get the law down on you."

"I can run from the law. I can get away."

Pap didn't answer me. He was quiet for a long time. "You'll be all right," he finally said. "I don't wanna hear any more about it."

# 4

I wrote Pap a letter that first night after I buried him.

*Dear Pap,*

*I'm going to see Mr. Abroscotto in the morning and ask him if he knows anything about getting to Alaska. Seeing as how I'll be leaving soon, I'll pull up the traps tomorrow and pack them in the boxes. I am going to take your watch and sell it to Mr. Abroscotto. I thought about keeping it for myself, but I don't need it and you were never much on things a person didn't need. I'm scared, Pap, but I know I can lick most anything three times my size. I know I can survive on my own and keep away from the government. I'm lonely, too, but you said that will go away after a while. It doesn't seem like a feeling that goes away easy. But you always knew about things, so I'm not worried.*

*Love, Moon*

I burned the letter in the woodstove and then walked to the back corner of the shelter where Pap kept his personal storage. It was a metal ammunition box containing his watch and a few other things he called his "valuables" and never let me see. The first time he brought out the box was when Momma died. He showed me the watch and said she gave it to him when they were married. It had "Mr. and Mrs. Oliver Blake—1968" etched into the back. On my eighth birthday I asked about the watch again. I think it made him remember Momma, and he let me study it. He told me that one day it would be mine.

When I got the box out that night, I realized that Pap hadn't told me where the key was that opened it. I didn't want to bust it in case I damaged the watch and anything else in there that I might be able to sell. I searched under Pap's bed and up in the roots of the ceiling. I felt around the hole that led to the stage-two area. After a while, I gave up and sat with the box between my legs on the hide pile.

The fire in the stove went out, and I didn't feel like starting it again. The shelter grew cold and damp and dark. I thought I would have nightmares if I slept, so I tried to stay awake and imagine what it would be like in Alaska. But I got so lonely that I decided nightmares were worth it. I closed my eyes and slept.

The next morning I woke before daylight and went to pick up the traps and release or throw away anything that was caught in them. There were two dead coons with stiff, matted hides. I pulled them from the steel jaws and tossed them into the brush because the meat was spoiled. When I returned, I packed the traps in the two wood boxes we used to store them and stacked them beside the shelter.

After watching Pap die, I found that his finally being gone

had made things easier on me. I still felt a deep, lonely hole, but as much as I missed him, I could now concentrate on what he'd told me to do and get started to Alaska.

## 5

I put my box on the floor of Mr. Abroscotto's store and sat on it. I was tired and breathing hard.

"You all right, Moon?" Mr. Abroscotto asked me.

I nodded at the floor.

"You carry that box all the way from your place by yourself?"

I nodded again. Finally catching my breath, I looked up at him. "I was hopin' you might wanna buy the stuff in it."

"Where's your father at?"

"He's dead."

Mr. Abroscotto put his hands on the counter and leaned towards me. "Dead!"

"Yessir."

"When?"

"Yesterday."

"How?"

"He broke his leg and it got infected."

Mr. Abroscotto frowned and shook his head. "I guess he didn't want you comin' after a doctor."

"Nossir. He always said when it—"

"I know what he always said. You wait here while I call the constable."

"You don't need to worry about that, Mr. Abroscotto. I already buried him up in the cedar grove near Momma."

"Moon, you can't just go off buryin' somebody without lettin' the law know about it."

"Pap wanted it that way."

"Well, your pap wanted lots of things that don't make sense. I don't mind tellin' you that." Mr. Abroscotto walked over to the wall and lifted the telephone receiver.

I stood and grabbed my box off the floor. "If you call the law, they'll take me away. I don't aim to go with 'em."

He watched me for a moment and then put the receiver back on the hook. He shook his head and rubbed his eyes. "Put your box down," he said. "Get that chair behind you, and pull it up here."

I did as he said.

"What do you want to eat?" he asked me.

"I don't have money for extras. I gotta save it."

"That's all right. It's free."

"Bologna and cheese."

"Mustard?"

"No thanks. That's all."

Mr. Abroscotto began to fix me a sandwich. My mouth watered at the bologna, cheese, and bread that I only saw when I came to his store.

"I'm sorry about your father, Moon. I didn't mean to sound like I wasn't."

"That's okay. He said I'd feel better after a while."

"Where you headed when you leave here?"

"Alaska."

"How you plan on gettin' to Alaska?"

"Sell the watch and things in this box. And I've got the money left over from last time we were here."

"I see. What are you gonna do when you get there?"

"Pap said there's other people like us there. He said you can get away from the government up there. Said you can homestead."

"That's what he said?"

"Yessir. So that's where I figure I'll go."

Mr. Abroscotto handed me the sandwich and leaned on the counter watching me eat.

"You know how cold it is in Alaska?"

I chewed and shrugged my shoulders.

"You're not worried about freezin' up there?"

"Pap said there's a lot of people like us in Alaska that I can stay with. He said there's more than ever these days."

"You ever thought about school, Moon?"

"I study my books almost every day."

Mr. Abroscotto shook his head. "That's not what I mean. With other children?"

"Pap said he could teach me better than any school."

"You know how to read?"

"Sure I know how to read. I can whip somebody three times my size, too. And I know everything I need to know to live on my own."

He bit his bottom lip. "Uh-huh . . . Tell me, what type of people are you lookin' for in Alaska? What does your father call the type of people that are like him?"

"People that hate the government."

"And he just expects you to make it from here to Alaska and find these people on your own?"

I nodded.

Mr. Abroscotto sighed and looked out the store window, then back at me. "I'm gonna tell you somethin', Moon. Your pap was an unreasonable person. Anybody that expects their ten-year-old son to try and make it from the middle of Alabama to Alaska on just a few dollars is either crazy or plain mean. You need to find a home with a good family that doesn't live out in God-knows-where with a dirt floor. You've—"

I felt anger flash through my head. I jumped up on the seat of my chair and leaped across the counter to land on Mr. Abroscotto. He fell back into the shelves behind, and I started hitting him with my one hand that wasn't holding on to him. I pounded him on the cheek over and over as fast as I could. Once he got his balance, he clamped his arms around me so that I couldn't move my fists.

"Moon!" he yelled at me.

I kicked him in the knee. "Mother mercy!" he yelled.

"I don't mind the way we lived!" I yelled at him. "Pap and I always got along!"

Mr. Abroscotto twisted me around and held me out by the shoulders so I couldn't see or kick him. "God, that hurt!" he said.

"Me and Pap were good friends!" I yelled. "Best friends."

He held me there for what seemed like a long time. I heard him catching his breath behind me, and I stared across the store. Finally, his breathing slowed again, and he talked to me.

"You gonna settle down?"

"If you stop talkin' about my pap like that."

"I'm gonna turn you loose now, okay?"

"Okay."

"You're gonna sit back down on that chair, okay?"

"Okay."

"I'm gonna set you down now."

"Okay."

Mr. Abroscotto put me on the counter and I climbed back down into my chair. He ran his hand through his hair and rolled his head around on his neck. He took a deep breath. "Man my age can't take somebody jumpin' on him like a wild monkey. What's gotten into you, Moon?"

I picked my sandwich off the floor and stared at it without taking a bite. I was nervous. I'd never acted like that to Mr. Abroscotto. "Don't talk like that about Pap," I said to the floor.

"Listen, Moon, I'm not tryin' to be disrespectful of your father; I'm tryin' to help you out. I'm worried about your sense of reality."

I thought about what he was saying and made sure there wasn't anything I didn't like about it.

"You don't know any better," he said. "If your pap just up and dies of a broken leg because he won't see a doctor, what do you think would've happened to you if you'd have broken your leg? It's things like that that aren't reasonable, Moon. Refusin' to see a doctor when you've got the responsibility of a son to take care of—there's somethin' wrong with that. Now he's dead, and you're out walkin' around on the highway wantin' to go to Alaska."

I stood and took a step backwards. My hands were shaking and I didn't know what to do. "Nobody's ever said anything bad about Pap," I said.

"Heck, who would? Who did he ever let you see that might say it?"

I set the sandwich down. "Are you gonna give me money for this stuff or not?"

Mr. Abroscotto shook his head. "Suit yourself."

I waited while Mr. Abroscotto walked to the back of the store to get a chain cutter. My head spun in confusion, and my hands still shook from being nervous. It was hard to think straight, so I walked to the front of the counter and stared at the box.

When Mr. Abroscotto returned, he clipped the lock from the box and opened it. He pulled out a small roll of money, some photographs, and the watch. There was nothing else to sell. He thumbed through the photographs and studied each one, back and front, for several seconds. He finally showed one to me and asked if I knew any of the people in it.

"Nossir."

He looked at the picture again. "This fellow here looks an awful lot like your pap. I'd even say it was his brother if I was to make a guess at it. He ever tell you that you had an uncle or talk about his brother or anything like that?"

"Nossir."

"He ever talk about any family?"

"Said I had a grandpappy that died. Talked about Momma a lot when he didn't think I was listenin'—when he was workin' on stuff and talkin' to himself."

"Maybe you've got other relatives that hate the government. You might have someplace to go."

"I just want the money for that watch there."

Mr. Abroscotto raised his hands in the air. "All right," he said. He opened the register and took some money from it. He put the bills, photographs, and the watch back in the box and shut the lid. "I'm not gonna take that watch your pap left you. I stuck some money in there with the rest of it. That should help you out. You can pay me someday when you get back from Alaska."

"Thank you," I said.

"Anything you need in the way of supplies before you get goin'?"

"Nossir. I can get most everything I need from the forest."

"I reckon you can, Moon."

"I'll see you later, then," I said.

"You be careful."

I nodded.

I saw Mr. Abroscotto through the store window as I walked back up the road. He had picked up the phone and was talking and watching me leave. I figured he called the law, so I tucked the box under my arm and ran for the trees.

# 6

Dear Pap,

I think the law is after me now, so I am going to start for Alaska tomorrow. I meant to ask Mr. Abroscotto if he had a map, but I had to whip up on him for talking mean about you. I'm afraid if I go back again the law will be there waiting for me.

Before I left he gave me some money and I added it to the money that you already had in the box. I don't know how much it is because I haven't counted it, but I didn't have to sell your watch.

He said you might have a brother, but I know you would have told me about that. He said you might have let me die if it was me that had broken my leg, but I know that's not true, either.

I'm trying to listen to the sounds outside, but I don't think I'm as good at it as you are. I went out to take a leak a few minutes ago and there was a coon swimming around in the curing barrel. You'd have thought I'd have heard that.

I wasn't lonely today, but I am tonight. I wish there was someone else out here to talk to. Maybe you can talk to me soon if you get a chance.

Love, Moon

That night I started a small fire in the woodstove and burned the letter. After the letter was just ashes, I put out the fire so that no one would see the smoke. The only light left was that of the grease lamp we'd made in a can that flickered and put shadows on the walls. I wondered if I'd ever have a place as nice when I got to Alaska. Then I tried to imagine what the person I would live with looked like. I wondered if any boys my age were there. I felt the loneliness creeping over me, and lay on the hide pile with my jacket covering me and my hat pulled down low. I hugged my knees to my chest and listened to the night sounds.

Eventually the grease lamp went out and it was so dark that I couldn't see my hands in front of my face. At one point I heard something moving outside and fear bolted through me and I hugged my knees tighter. It wasn't like me to be scared of creatures moving in the night, but I wasn't myself with all the loneliness in that dark hole.

"Pap," I whispered, thinking that maybe he was out there. Maybe he was going to talk to me and make me feel okay again. I took off my hat so I could hear better and held my breath and listened. Whatever creature had been moving outside stopped.

"Pap, can you hear me?"

I heard the creature scurry off through the leaves. Then I started thinking about the good times I'd had with Pap when we'd swim in the creek and make flutter mills and scratch tic-tac-toe in the dirt. All these memories poured on me like a waterfall until I was shaking and crying. Then I couldn't take it anymore and leaped off the hide pile and ran out into the night. "Stop!" I cried after the creature. Even if it was just a coon or an armadillo, I wanted something to be with me that night. "Don't leave! Come back!" But my shouts made the rest of the forest creatures duck away and grow silent. I was left standing in the clearing with only the sound of the wind in the treetops. Then I imagined that the law was all around me. I started breathing hard and staring into the darkness beyond the trees. Suddenly I was running as fast as I could. Spiderwebs covered my face and tree branches slapped my cheeks. Every time I thought about slowing, I imagined people running behind me. I wasn't taking any trail that I knew of, but following the gaps in the trees. Sometimes the ground would fall from under me and I'd roll down a hill, only to get back up at the bottom and keep going. I crashed through a creek and climbed up a steep bank by clutching tree roots. At the top of the bank was a clearing that I dashed across and then ran on again beneath the tall pines.

Eventually, I broke from the trees onto the lawyer's new road. It felt better to have clear space around me where I could see that nothing was hidden and watching me. I started down the road, and the air whistled past my ears and my moccasins padded on the soft dirt. I kept on until the new lodge rose in front of me. The sight of it made me stop and stare up at the windows on the second floor.

"Hello," I said, but not loud enough for anyone to hear.

The lodge was dark except for one lit room on the corner. I stepped sideways across the clearing and saw a man sitting in the room reading a book. I sucked in deep breaths to calm myself the way I always did before I pulled the trigger on a rifle, and my panic began to go away. It made me feel better to watch the man, even though I didn't know him and didn't want him to know I was outside. I could see there was at least one other person in the world besides me.

I sat against a tree at the edge of the clearing. The wind rustled the treetops and reminded me that I'd left the shelter without my jacket and hat. I pulled up my knees to keep warm and watched the room.

It was just breaking day when I opened my eyes and saw the man standing over me with a rifle. I leaped to my feet and stared at him.

"What are you doing out here?" he said.

I was too startled to reply.

"Are you lost?"

I shook my head.

"You're the boy who buried his father, aren't you? The constable's been out here looking for you."

"I didn't do anything wrong."

"I didn't say you did. I was just about to step off into the woods and do a little hunting. I saw you sitting here."

"I'll go now."

He put his rifle over his shoulder and motioned towards the lodge. "Come on inside. I'll fix you something to eat. I can go hunting tomorrow."

"I better not. The law's gonna be after me soon."

"I've got a chime that goes off if anyone drives through my gate. I'll know if somebody comes for you. Besides, from what those surveyors said, it would take an Indian chief to find your shelter."

I didn't know what a chime was, but it made me feel better to hear that the constable wasn't close.

"Are you Mr. Wellington?"

"I am."

"I got scared out there last night. I shouldn't be here."

"Do you like sweet rolls?"

"I never had any."

"Let's go get some, then. I've got one left on the counter that I didn't eat."

I thought about it and watched his face. I didn't know Mr. Wellington, but my lonely sickness was less at the sight of him. I didn't see anything in his expression that told me I shouldn't trust him, and I still needed someone to tell me about getting to Alaska. Even though my instincts were against it, I stood and followed him.

Once we entered the lodge, I saw Mr. Wellington better in the light. He wore fancy hunting pants and a hat with a turkey feather in it. His face was tight and clean for someone his age. The only way you could tell he was older than Pap was by his eyes. They looked tired past his silver hair.

The lodge was warm inside and smelled of cut cedar and pine. The ceiling was high and I saw the second story was just windows halfway up the wall. I followed him into the kitchen, where he gave me a napkin and the sweet roll off the counter. I bit into it and the sugar tasted so good that I almost closed my eyes while I chewed.

I followed him into a larger room just outside the kitchen. "Sit down in that chair over there," he said. His hand pointed to a wood chair against the wall. I was disappointed that it wasn't one of the soft chairs in the middle of the room, but I went over to it and sat. Mr. Wellington walked around in front of me and pulled up another, more comfortable chair and sat down. He crossed his arms on his chest.

I finished the sweet roll and looked around at the light fixtures and the nature paintings on the walls.

"I talked to that friend of yours who owns the store up the

road and he said you all have been out there for about eight years."

"He's not my friend," I said.

"Okay."

"Pap said you'd run us off," I said.

"Well, I just wanted to find out who was living on my property."

I studied a painting of an Indian kneeling by a waterfall and didn't respond.

"The surveyors said they found a primitive dwelling of some sort. I suppose that was yours."

"It's a shelter. It's built like that so people won't find it."

"I see. What kind of pants are those?"

"Beaver britches."

"Did your father make those for you?"

"Nossir, I made 'em. Made a deerskin hat, too, but I left it at home."

"Interesting."

Mr. Wellington must have seen me look over at his television, because he said, "Would you like me to turn it on for you?"

I watched his face to see if I could read anything in it. I thought about how lonely it was back at the shelter. I thought about how warm and dry it felt inside the lodge. "You gonna call the constable on me if I stay?"

Mr. Wellington paused for a moment. "No, I'm not going to call the constable. I'm not sure I like his kind."

"Can you tell me how to get to Alaska?"

"I probably can. I may have some maps in one of those

back rooms. Why don't you sit in this chair right here while I see what I can find."

I looked at the soft chair he was pointing to. "Okay."

Mr. Wellington turned on the television and then walked away. "I'll be back shortly," he said.

I'd only seen television a few times. Mr. Abroscotto had a set in his store over the counter. I got up and moved over to the cushion chair and sank down until my chin touched my chest. I'd never felt a more comfortable chair in my life. There was a show about lions playing. I'd only seen them in picture books and couldn't take my eyes off them. Daylight soon slipped through the windows and I grew groggy and lazy.

An hour must have gone by when I heard someone knocking on the door. Mr. Wellington walked out of one of the back rooms and went to answer the knock. When he opened the door, I saw a man in a suit standing there. I knew right away that he was there to get me. It was how he looked at me when he stepped inside. I leaped from my chair and ran towards the back rooms where Mr. Wellington had gone earlier. But as soon as I reached the hall, a man in overalls stepped out and grabbed me from behind. He pulled me to his chest and bear-hugged me so that I couldn't do anything but kick. I kicked backwards at his knees so that he had to walk me into the main room with his legs spread. He took me over to the man who had come for me and held me out.

"He's all yours, if you can hold him," the man in overalls said.

"Mr. Hill's my caretaker," Mr. Wellington said to the man

in the suit. "He came in through the back door. We figured the boy would make a run for it."

"I appreciate the help," the man in the suit said.

I looked at Mr. Wellington. "Liar!" I yelled at him.

"Mr. Gene's not the constable," Mr. Wellington said calmly. "He's from the boys' home. He'll treat you a lot better than that constable I met yesterday."

"Take it easy," Mr. Gene said. "Nobody's going to hurt you, Moon."

I started bucking, kicking, and pounding my arms against Mr. Hill. I thought I was about to slip out once, but he joggled me back up and squeezed me tighter.

"Boy needs a bath and a haircut," Mr. Hill said. "I can't stand the smell of him."

"I didn't do anything wrong!" I yelled.

"Moon!" Mr. Gene shouted.

I kicked at the air again. "I haven't done anything to anybody!"

"Moon, calm down. Just bring him outside and put him in the car. We'll take him to the home and get him cleaned up."

Mr. Gene hurried out to the car and opened the back door while Mr. Hill carried me behind him and Mr. Wellington followed. When we reached the car, Mr. Hill leaned over and shoved me in. Before I could turn around, I heard the door slam shut behind me. It only took a second to look up and see that there were no handles and a plastic shield between me and the front seat. I knew I was trapped. "Liar!" I yelled at the floor.

I had never been in a car. The only time I had ridden in anything was when Pap came down with a fever once on the way to Mr. Abroscotto's store. He let Mr. Abroscotto ride us in the back of his pickup truck to a place up the road, where we went on foot the rest of the way to the shelter. But it was different then. We were in the truck bed, where the fresh air brushed our faces. It wasn't much at all like being shut up; it was more like flying.

I lay down and pulled my knees up. The three men talked outside for a few minutes and then Mr. Gene got in and started the engine. My ear was pressed to the vinyl seat and I could soon hear the dirt road passing under the tires. After a minute I felt the car slow and swing onto the highway. I grew woozy as I listened to the hum of the asphalt. I tried holding my breath to make it go away.

"You can sit up, you know."

I didn't answer. I stared at the back of Mr. Gene's seat and concentrated on the queasiness in my stomach.

After a moment, I heard him turn. "You okay back there?"

I closed my eyes and took a deep breath. I heard the crunch of gravel as the car slowed and pulled onto the side of the road. I heard Mr. Gene's door opening. A steady dinging sound came from the front part of the car. My door opened and Mr. Gene grabbed me by the shoulder and shook me gently. I felt the contents of my stomach lunge forward and splatter against the back of his car seat.

"Gyaaa!" he yelled as he jumped away.

He jerked me out and dragged me down into a grassy ditch where he held me under one armpit and let my head dangle. I stared at the ground and thought of nothing except how grateful I was to be out of the car. I breathed the fresh air and felt my stomach easing.

"Are you done?"

I didn't answer. I moved my eyes and stared at the tips of his shiny leather shoes. He shifted his feet. "Are you feeling better?"

I thought about it. I felt better. My stomach was back to normal. I let my eyes creep slowly past the tips of his shoes and up his pant leg. Then I looked down at my left hand, which rested on one slightly bent knee. I remembered something Pap had told me. *Moon, there's no faster way to take a man down than to punch him between the legs with everything you've got. If that doesn't work, take a stick to him.* I took a deep breath, balled my fist, and socked him in the crotch. Before I even looked up, he'd let go of me. I jerked away and took two quick steps towards the car. Mr. Gene drew himself inwards like a turtle. He closed his eyes and sank to the ground and rolled over onto his side. He pulled his knees in tight as a baby and moaned curses at me.

"Don't you . . . don't you even . . . even think about running off . . ."

I looked in both directions on the road. It was empty. I wiped my mouth on my shoulder, crossed the blacktop, and ran into the forest.

## 7

I made it back to the shelter that evening. The dark hole that had seemed so terrible the night before now made me feel safe again. I figured the outside world was just what Pap had warned me about. Everybody was out to get us, and hiding in the forest was the only way to stay safe. Loneliness was something I'd have to wait on to pass, like Pap said it would.

I sat on the hide pile and put on my jacket and hat to warm up. Then I pulled some dried venison off a hindquarter that hung from the ceiling and chewed it slowly while I listened to the forest sounds. I figured I could spend at least one more night before the law could get with the surveyors and track me to the shelter. It was too far and too dangerous to try it after dark, so they wouldn't start out until morning. The closest paved road was three miles to a bird. With all the gulleys and swamps, though, not even I could travel that direction in less than half a day.

When I woke at daybreak, robins were scratching in the leaves, and a blue jay complained from nearby. I lay still and listened to the forest for several minutes until I was sure that I heard nothing unusual. When I was satisfied that no one was outside, I slid off the hide pile and got my rifle from the place I kept it in the ceiling. I grabbed some bullets out of the paint can and poured them into a cheesecloth that I tied together. Then I quickly gathered other things I thought might be useful for the trip and packed them all in the wheelbarrow: my rifle, bullets, traps, several hides, dried coon meat, extra clothes, Pap's personal box, some rope, a cooking pot, and a hatchet.

When I was done, I threw a rain tarp over everything and used some twine to secure it. After one last look around, I stuck my deerskin hat on my head and set out for the river. I'd take a trail we rarely used that went north to the high ridges of the Noxubee River and then cut west to the blacktop. It was a longer route, but the river bottom was open and free of brush, so I could more easily push the wheelbarrow and see anyone that might be after me. Once I made it to the blacktop, I would be at the bridge that crossed over the river. I'd have to push my wheelbarrow over the bridge and then get back into the trees again on the other side. I thought about what Pap said about only traveling at night, but I reasoned it was more important for me to get off Mr. Wellington's property as fast as I could.

Between wrestling the wheelbarrow through the forest and resting, it took me close to six hours to get to the highway. Besides the river bottom, I had to get through two sloughs, a thick cedar grove, and a quarter mile of swampy cane thicket. When I got to the blacktop, I stayed just inside the trees and lay down to rest. I felt my legs throbbing and watched my stomach move up and down. A breeze chilled my forehead where the sweat clung to my bangs. I reached over and pulled some coon meat from beneath the tarp, lay back, and chewed it slowly. I wanted to close my eyes, but I knew there was no time to sleep. Then I heard a car whoosh by, and it reminded me to get on my way again.

I stood ready in the trees and listened and watched the road. When I thought it was safe, I pushed out and up onto the blacktop and started running behind the wheelbarrow.

I'd never been on the bridge before. I'd only seen it from upriver. It was longer and higher than I thought and I felt myself growing a little dizzy. The solid rubber tire of the wheelbarrow hummed across the asphalt and far below the water swirled and passed under me. The air was much colder coming down the river, but with the panic that was rising in me, I hardly noticed.

When I heard the car, I didn't turn around to look. I pushed my legs to go even faster and felt my neck hairs rise with fear. The end of the bridge was only thirty yards away, but if it was the law, I'd need time to escape into the forest with my wheelbarrow at the other side, and that seemed impossible. I heard the car speeding up just as I came to the end of the bridge. Then my breath almost left me when I saw what I was up against. The road dropped off steeply to a swamp on both sides. There was nowhere to go. I stopped the wheelbarrow and spun around and spread my legs for balance like Pap had shown me to do when I was about to fight.

I recognized the police car from pictures. It had a light on top and a badge painted on the door. It skidded to a stop in front of me and I watched the constable watching me and putting on his hat inside the car. When he stepped out, I could see he was taller and heavier than Pap. He wore his clothes tight and moved with his chest out so that he reminded me of a flared turkey. He nodded at me from behind dark sunglasses and then looked over at the wheelbarrow. "What you got there, boy?"

"Livin' stuff."

He stared at the rifle barrel sticking out of the tarpaulin. "You doin' some huntin'?"

I shook my head. "Nossir."

"What you doin' with that rifle?"

"It's mine."

"What's that on your head?"

"Hat."

"You make it?"

"Yessir. Out of deerskin."

He walked to the wheelbarrow and lifted a corner of the tarpaulin. He set it back down. "You that Blake boy?"

I didn't answer.

"You're him, ain't you?"

I looked quickly at the gulley behind me. I glanced down at my rifle.

"Don't try it," he said, like he knew what I was thinking. "I'll be all over you before you know it."

"I'm not doin' anything to anybody."

"Well, you better stop bowin' up at me. Come over here and get in this car."

I glanced over at the rifle. Suddenly the constable stepped towards me. "Boy, you look at that rifle again and I'm gonna knock you sideways."

I swallowed hard.

"Damned if you ain't the mean little cuss I thought you were."

I looked at his holster and the giant chrome pistol that was stuffed into it. I thought about how long it would take him to pull it out and shoot me. A second later, I spun around and leaped out into the air.

I hit the ground about halfway down the slope and rolled the rest of the way to the bottom and splashed into the shallow water of the swamp. When I tried to stand, my feet punched into the soft mud, and I tripped and landed face-first. Then the constable crashed up against me and I heard him grunt. I quickly got to my knees and started to crawl, but I felt him grab my ankle and hold it as I pulled handfuls of weeds and muck. Suddenly, I slipped free, and I scampered almost five feet before I heard him splat in the mud behind me and felt my ankle gripped again.

"Little bastard!" he yelled.

I looked over my shoulder and saw him lying on his stomach. His sunglasses were gone, and his face was red and twisted with frustration as he slapped at me and pulled his boots from the mud. I made a last desperate leap to get away, but I wasn't able to break his hold. I sat up and kicked his hand and he rolled over, cursing me. Like someone doing the backstroke, he threw his free arm into the air and down into the mud and grabbed my other foot. I twisted and rolled like an alligator, but it did no good. He pulled me towards him in little jerks.

"Don't you"—*jerk*—"make me"—*jerk*—"have to"—*jerk*—"shoot your ass." And he sat up and pulled me into his lap. "Boy!"

I punched him in the face as hard as I could.

"Unh," he grunted. He stood up with me and crushed me against his chest. For a moment I couldn't breathe, and I felt that my shoulders were about to snap. He slopped out of the swamp and walked sideways with me up the embankment, his shoes wheezing and him spitting at the ground. He kept me squeezed so tight that I couldn't think over the pain.

When we got back to the top of the embankment, the constable paused for a few seconds and caught his breath.

Then he carried me over to the car and dropped one arm to pull the door handle. With the pressure off me, my senses came rushing back and I spun around and bit him on the tit. He yelled and pulled my head from his chest.

"Juvenile center my ass! Jail's more like it. Crazy little long-haired bastard!"

He slapped my deerskin hat from my head, and I saw it roll across the road. I tried to cry out, but I felt weak and dizzy. He opened the door to the police car and shoved me across the backseat and slammed the door. I lay there until I caught my breath and the dizziness went away. When I sat up I saw the constable standing beside the car with his mud-covered arms out like a scarecrow, cursing and flapping them to fling the mud off. He kicked his legs from side to side and slung large chunks of mud and grass over the road. Then he noticed the black box clipped to his belt. He stopped and stared at it. He gently pulled it loose and shook it. He walked behind the police car and hurled it at the asphalt, where it shattered and spread across the highway in little black and silver pieces.

After almost ten minutes of pacing and cursing on the side of the road, he threw my things into the trunk. When everything was out of the wheelbarrow, he picked it up and tossed it over the embankment, where it arced out and stuck straight up by the handles in the swamp below. He spit after it, then came around and sank into the driver's seat and glanced at me briefly in the rearview mirror.

"I hope I busted those sunglasses good, too," I said.

# 8

I leaned up in my seat and pressed my face against the glass as the car crossed back over the bridge and picked up speed towards Gainesville. Mr. Abroscotto's store flashed past and I stared ahead at the green traffic light, not believing that I'd actually get to see it up close. When we passed under it, I tried to look up and then spun in my seat and watched it fall behind. Then I saw a car rush past us from the other direction. I spun around again, my heart racing. Buildings came at us on each side, all of them bigger than Mr. Wellington's lodge. We sped past them and then I sat back as we started up another bridge. There was only blue sky in front of me through the front windshield. I felt the sickness creeping back into my stomach like I'd felt in Mr. Gene's car. I took a deep breath and held it, but the nausea sat in me like poison. I lay on the seat and drew up my knees and closed my eyes.

It seemed like the ride would never end. Sometimes we would slow down or even come to a stop, but then we'd start moving again. The constable didn't say a word to me, and all I could hear was the road through the vinyl seat and other cars passing us. I was able to keep from getting sick by continuing to take deep breaths and holding them.

After what seemed like an hour, we finally stopped. The constable got out of the car and left his door open. I sat up slowly and looked around. We were parked in front of a brick building that said LIVINGSTON POLICE DEPARTMENT across the front.

The constable came back a minute later, opened my door, and dragged me off the seat. He pulled me by the arm and I hopped along on one foot beside him, staring at all of the shiny cars in the parking lot.

"What about my hat?" I said. He squeezed my arm tighter and jerked me forward. Once we were through the door, he let loose and walked out again. "Clean him up, Earle," he said over his shoulder.

Earle had on a different-colored uniform and was a lot younger than the constable. His hair was slicked back and as tight on him as his shirt and trousers. He looked at me, shook his head, and said, "Jesus." I could tell he was nervous about something.

He pointed me into a bathroom where they had a shower. He had me strip naked and stand under the shower head with a big brush in my hand while he turned the knobs. It was the first time I'd ever taken a shower and had so much warm water over me. I shut my eyes and hoped I could stay there for a while.

"You gonna be trouble to me?" Earle said.

I opened my eyes. "I didn't do anything."

Someone called from the next room over. "You all right in there, Earle?"

"Yeah, I'm all right, Bob. Is Sanders gone?"

"He's gone."

"You'd think this was his police station the way he just comes in here and tells us what to do."

"His daddy's the judge, Earle."

Earle shook his head. He looked back down at me. "Start scrubbin' yourself. I ain't doin' it."

After my shower, Earle made me put on new clothes that were too big and smelled like Mr. Abroscotto's soap shelf. "I barely found those for you," he said. "I don't have anything to fit your feet, so you'll just have to walk around in those socks."

He led me back to where they locked people up and I did my best not to trip over my pant legs and slip on the waxed floor. Pap had told me about jails, so I wasn't surprised when I saw the cages. Earle unlocked an empty one and motioned me inside. "You just stay quiet in here until somebody comes for you," he said. I nodded to him and he locked the door and walked out.

Jail was the best place I'd ever been. They had good food and a comfortable bed and a sink with running water and a flush toilet.

The only other person in a cage, across the hall from me, was a man who told me his name was Obregon. He said they locked him up for being too drunk and wrecking his car. He was lying on his bed talking at the ceiling and picking scabs on his face.

"What they got you in here for?" he asked me.

"I don't know."

"Where you live at?"

"At a hole in the ground in the forest."

"You say you live in a cave?"

"No. It's a shelter that trees have grown over."

"I seen the story on TV. Your daddy's the one that lived out in those woods, ain't he?"

"Both of us did."

"What you eat out there?"

"Lots of stuff. Stuff I trap and kill mostly. Some stuff Pap and I used to grow."

Obregon grunted and laughed to himself. "By the looks of him, you sure gave Sanders a hard time."

"I told him I didn't wanna go."

"He's liable to keep you in here for a while, riled up as he is. He's not one that likes to be made a fool of."

"I don't mind. I like the food here."

Obregon sat up and yawned. "I imagine you do. You don't look like you get much to eat."

"I think I could live here for a little while. They let you go outside some?"

"Yeah, they'll let you out to walk around. Least they let me out. They might be too scared of you."

I smiled at him. I knew he was kidding me. "What're they gonna do with my stuff?"

"They got it stored up front."

"They stripped off all my clothes."

"They'll keep those for you, too."

"I had a wheelbarrow that Sanders threw off into a swamp. I had that wheelbarrow ever since I can remember. I hauled my dead pap around in it."

"You what?"

"Loaded Pap and took him up to our cemetery in it."

"Got some special meanin' to you?"

"It's the only way I've got to get stuff around."

"I never thought of a wheelbarrow meanin' much to anybody."

"Had a deerskin hat, too. I made it myself, but Sanders threw it away. You think they'll let me have some more pie?"

Obregon shouted towards the door. "Hey, Earle! Earle!"

Earle came through the door. "What?"

"The little feller says he wants more pie. You got any in there?"

Earle looked at me and shook his head. "One more person tells me what to do . . ." He left the room and shut the door behind him. He came back a few seconds later with the pie and stuck it through the bars to me. "This is all you get, you hear?"

I took the pie. "You gonna let me stay in this cage tonight?"

"Let you?"

I nodded. "On this bed here."

"That's up to Mr. Sanders. He's in charge of you."

"Where'd he go?"

"He went home to Gainesville. Said to keep you here until he got back."

"Then what's he gonna do to me?"

"I reckon he'll haul you over to the juvenile home in Tuscaloosa."

"He said I was more fit for jail."

"Well, I don't know. We'll just have to see. I just do what I'm told."

"You're spineless, Earle," Obregon said.

"Shut up, Obregon."

"You can tell Mr. Gene and Sanders both that I don't aim to go with 'em anywhere. Tell 'em I can whip a man three times my size. Maybe two at once."

Earle shook his head. He leaned into the bars of my cage. "I'm gonna give you some advice, kid. You're already in a lot of trouble and don't have to be. You'll be lucky if they don't come down on you for assaulting a lawman. You need to tame that temper of yours and cooperate, or you're gonna end up in a lot of places you won't want to be."

"Let the kid be," Obregon said.

"Shut up, Obregon."

"I just want people to leave me alone," I said.

"It doesn't work like that. You can't live by yourself until you're older, kid. It's the law."

"Pap said go to Alaska," I said quietly.

"What?"

"Never mind," I said.

# 9

The next morning another policeman brought me bacon and eggs and a biscuit for breakfast. Obregon said I ate it all like a wild dog. I told him it was the best breakfast I ever had. Not long after I finished, I heard Sanders talking about me beyond the door.

"Where's that little pissant?"

"He's back there," someone on the other side of the door said. "He's not too upset about it, either."

"He been givin' y'all any trouble?"

"No. He's been eatin' up everything we bring him. He and Obregon are good buddies now."

I heard Sanders grunt, and then footsteps came towards the door. He came in the room and looked around until he saw me in my cage. "You ready, boy?"

"Where we goin'?"

"Takin' you to Tuscaloosa. Gonna reintroduce you to your old friend Mr. Gene. Get up."

I set my jaw and shook my head.

"Don't you shake your head at me, boy!"

I went to the back of my cage and sat in the corner. I drew my knees up to my chest and hugged them there possum-style. Sanders reached to his belt and pulled away a set of keys. He unlocked the door and stepped inside. "I said to get up!"

"That child can't be more'n ten years old, Sanders," Obregon said. "He got you jumpy?"

"Shut up, Obregon!" Sanders put the keys back on his belt and unsnapped a leather case that held a pair of handcuffs. "Hold out your hands, boy."

"What's your problem, Sanders?"

I quickly pulled my hands away from my knees and sat on them.

"This ain't none of your damn business," Sanders said to Obregon.

"Don't tell me you gotta handcuff him?"

Sanders turned around and looked at Obregon. "I thought I told you to shut up."

Obregon smiled. "I'll bet you used to have bullies on you like wild dogs on meat when you was in school. Never mind, I forgot. You didn't make it past eighth grade, did you, Sanders?"

Sanders ignored Obregon. "Get up!" he said to me.

I shook my head.

"Now!" Sanders yelled.

I didn't move. Sanders reached down and grabbed me by the back of my shirt. He lifted me, still balled up, but with my arms around my knees again. Obregon stood in his cell and clung to the bars. "You hurt him and I seen it all," he said.

I smiled at Obregon. "It doesn't hurt," I said.

"At least put some shoes and a jacket on the kid!" Obregon called after us.

Sanders carried me out of the cage, through the main office, and outside. He opened his car and tossed me in the back like I was nothing but a sack of coon hides. He slammed the door behind me and went back inside.

When Sanders returned, I had come out of my ball and was sitting up in the normal way. He glanced at me once and then got into the driver's seat and started the engine. I knocked on the plastic shield between us, but he acted like he didn't hear me.

"Sanders?" I said.

No answer. He pulled onto the road and sped up.

"Sanders?" I said again.

"What!"

"Where are we?"

"First of all, it's Constable Sanders to you. And we're in Livingston."

Suddenly the window beside me slid down a few inches and the cold air came rushing through and blew against my face.

"Little chilly back there?" Sanders said as he chuckled to himself.

I didn't say anything. I wanted the window down to keep me from getting sick again. As I watched the countryside pass by, I thought about escape. But I'd not been farther than Mr. Abroscotto's store that I remembered, and I knew we weren't anywhere close to that. I reasoned that even if I could get out of the car, I wouldn't know where to go, and I wouldn't have any of my supplies.

"When do I get my things back?"

"You'll get 'em when we're good and ready. Everything except the rifle and bullets you were totin'."

I felt my face grow warm. "You can't take my rifle!" I shouted. "Pap gave me that rifle!"

Sanders seemed to like it that I was getting upset. He shook his head and smiled. I slammed my fists into the plastic shield.

"Hey!" he yelled. He looked in his rearview mirror at me. He wasn't smiling anymore. "You scratch up my new patrol car and we're gonna have a go at it. I spent two hours cleanin' your stink out of it last night."

I sat back and looked down at my knees. We drove along without talking for a long time. I thought again of ways to escape, but the situation seemed hopeless.

After a while, Sanders pulled over at a gas station and filled the car. When he came back from paying, he was popping a flat round can against his thumb. He got into the car and opened the container by cutting it with his teeth.

"What's that?"

"Copenhagen chewin' tobacco. Now shut up."

"I've gotta pee."

"Hold it. You ain't gettin' out of this car."

He put some of the tobacco between his front lip and his gum and flicked his fingers at the floor. He closed the door and started the engine. As we pulled onto the highway, I watched him move his lip around and spit into an RC cola can. He caught me staring. "I can't help but think I'll be seein' you in and out of jail all your life, kid."

I looked away and didn't answer him.

"You ain't nothin' but white trash. You worse than white trash. You ain't even trailer trash. You know what you are?"

I shook my head against the car window, still watching the fields pass by.

"You're stinkin' militia trash, is what you are."

I didn't know that word "militia." I kept staring out the window while he talked to me. He spat into the can and then scraped it against his chin to catch some dribble. Spat again. "Your daddy ain't never owned a thing in his life. He trespassed and poached for a livin'. Some dirty low-life you'd see walkin' down the highway with animal furs wrapped around him."

"You don't know my pap!"

"The hell I don't. I've seen him."

I felt my face go hot again and balled my fists on my knees. I knew there wasn't anything I could do, so I stayed quiet.

"You'd have never been nothin', boy. That man didn't care a lick about you."

I couldn't hold the anger in any longer. I slammed both

my fists into the plastic shield and shouted at him. "I've got another gun, you know! I've still got Pap's hidden away with some bullets! You'll be lucky if I don't shoot you dead!"

"Here we go," he said.

Sanders veered off the road and skidded to a halt. He racked the gearshift into place and flung the car door open. I crouched on the seat like a frog. When he opened my door, I jumped at him. He didn't expect me to come at him like I did. By the time his hands stretched out to grab me where I would have been on the seat, I was already clinging to him with my legs wrapped around his stomach and my arms under his armpits. I bit into his shoulder and chewed at it like it was tough gristle. Sanders started yelling and backed away from the car while I worked in three or four chews. He grabbed me around the waist with both hands and squeezed so hard that my body shot with pain and I had to throw my head back and cough at the sky. I felt my pants grow wet with pee flowing down my leg.

"Damnit!" he yelled. "How about this! You feelin' this?"

I tried to nod so that he would stop, but I couldn't.

"I ain't the man to mess with, boy. My family's owned land in Sumter County for a hundred years. You wouldn't know anything about ownin' stuff, now, would you?"

I coughed again and my eyes felt like they were about to burst.

He squeezed me harder. "Would you!"

Everything I saw was blurry. A truck whooshed by. I heard the dinging of the police car where the door was still open. Suddenly he released me and dropped me to the asphalt, and I heard him spit and walk away. I rolled over and got sick onto the ground. I hoped that he'd let me lie there until I felt better. I wanted to stay until it became dark out and I heard owls calling. I lay there for what seemed like a long time, staring at the loose gravel, until he grabbed me by the shirt and lifted me and threw me back into the police car. He said something to me, but I couldn't make it out.

I lay across the backseat, taking deep breaths and waiting for the pain to go away. I felt the gentle motion of the cruiser through the vinyl.

It wasn't long before the car slowed, and I heard the tires on a gravel road. "Want you to pay attention to somethin'," Sanders said.

The car stopped and I saw Sanders's window going down. "Billy!" he yelled. "Go tell your daddy to get out here."

I heard a screen door slam somewhere outside. Sanders began to pack his Copenhagen with dull thumps against his thigh. "Show you what it's like to own things, boy."

He turned and looked at me as he shoved another pinch of tobacco into his mouth. I watched his face as he stared at me and worked the tobacco around with his tongue. Then I heard another man's voice outside.

"How you doin', Davy?" the man said.

Sanders turned away from me and peered out the window. "What did I tell you last month, Allen?"

"Davy, you know how things have been around here. I talked to your daddy about it. He said we could get settled with you in two weeks. I got disability comin'."

Sanders shook his head and stared straight out over the steering wheel. "Allen, lean in here," he said calmly.

I heard footsteps outside the car.

"Come here," Sanders said again. "I wanna tell you somethin'."

"Well, I can hear fine from right here, Davy."

"Lean in here. No sense in little Billy hearin' this."

I heard the footsteps again and saw the man's head appear at the window and his hands rest on the driver's door. His face was long and sunken and smudge-streaked. He reminded me of a blue heron. He swallowed and I saw his Adam's apple move up and down. Sanders suddenly let go of the steering wheel and backhanded the man across the jaw. It happened so fast I jumped in my seat. The man's face was knocked around as if he'd looked away to stare at the back tire. He slowly wiped his mouth and continued looking downwards.

"My granddaddy didn't leave this land to my daddy, did he?"

The man didn't answer. His face was beet red.

"Did he?" Sanders repeated.

"No. He didn't."

"See what you can do, then. I know plenty of people that would love to take over this house you built on my property." Sanders rolled up his window and began to drive forward. The man's hands slipped away from the car and his face passed by my window. He never looked up.

"That's white trash," Sanders said.

# 10

When we got to the boys' home, there were people in the driveway with cameras to take pictures of us. Sanders opened the back door and the people crowded close and shouted questions, but my chest and head hurt too much to answer. I balled up on the backseat.

"Where's your daddy, kid?"

"How long have you lived in the cave?"

"We heard you buried your father. Tell us about it."

Sanders grabbed me under the armpit and lifted me onto my tiptoes. He leaned down close to my ear. "You screw up, kid, I'll squeeze you until your head pops off."

I watched the sidewalk pass under my feet while Sanders pulled me along. Cameras flashed and people yelled at me.

"Officer, can he talk? Has he been educated at all?"

I heard Sanders reply. "He's a little militia kid. He don't know much of anything."

"Your daddy ever kill anybody, kid?"

"Does he have any relatives?"

"Hey, kid! Is it true you lived in a tree?"

We were soon inside the boys' home, and the flashbulbs and the shouting of reporters faded away behind the front door. Sanders stopped and my eyes saw the tips of shoes in front of me. I looked up to see Mr. Gene.

"Moon?" he said.

I didn't reply.

"You best get some restraints on this boy before I let loose," Sanders said.

"I don't think he's going anywhere," Mr. Gene replied. "Unless he knows how to buzz that front door open, he can bounce off these walls all day long."

Sanders released me, and I dropped to the floor. "He's all yours, then. Kid's an animal. He pissed his pants and I got to clean my backseat of him for the second time."

I tried to rub my shoulder where Sanders had been squeezing me, but the constable slapped my hand away. "Don't you move a finger!" he spat. Sanders looked back at Mr. Gene. "I'm tellin' you now, this kid'll be on you like a wet cat, you don't tie him down."

My stomach felt queasy and my head was still throbbing. I wanted to lie down and sleep. "I'm not gonna whip up on anybody," I said to the floor.

Sanders left and Mr. Gene took me to a back room and stood me in front of a giant black man.

"This is Mr. Carter," he said. "He's the watchman here at Pinson. He'll take you from here."

"My stomach hurts," I said.

"I'll bet it does," Mr. Gene said like he didn't believe me. "I know all about that stomach. We've seen just about every trick in the book at Pinson. Isn't that right, Mr. Carter?"

"That's right."

"Mr. Carter, will you get this boy a uniform and show him to the shower room? After that you can show him to his bunk."

Mr. Carter nodded and began to lead me away.

"And Mr. Carter," Mr. Gene said. We stopped and turned

around again. "Moon will be wearing our special color for the time being."

"I'll fix him up," Mr. Carter said.

Mr. Carter pointed me through a door on my right and then we turned left down a hall. Soon we came to a closet where we stopped. He opened the door and, from a top shelf, got a one-piece uniform that was the color of orange flagging tape. He handed it down to me. "You don't give us any trouble and we'll let you wear a white one. What size shoes you wear?"

"I don't know."

He knelt down and dug into a cardboard box and pulled out some white canvas tennis shoes. "Take these with you and we'll swap 'em out if they don't fit. I'll round up a jacket for you and put it in your locker later on."

I took the shoes and backed up as he came from the closet and shut it. We continued on until we came to a steel door that Mr. Carter had to unlock with keys that hung from his belt. Once we passed through I heard the sound of boys shouting. He locked it behind us and we turned right and kept walking. "You have boys in cages here?"

"Cages?"

"Like jail."

"No. No cages like jail."

We turned left again and walked down another hall until Mr. Carter pushed open a door and motioned for me to go in. "Get a shower and get dressed. There's towels above the sink in there. I'll be out here when you're done. You had lunch yet?"

"Nossir."

"The rest of the boys already ate, but I'll see what I can find for you."

I walked into the empty shower room and looked around. I saw the stall and remembered how Earle had turned the silver knobs to get the water out. After placing my new clothes on the floor, I stripped naked and stepped under the shower head. I watched the nozzle as I turned the knob and suddenly icy-cold water pounded my face. I sucked in my breath and let the water run over me for a few seconds before I reached up and turned it off.

When Mr. Carter came back I was waiting in the middle of the floor with my new uniform and shoes on. He gave me a sandwich and bent over and picked up the clothes Earle had found for me. When we walked back out into the hall, he tossed my jail clothes into a trash can and wiped his hands on his pants.

The next room he took me to was full of numbered bunk beds, each one with two lockers next to it. There was a door against the far wall that led outside to a play yard with trailers in it. There was another to my right that I reasoned would open back into the shower room. Out the windows I saw boys running about and playing.

"We've got twenty-one residents here, so chances are you're gonna find a friend. It ain't so bad if you follow the rules."

I nodded.

"You know how to read, kid?"

I nodded again.

"Then go find bed eighteen. That's gonna be your home for a while."

He walked out, and I wandered along until I found bed eighteen. It was a top bunk and I crawled up onto it and unwrapped my sandwich. I chewed it slowly and watched the boys. I was hungry, but it wasn't long before the loneliness started creeping up over me again and I wrapped what was left of the sandwich and lay down to sleep.

Mr. Carter came back into the room after an hour. He shook my shoulder and pain shot down my arm. I leaped back.

"Somethin' wrong with your arm, kid?"

"Sanders squeezed it," I said.

"Lemme see."

I sat up and unzipped my uniform and pulled it to my waist. He studied my shoulder for a moment, then reached out and touched the blue areas with his finger. Where he pressed, the skin turned red and then blue when he pulled his finger away. He shook his head. "That Sanders, he's trouble. I've got some cousins in Sumter County that say he ain't easy to deal with. You want some ice to put on it?"

"Nossir. I'm okay."

Mr. Carter watched me while I zipped up again. "Boy, you're built like a squirrel."

"Pap said I could climb like one, too."

"Bet you could. I ain't seen many white boys with muscle like that."

"From workin'."

He picked up the sandwich I hadn't finished. "Must not be from eatin'."

"I'll finish it later," I said.

He tossed it a few feet into a trash can. "That's all right.

We got supper comin' pretty soon. You'll get all you can eat then." He leaned against the bunk behind him and stuck his hands in his pockets. "You're all over TV, you know."

I shrugged.

"They say you're mean as a snake. You don't look too mean to me."

I lay back down on the bed and pulled the blanket up to my chin. "People keep tryin' to catch me all the time and I haven't done anything. Before my pap died, he told me to head to Alaska. Said there were more people like us up there."

"More squirrelly people with long hair?"

"Nossir. More people that hate the government."

Mr. Carter smiled and nodded. "Gov'ment haters. That's right. All those gov'ment haters up there."

"That's what he said."

"How you gonna get to Alaska?"

"Walk, I guess."

Mr. Carter laughed. "You ain't off to such a good start."

"Soon as I get out of here I will be."

Mr. Carter smiled and shook his head. "You don't get it, do you? They ain't gonna let you out of here unless somebody comes for you."

"I figure I won't have much of a problem bustin' out once I get to feelin' better again."

Mr. Carter's face grew serious. He pulled his hands from his pockets and took a step towards me. "Listen, no more foolin' around. Don't you be talkin' like that anymore. You're gonna get yourself in a heap more trouble'n you're already in."

"All right," I said.

"All right what?"

"I won't talk about it anymore."

## 11

The rest of the boys came crowding into the room just after Mr. Carter left. I lay quietly on my bunk and watched them file through the play yard door and spread out towards their own beds. One of them happened to glance up and see me. He stopped and his eyes grew wide. "Hey!" he yelled. "It's the cave boy!"

The rest of the boys heard him and they all looked at me. I lay there and didn't move.

"It *is* him!" someone else yelled. "The kid they talked about on TV!"

"It's the wild boy!"

I watched as everyone gathered around me. I paid the most attention to the tallest boy, who seemed to be moving through the others to get closer. In a moment, he was standing before me, staring at my face poking from the blankets. "You that wild kid?"

"I don't know," I said.

"You the one got arrested yesterday?"

"Yeah."

He turned to the others and then to me again. "You don't look so tough."

I sized him up. He was about twice my weight and height. "I can whip *you*," I said.

His face went red. He reached out to grab me, but I was ready for him. I swung my arm from under the blanket and hit him open-handed across the face. At the same time, I leaped up and stood on my bunk. The boys cheered and began gathering closer. The big kid recovered and grabbed for my feet. I danced around the top of the bed and avoided his hands for a few seconds, but he finally got me and I fell onto the mattress. He dragged me towards him. I took my free foot and slammed it against the other, knocking his fingers between the knobs of my ankles. He yelled and let go. About that time, I heard something smack against the hall door, and the crowd grew silent. I rolled onto my back and propped myself on my elbows and looked in the direction of the sound. Mr. Carter stood there holding a club.

"Everybody to their bunks. Now! You'll stand there until suppertime if I hear another word."

Everyone began to find their beds. The boy who'd come after me was three bunks towards the door on the bottom. He turned and gave me a mean stare.

"Hal Mitchell," Mr. Carter said. "I want you in the center of the floor."

Hal moaned and stepped to the middle of the room and faced Mr. Carter with his jaw set tight. It looked like somebody had painted a red hand on his cheek.

"What happened?"

"The little runt popped me across the face."

"Who?"

Hal rolled his eyes at the ceiling. "The cave boy."

"His name's Moon."

"Whatever."

Mr. Carter walked towards Hal. "Why'd he slap you?"

Hal raised one shoulder like he didn't care. "I don't know."

Mr. Carter towered over him. "I don't imagine you were provokin' him?"

Hal shrugged.

"You sleep outside tonight. No supper."

Hal set his jaw tightly and stared at Mr. Carter. "What?"

Mr. Carter didn't change his expression, but pointed to the door leading into the play yard. "Outside."

"Are you serious!"

"Now."

"You can't do that!"

"Says who?"

"Says . . . Well, you just can't."

"Now!" Mr. Carter's voice boomed and I thought I saw Hal jump a little beneath his uniform. Hal began to walk towards his bed.

"Where you goin'?"

"Get my blanket and pillow. It's cold out there."

"Next time you ask me first, you hear?"

I saw Hal's face go red. "I might."

The room was silent. Hal reached out for his pillow, but Mr. Carter took two steps and grabbed him by the shirt collar. He lifted Hal like a scarecrow and dragged him across the room. He hung there, red-faced and coughing against the shirt that pressed into his throat. In less than two seconds, the door was flung open, and he was shoved outside. Mr.

Carter walked over to the bed and grabbed the blanket and pillow. He returned to the door and threw them out into the yard, pulled the door shut, and turned to face the room. He pressed his fingers together and cracked his knuckles. "I catch any of you lettin' him back in here, you'll be spendin' the night out there, too. Now, go back to your business. Mrs. Broomstead said she'll ring the supper bell in ten minutes."

Mr. Carter walked out and I lay on my side and watched everyone. I'd never been with so many people my age. All their talking and moving around made me dizzy. I rolled over and stared at the ceiling until I heard the bell ring.

I climbed off my bed and followed the other boys through a hall and into a large room with two long tables. On the left side was the kitchen, all caged behind thick wire. Mr. Gene stood on a platform and began to say some stuff into a microphone. Halfway through his speech the boy next to me poked me in the ribs with his elbow. "It's a prayer," he said. "Look down and shut your eyes."

After the prayer, two boys I had seen earlier took bowls of food from a slot in the kitchen wire and set them on the tables. There was even more food in the boys' home than in jail. We had mashed potatoes, ham, rolls, salad, and iced tea. You ate as much as you liked. If you ran out, there was always more.

"I've never seen somebody eat so much," the boy next to me said.

I kept eating and didn't answer.

"My name's Kit Slip," he said. I turned to him and sized him up. He was even skinnier than me and so fair-skinned that he reminded me of a bull minnow. I might have thought he was sick if he hadn't been sitting up and talking to me like he was. The thing most unusual about him was that he barely had hair. What hair he did have was as white as spider-weaving and seemed that it would blow away like dandelion seeds if you got him in the wind. When I was finally able to swallow everything, I said "Moon Blake" to him.

I didn't notice when the other boys started returning their plates to the kitchen. Kit had to tap me on the shoulder.

"Come on, Moon," he said. "It's time to go."

My plate still had some mashed potatoes left. I saw the others walking past me and out of the dining hall.

"Do we have to? I've still got some left."

"Most boys go to the rec room now. We can play Ping-Pong or watch television."

I took one more quick bite, then got up and returned my plate, too. I followed Kit to the rec room. But when we passed through the door that led out of the dining hall, Mr. Carter tapped me on the arm. "Come with me, Moon. Mr. Gene wants to see you."

"What for?" I asked.

"I don't know. He's the boss. I don't ask questions."

"You scared of him?"

Mr. Carter scrunched his face. "Come on," he said.

# 12

To get to Mr. Gene's office Mr. Carter had to unlock the steel door again. After we passed through, he locked it back and motioned for me to keep moving. I followed behind and tried to match my steps with his until he stopped and turned and stared at me. "Don't you be makin' trouble," he said.

"I'll bet you can run fast," I replied.

"You bet I can."

We started walking again, and he went slower and I got up beside him. "Why'd you send Hal outside?"

" 'Cause he's mean to you and everybody else."

"What's wrong with him?"

"Got a bad attitude. He's been like that ever since he got here."

"Why don't you send me outside? I'll stay under a tree and everybody else can stay in here."

"Gonna be chilly tonight."

"Cold doesn't bother me. All you need's a blanket and fire."

"Ain't gonna be no fires around here. No matches allowed."

"I don't need matches. I can rub sticks and make fire."

Mr. Carter didn't answer, but started shaking his head. Soon we came to a door and Mr. Carter knocked on it.

Mr. Gene's office had thick carpet and a big desk with two chairs in front of it. He was pouring himself a glass of water when we walked in. His face was drawn like he worried a lot and didn't get much sleep.

"Thank you, Mr. Carter," he said. "Moon, why don't you take a seat in one of those chairs."

I sat down. Mr. Gene went around the other side of the desk and got in his chair and placed his drink down in front of him. I turned to see if Mr. Carter was still there, but he'd already gone. Then I started to feel sick from all of the food I'd eaten. I took a deep breath and crossed my arms over my stomach.

"How was your supper?" Mr. Gene asked me.

"Good," I said. "Better than jail." I watched my stomach rise and fall because it felt bigger than usual.

"Mr. Carter says Sanders roughed you up."

I shrugged.

"You know, we've had trouble with him before."

"I'm okay."

He studied me for a moment, then took a sip of his water. "Very well. Are you still planning on busting out of here?"

"Yessir."

"Don't you think you'd rather be inside and warm than out in the cold alone with people like Sanders?"

"I'd rather be on my way to Alaska."

"Ah yes, Alaska. Mr. Wellington told me about your Alaska plans."

"There's people like me up there."

"Yes?"

"That's why I'm bustin' out."

"It seems you've got your mind pretty much set on what it is you want. Since that's the case, let me tell you how it's going to be." Mr. Gene sat up in his chair and set his drink back down. His face tightened and became serious. "First of all, you're not going to bust out of here. We've never had anyone escape from Pinson. That talk is nonsense and you may as well get it out of your head. Second of all, there's a possibility that you have relatives." Mr. Gene bent over and brought Pap's box from the floor and set it on the desk.

"Where'd you get that?"

"We've got all of your things in a safe place for you."

"What about my rifle and bullets?"

"The police in Livingston have them."

"What about my wheelbarrow and my clothes?"

"I don't know anything about a wheelbarrow and clothes."

"Well, then, you don't have it all. Sanders threw my wheelbarrow in the swamp and he threw my deerskin hat in the road. They took my moccasins and my jacket at the jail. Said I wasn't gettin' my rifle back."

"We'll look into all of that. However, your friend Mr. Abroscotto—"

"He's not my friend."

"Fine. Mr. Abroscotto told me about these pictures. He—"

"That's why he's not my friend."

Mr. Gene held up his hand. "Will you let me finish?"

I didn't answer him because my stomach suddenly started hurting bad. I took a couple of deep breaths.

"Mr. Abroscotto said one of these men here looks a lot like your father. If anyone turns out to be a relative of yours, then he can claim you. If not, you'll remain the property of the state. If you behave yourself, we may eventually find a foster home for you. Otherwise, you'll remain here until you're fourteen years of age, and then you'll be moved to Hellenweiler, our facility for older teenagers. You understand all of that?"

My stomach hurt so much that I didn't care what he said. I nodded my head and took another deep breath.

"Any more incidents like the one you had with me a couple of days ago and your stay here will not be pleasant. Do you understand that?"

I nodded again.

"Good. First thing you'll need to do here at Pinson is get that mess of hair cut out of your eyes. You can do that tomorrow after breakfast. Report to the back of the kitchen and Mrs. Broomstead, the cook, will take care of it." He shoved a pile of books from the corner of his desk at me. "And these will be your schoolbooks. We have school every weekday from seven thirty until three. You'll be in trailer two with Mrs. Crutcher. Understand?"

"Yessir."

"Very well," he said. "We'll see you in the morning."

I stood up and grabbed my books.

"You know how to get to the rec room?"

I shook my head.

"After you put your books in your locker, go back out to the hall and take a left. It's the last room at the end of the hall. You'll see everybody in there."

"Yessir," I said.

"Who taught you to say 'yessir'?"

"Pap did. Taught me everything."

"That's good," Mr. Gene said. "Keep it up."

Mr. Carter was waiting outside the office. He walked back with me far enough to unlock the steel door and let me through. "Don't you cause any trouble back there," he said.

"I won't."

On the way to the bunk room I noticed that all of the windows had wire inside the glass. Every door that led out of the building had alarm signs on it. Unless there was some way to get out of the play yard, I understood why no one had ever escaped from Pinson.

I heard the sound of the other boys down in the rec room, but I felt so bad that I decided to go to my bed and lie down. When I walked into the bunk room, I heard someone tapping on the window. I turned sideways and saw Hal pointing at me. "You're dead," I heard him say. I looked away and continued to my bunk. I put my books in locker eighteen and saw a new blue jacket hanging in there. I ran my finger over it and thought about how much I missed the deerskin one that Pap made me. "Gonna get my stuff back, Pap," I mumbled. I shut the locker and climbed up to my bed and slept.

My stomach had started to feel a little better by the time the rest of the boys came back. Kit saw me on my bed and came over. "Why didn't you come to the rec room?"

"Stomach hurt," I said.

"You ate too much."

I didn't answer.

"Hal came and talked to us through the window," Kit said. "He said he's gonna tear into you as soon as he gets a chance."

"I'm not scared of him."

"You oughta be. He's the toughest one in here. He's almost fourteen. They're gonna send him to Hellenweiler in a couple of weeks. One time, he hit a guy in the gut so hard he threw up."

"Pap says I can whip anybody three times my size."

"That's a good thing."

"I know. I've been learnin' that."

Some other boys walked over and stood behind Kit. They all watched me. One tall boy with red hair and freckles said my name.

"What?" I said.

"What's it like to be famous?"

"I don't know."

"They've got you all over the TV. We watched it in the rec room. They said you beat up a constable."

"I didn't beat him up good enough. He still got me. Threw my wheelbarrow in the swamp. Threw my hat in the road. Took my rifle and all my livin' stuff."

"Do you really live in a cave?" another boy asked me.

"No, it's a shelter that's built low to the ground."

"What did you eat out there?"

"Coons and deer and stuff we grew. Things that came out of the forest."

"Did you have to go to school?"

I shook my head. "Pap got me some books. I learned with him."

"Can you read?"

"Yeah."

"Write?"

"Yeah. Morse code, too."

"They gonna take you to jail, or you stayin' here?"

"I'm gonna bust out as soon as I find a way."

"You can't bust out of here," Kit said.

"I can get out of most anything. Pap used to trap me like I was a coon and snare me twenty feet up in a magnolia tree. I'd be up the rope and down the tree before he could go touch the shelter and get back."

"Must have been fun living out there!"

"Better than being in here like a penned-up bird dog."

"Hal's gonna kill you," another boy said.

"Kit already told me about it."

Suddenly we heard Mr. Carter standing at the entrance to the bunk room and hammering on the wall with his club. "Lights out, everybody! Get in your bunks."

Some of the boys mumbled complaints as they made their way back to their beds. I looked over at the window, and Hal was still there, staring in at me. I turned my head and went to sleep.

## 13

Mr. Gene woke us by beating on the door just after daybreak. I reached to my feet and grabbed my uniform, which I'd balled up under the covers, and jumped down. Kit came over and stood in front of me.

"We've got showers now," he said.

"I already took one yesterday."

"We have to take them every morning."

"Okay," I said. "I don't mind."

I stripped down like all the other boys and followed Kit into the shower room. I waited in line until it was my turn to walk under the water. It was warm this time and I let it run over me. Kit stepped under the shower beside me and tapped me on the shoulder. He pointed to the soap. "Rub that on you," he said.

I took the soap and rubbed it on my arms and chest like Kit. Then I closed my eyes and let it rinse off.

"Hurry up!" somebody behind me said.

Kit tapped me on the shoulder again and I opened my eyes. "Come on," he said. "The breakfast bell's gonna ring soon."

We wrapped ourselves in towels and returned to our bunks. I grabbed my uniform off the floor where I'd left it.

"We've got lockers, you know," Kit said.

"I know. I put some books in there."

"You're supposed to keep your clothes in it, too."

"I don't care. I'm not gonna be here long enough to need a place to put clothes."

"Can I come with you?"

"I don't care who comes."

"Where are you going?"

"Alaska."

Kit's eyes grew wide. "Man!"

I zipped up my uniform and sat on the edge of the bottom bunk. "Gonna find more people that don't like the government."

"Are there lots of them up there?"

"That's what Pap said."

"Why do you hate the government?"

I thought for a second. "Because they never gave me anything," I said. "And they think we owe 'em somethin'."

"Sounds like it would be fun to live on your own."

"Then you should come with me."

"How are we gonna get out of here?"

"I don't know yet. Where's Mr. Carter?"

"He comes at lunch and leaves at midnight."

"Good. I think he might be able to outrun me . . . Mr. Gene here the rest of the time?"

"He lives here. His house is connected to the back of the building."

Mr. Gene walked into the room again and crossed the floor. He opened the door to the play yard and Hal came in. His clothes were dusty and his hair was cowlicked over to the side. He glared at me as he walked to his bunk.

"You're in for it now," Kit said.

Mr. Gene watched Hal. "We don't want any more trouble out of you, Hal. You hear?"

Hal didn't answer.

"Hal, don't make us punish you again!"

"I hear you," Hal said.

Mr. Gene shook his head and walked out of the room. Hal spun around and looked at me. "I'm gonna get my chance at you," he whispered.

"All right," I said.

Hal glared at me for a second longer and then headed for the showers. I stood and followed Kit to the dining hall. We sat next to each other and ate a breakfast of eggs, bacon, grits, toast, and orange juice.

"They always have food this good?"

"Most people don't think it's so good."

"I think it's the best I've ever had. Better than jail."

"Don't eat too much again."

"I'm tryin' not to, but it's hard. I've never had people cookin' me all I could eat."

Mrs. Broomstead walked up to our table and gave Kit a

small cup with a white tablet in it. Kit dumped the pill on his tongue and washed it down with water.

"What is that?"

"My medicine."

"How often do you take it?"

"Every day."

"What does it do to you?"

"It helps me stay well. I won't need it much longer." He shrugged, then asked, "What trailer are you in for class?"

"Number two."

"Me too. Are they gonna make you cut your hair?"

I nodded with my mouth full.

"How'd you cut it when you lived in the forest?"

I chewed fast and swallowed. "Pap jammed his hat down over my head and burned around the edges with a candle."

"Hurt?"

"No, but it stunk real bad."

"You didn't have scissors?"

"Yeah, we had scissors. We had most everything you'd need to cut and sew things. Sometimes he'd cut my hair with scissors when it got too thick."

"You know how to sew?"

"I can make some beaver britches that'll keep rain and stickers off. I made my own deerskin hat."

"I've always wanted a coonskin hat. Is it like that?"

"Yep. Tail and all. Soon as I get out of here, I'll get a deer and make you and me one."

Kit smiled. I could tell he was thinking about the deerskin hat. I caught myself eating too fast again and set my fork down. I heard laughing and looked up to see Hal coming into the dining hall. His hair was wet and he smiled like he didn't care that he'd gotten into trouble. He didn't look at me, but sat down with another group of boys across the room.

"What did he do to get in here?" I asked Kit.

"Most people didn't do anything. Most of us just don't have parents. I think Hal's got parents, but they won't let him stay with them."

"The government?"

"Yeah."

"How come?"

"I don't know."

"What about you?" I asked.

"I didn't ever know my parents."

"You lived here your whole life?"

"No, I've lived lots of places," he said. "I saw on the news that your daddy died. What about your momma?"

"She died when I was little. I don't hardly remember her. Sometimes yellow finches remind me of her."

Kit thought about that for a minute, then went back to his breakfast. Before long, Mr. Gene told us to go to our lockers and get our things for school. I said goodbye to Kit and headed for the kitchen. Not far from the serving slot was a door of the same thick wire that made up the rest of the kitchen wall. I walked through the door and saw Mrs. Broomstead making a list at a small table in the back of the kitchen. When she saw me, she stood and pointed in the direction I'd come from. "Nobody steps in this kitchen without me knowin' about it first," she said.

"Mr. Gene told—"

"Get back out there and wait until I call for you," she snapped.

I did what she said and returned to the dining hall. In a few minutes she appeared again and motioned for me to follow her through the kitchen. We ended up in a small room with no windows and boxes of food stacked against the wall. At the opposite end of the room was a steel door with no alarm signs. Mrs. Broomstead grabbed a metal chair and set it out for me. She motioned for me to sit, then got beside me and pulled scissors from her apron pocket.

"You're that boy that lived in the forest, aren't you?"

"Yes, ma'am."

"They say you're mean."

"I'm not mean."

"That's good. You sit still and stay that way."

"Okay."

"I ain't never seen such hair," she said.

"Me and Pap wear it long in the winter to keep warm. We wear it short in the summer so bugs don't get in it and so we keep cool."

She got behind me, and I felt her fingers moving through my hair and gathering it. "Better not be bugs in there now," she said.

"There's nothin' livin' in there."

"Hmph."

I heard the scissors snipping and felt my hair getting tugged. Mrs. Broomstead smelled like something in Mr. Abroscotto's store. I was trying to figure out what it was when the steel door opened from the outside and a man entered the room carrying a box.

"Where you want it?" he asked.

Mrs. Broomstead put the scissors back in her pocket and showed the man a place to put the box. "You do haircuts, too?" he asked her.

She frowned. "Seems like I do most everything around here. What else have you got for me?"

"Milk, eggs, flour, cheese, peanut butter. We've got some boxes of mashed potatoes we'll bring later."

Mrs. Broomstead waved her hands in the air. "Just put it wherever and I'll arrange it all later on. I've got too much to do right now."

"Yes, ma'am."

"And don't forget to pull that door shut when you leave."

The man continued to bring boxes of supplies through the door while Mrs. Broomstead finished my haircut. When she was done, she brushed her palms against her sides and told me to put my chair against the wall, get my books and jacket from my locker, and go to my classroom trailer. On the way back I rubbed my hand over my new haircut and buzzed with excitement. Short hair was fine with me. I'd just discovered a piece of my escape plan.

## 14

I was fifteen minutes late for class when I walked into the trailer. There were eight boys in the ten- and eleven-year-old group, and they laughed when I came in. I felt my new haircut and smiled back at them. Mrs. Crutcher stood at the front of the room before the chalkboard and waited for me to find a chair. She was young and pretty, with her hair pulled into a ponytail.

"Everyone get quiet," she said. "This is our new student, Moon Blake."

"They all know me," I said.

"Very well, Moon. I'm Mrs. Crutcher. Why don't you go ahead and sit down and tell us about yourself."

I sat in the chair and put my books on top of the desk. Everyone was staring at me, and I felt jittery. "What do you wanna know?"

"Where are you from?"

Everyone started to laugh again until Mrs. Crutcher held up her hand for them to be quiet. "The forest," I said.

She got a surprised look on her face. "The forest?"

"Yes, ma'am."

"Let's don't be silly, Moon."

"He is from the forest," Kit said. "He's the one on TV."

Mrs. Crutcher put her hands on her hips and narrowed her eyes at me. "They sure did clean you up," she said.

"Took three showers. Got my hair cut by Mrs. Broomstead."

Mrs. Crutcher walked to my desk and looked down at my schoolbooks. "When was the last time you attended school?" she asked suspiciously.

"This is my first time."

The other kids began laughing again as Mrs. Crutcher's eyes grew wide. She turned in a circle with her finger to her lips and they grew quiet.

"Well," she continued, "we've got our work cut out for us. Do you know how to read?"

I nodded. "Read to myself and write, and I know most anything you can ask me about animals. Pap said he taught me more than I'd get at school."

"Very well, why don't you help us out by turning your reader to page sixty-seven and reading the first page to us."

"Okay," I said. I opened the book to page sixty-seven.

"Do you mind reading out loud from the front of the room?"

"I don't mind readin' from anywhere." I went to stand before the chalkboard and read about a boy and his yellow dog. I enjoyed the story and smiled as I read it. When I was done, Mrs. Crutcher nodded. "That was very nice, Moon."

"Pap said people have to know how to read and write."

"How are your arithmetic skills?"

"Not good. Pap said he didn't know a lick about math. I can add and subtract, but I don't know division or multiply tables."

"We'll have to work on that, then."

"Might not wanna waste your time on me. I'm gonna be out of here before long."

The class laughed again. "I see," Mrs. Crutcher said. I could tell she didn't believe me. "Well, for now, Mr. Moon Blake, why don't you return to your seat and try to focus on learning some things in here."

I shrugged and went back to my desk. The other students took turns standing in front of the chalkboard and reading from the story about the boy and his yellow dog. I put my chin on my desk and listened.

When reading period was over, we worked in our arithmetic books. Mrs. Crutcher told me to follow along as best

I could. She scribbled multiplication problems on the blackboard, and I thought they made no more sense than turkey scratch.

After a while, it began to rain outside. Mrs. Broomstead brought in a box of sandwiches and drinks so that we could have lunch in the classroom and didn't have to get wet and track mud in her dining hall. We sat on the floor in a circle and the boys wanted me to tell them about living in the forest. Mrs. Crutcher sat at her desk and watched us. She seemed tired, but every once in a while she smiled at me.

When Mrs. Crutcher dismissed us that afternoon, the rain had stopped and the play yard dripped under gray skies. We were the first trailer to be let out, so Kit and I stood under a tree and waited for the rest of the boys. After a minute, Kit told me he needed to use the restroom and left me alone. He wasn't gone long before the door to the twelve- and thirteen-year-old trailer opened and I saw Hal come down the steps into the yard. He saw me immediately and began walking towards me with some of the other boys following.

My eyes searched for a stick, but there were none nearby. Hal was walking faster, and he seemed to have something in mind for me. I stood up and got into my fighting stance. He never stopped walking, but stomped right up to me and swung his fist. I ducked and felt his hand lift the hair on my head. While I was crouched down, I hit him as hard as I could in the crotch. Then I covered my face with my hands and started rolling across the ground.

When I looked up, I could see the other boys standing around Hal. He was lying on his side and moaning. Kit came running and grabbed my arm to help me. I stood and brushed off my pants and pulled the pine needles from my hair.

"You better get up, Hal!" I heard somebody say. "Here comes Mr. Carter."

But he didn't get up. When Mr. Carter broke through the crowd, Hal was still moaning and holding his crotch. Mr. Carter watched him for a second and then turned to me. "What'd you do to him?"

"I knocked him in the balls about as hard as I could."

Mr. Carter shook his head. "Hal, I'd think you'd learn to leave this fellow alone by now. You lay there as long as you like. You'll be out there until tomorrow mornin'."

Hal moaned and a few of the other kids started laughing. I looked at Kit, and he was smiling at me. "How'd you do that?"

"I just hit him real good. He curled up like that all on his own."

# 15

We went to the rec room after supper, and Kit showed me how to play Ping-Pong. I wasn't very good. He said I hit the ball too hard, but I didn't care. Something inside me made me feel like things were wrong. I was worried that I hadn't escaped yet. I felt so penned up that my skin was beginning to itch.

"I can't play anymore, Kit."

"How come?"

"I don't feel good. I'm gonna go in the bunk room and lie down and look out the window."

"You want me to come with you?"

"You don't have to."

"I'm coming with you."

Kit followed me down the hall. It was dark outside, and I could hear the wind picking up in the trees. When we got to the bunk room, we heard tapping on the window. It was Hal. When he saw that it was us, he frowned and walked back out into the play yard. I looked at his bunk and noticed that his blanket and pillow were still on it. I thought of what Pap would tell me if I were out there. *Boy, you'll catch pneumonia out in this cold. Go back and get somethin' to keep you warm.*

We lay on our sides on Kit's bottom bunk, with our heads at opposite ends. I put my hand through my hair again while Kit watched me.

"I'll bet it was fun out there in the forest with your father," he said.

I nodded.

"You could do anything you wanted," he said.

"You don't need anybody tellin' you what to do," I replied. "No government. Nothin'."

"And just you and your father all the time."

"That's right."

"I wish I had a father."

I gazed out the window where Hal had been earlier. "I wish I was busted out of here," I said.

"I've never had any friends like you."

"I don't know how long I can take this place."

"You know, I wasn't one of the ones making fun of you yesterday."

I looked at Kit. "I know."

"Most everybody wants to talk to me now because they know I'm your friend. They're scared of you."

"I'm not gonna whip up on anybody as long as they don't try and make me do things I don't wanna do."

"That's good."

"You know," I said, "Pap told me I could talk to him by writin' letters and burnin' 'em. He said you can talk to dead people that way."

"You ever do it?"

"A couple of times. I wish I had some stuff to write with and a fire right now."

"They won't let us have fires here."

"I know. I could start one up quick if we could. I like Mr. Carter, though, and he told me not to."

I gazed out the window again.

"What are you looking at?" Kit asked after a while.

"Nothin'."

"What's it like in the forest right now?"

"It's windy at the tops of the pines, but not enough for it to get down to the forest floor. There's a few clouds overhead but not enough to cover up the moon. There's a slice of moon out tonight."

"What kinds of animals are out when it gets dark?"

"Not too long ago the coons came down out of the oak and hickory trees and started walkin' around findin' stuff to eat. They like bugs and frogs and bird eggs. There's deer walkin' around. Owls callin'. Turkeys sittin' up in the treetops like big black nests . . . You can smell the dirt."

"You can smell dirt?"

I nodded. "You can smell everything out there. Especially at night when the air gets still. Just about the only thing sleepin' are small birds and people. Squirrels. Most things in the forest like the nighttime."

Kit nodded. I was still staring out the window. "He's gonna be cold," I said. "He doesn't have his blanket."

"Who?"

"Hal."

"He's got his jacket on."

I didn't reply, but got up and went over and got Hal's bedding and started for the door.

"Where are you going?"

"Take him his stuff."

"No! He'll kill you! There's not anybody around to help you right now."

"I'm not scared of him."

"Don't go out there, Moon!"

"I'll be okay."

I opened the door and stepped outside. A cold wind came across the play yard into my face, and I saw Hal huddled against one of the school trailers. I walked towards him and he took his hands from his pockets and crossed his arms tightly. "What the hell you doin'?" he said.

"Tradin' with you."

"Tradin' what?"

"I'm gonna sleep out here tonight. You can pretend to be me and use my bed. This is your stuff."

"Pretend to be you?"

"Yeah. Pull my covers up over you and pretend to be asleep when Mr. Carter comes in for lights-out."

"You crazy?"

"No. I just don't feel good."

Hal took a step towards me and jammed his hands down in his pockets. "Why're you doin' this?"

"It's nothin' to me to sleep on the ground. I'd rather be outside than in there. I think it'll make me feel better."

Hal shrugged his shoulders. "If you say so. If Mr. Carter catches us, he's gonna kick my ass. Maybe yours, too."

"Scrunch up good under those covers."

"Yeah. All right."

Hal bowed his shoulders in and ran towards the door with his hands still in his pockets. I looked around the play yard until I saw a big oak tree. I walked over to it and set my bed up on the downwind side. Even covered up completely, I still heard the wind and the night rolling over me. I felt my worries ease, and I lay there in the darkness and imagined that I was someplace else.

I woke before daybreak when the first birds made scattered calls. I lay under the blanket for a few seconds remembering where I was. Eventually, it came to me, and worry flooded me again. I peered out and watched my breath stream before me in the chilled morning. The wind had settled and the ground was covered with frost. The windows of the boys' home were dark and the only sound was the humming of streetlights.

I stood and wrapped the blanket around my shoulders and studied the play yard. I looked at the tall utility fence with barbed wire on top and then inspected each of the trees. None of them were close enough to the fence to allow anyone to climb up and jump over. I knelt and dug at the bottom of the fence with my hands until my fingers scraped cement. There was no way under. I stood again and walked over to the school trailers. They were set almost ten feet away from the fence. There was no way to leap from the roof. But I had not studied them long before I knew they were the second piece of my escape plan.

I slipped into the bunk room just as people started to stir in their beds. Radiators hissed and warmed the room from each side, and everyone was wrapped tightly in their blankets. I went to my bunk and touched Hal's shoulder. He opened his eyes and looked at me.

"Better get outside," I said. "Mr. Gene's gonna be here soon."

Hal rubbed his eyes and didn't seem to hear me. Suddenly, he sat up and threw off his blanket. "Crap!" he said, and hurried outside.

During breakfast Kit told me that some of the other boys had been talking about making me president.

"President of what?"

"Of Pinson."

"What does the Pinson president do?"

"He just acts like the president."

"What do presidents act like?"

"Like the boss of everybody."

"Who's president now?"

"Hal."

"Does he know about me gettin' his job?"

"No."

I looked over at Hal. He stared at me, but it wasn't a mean stare. He watched me curiously. "He's lookin' at me right now," I said. "I think he might know somethin' about this president stuff."

"No way he knows. Everybody except you is scared of Hal."

"Well, I don't wanna be president. I'm not gonna be here long enough to be a president."

"When are you leaving?"

"Tonight."

"Tonight!"

"That's right. I'm bustin' out of here. I can't take bein' penned up much longer. I think it's makin' me sick."

"Can I still come?"

"Yeah. I don't think I can do it without you anyway."

"Me?"

"Yeah. You're the one that's gonna let us out of here."

## 16

During our lunch break, Kit followed me to the corner of the play yard where Hal stood with some other boys. I saw them stop what they were doing and watch us.

"Hey," I said.

Hal looked around at the others and then back at me.

"Come over here with me and Kit," I said. "I've got somethin' to tell you."

Hal rubbed his palms on his uniform nervously. "You know I ain't mad at you anymore?" he said.

"I know. I forgot all about that. We've got other stuff to talk about."

Hal glanced at his friends and nobody said anything. "All right," he said.

I led the two of them to a spot in the play yard where no one would hear us talking. "You wanna help us bust out of here?"

"What?"

"I'm bustin' out. I need your help."

"How in hell you gonna bust out of here?"

"Kit's gonna let us out. I've got it all figured."

Hal pointed to Kit. "He's goin'?"

"What's wrong with Kit?"

"He's got to have medicine, for one. He can't do anything without gettin' sick."

"You worry about yourself, Hal!" Kit said. "You don't know about me."

"Whatever," Hal said. "Nobody's ever gotten out of Pinson, anyway. You can't get out of here, Moon."

"I can get out of most anywhere."

Hal studied me for a second and then shrugged his shoulders. "Well, sure," he said. "If you think you can do it, I'll help you. I wanna come with you, though."

"I told Kit, I don't care who comes with me."

"What do you want me to do?"

"You're gonna drive."

"Drive?"

"Yeah. You know how to drive?"

"I used to drive my daddy's truck a little. Just around the clay pit."

"Drivin's drivin', right?"

"I guess," Hal said.

"As long as you can see over the steerin' wheel, we can figure out the rest."

"I think I can do it."

"Good, because they'll catch us for sure if we start runnin' from right outside that fence."

I could tell that Hal was getting excited. His face twitched and his hands jittered against his sides. "When do we go?" he asked.

"Tonight. After Mr. Carter leaves and Mr. Gene's asleep in his house, I'll wake you up."

I climbed out of my bunk a couple of hours after lights-out. I passed by Kit and Hal, and both their eyes were wide open and watching me. "I'll be back," I whispered. "Wait here."

I slipped out of the bunk room and down the hall into the rec room. Then I crawled under the Ping-Pong table and used a penny I'd found in the play yard to unscrew a flat metal fastener that held the two halves of the table together.

I went back out into the hall with the fastener and crouched against the wall opposite the entrance to the rec room. From there I could hear the opening and closing of the front door. I sat still until I heard Mr. Carter leave at midnight.

When I returned to the bunk room, Hal and Kit were still watching me. "He's gone," I said. "Get dressed."

The two of them got out of their beds quietly, then all three of us put on our uniforms and jackets.

"I still don't see how you're gonna do this," Hal whispered.

"Come outside," I said. "We can talk where nobody hears us."

I pushed the door to the play yard open, and we stepped out into the night. I showed them the fastener. "You see this? Hal, you lift me and Kit up on the roof of one of those school trailers. I'm gonna unscrew a piece of that sheet tin with this Ping-Pong piece for a screwdriver. I figure that roof's about twelve feet wide and that trailer's about ten feet from that fence. Once I get that piece of tin off, we can lay it from the roof of the trailer to the top of the fence. Somebody light, like Kit, can slide right down it and out of Pinson."

Hal thought about it. "What's gonna happen when he falls off the other side of that slide? He's gonna break his leg."

I looked at Kit. "Kit, you know how to make a monkey-landin'?"

Kit shook his head.

"Like this," I said. I jumped up and landed with most of my weight on my knees, bent them slowly, then rolled across the ground. "You've gotta take the fall like that. Just sink to the ground when you land and roll over."

"I don't know if I can do it."

"You can do it. After you get over there, you're gonna go

around to the supply room door next to the kitchen where you get haircuts. When I was in there, I saw that you can get in from the outside without a key. They come in there to drop off food boxes. Once you get in, though, you gotta prop the door open so it won't lock behind you. Then there's gotta be somebody to open the kitchen door from the inside. We'll be there waitin' on you."

"How you gonna get through the kitchen to that supply room door?" Hal asked. "Mrs. Broomstead locks it every night and takes the key home with her."

"I got it all figured, Hal. Don't you worry."

"You better have. You got it figured what car we're gonna drive out of here?"

"I don't know yet. Whichever one has keys in it. Y'all ready?"

"I'm ready, Moon," Kit said.

Hal frowned and shook his head. "I guess. Jesus."

Kit and I stood on Hal's shoulders to get onto the roof, where I started unscrewing a piece of sheet tin. I went slow so I wouldn't make any noise and wake Mr. Gene. We could see every window of his kitchen from where we were, and the streetlight had us lit up like we were on a stage. I told Kit to keep a lookout for anything unusual going on in Mr. Gene's house.

It seemed that I took out nearly fifty screws and passed thirty minutes before I could lift the sheet tin. When I looked down, Hal was sitting against the trailer sleeping. "Hal," I said. He jerked awake and rubbed his eyes. "Get ready. Go stand under this slide I'm about to make in case Kit falls."

"This better work. I'm tired."

"Hurry up," I said.

Hal stood and walked around the other side of the trailer near the fence. "You ready, Kit?"

"I think so."

I lifted the tin and walked to the edge of the trailer. My plan was to stand it straight up in the air and let it down slowly to the top of the fence, but when I had it up, a breeze came and blew against it. I almost slid off the roof trying to hold it.

"Kit, come help me! I'm about to fall off here!"

Kit jumped up and grabbed one side of the tin. The breeze came again and blew against it. We held on the best we could, but we weren't strong enough. The tin slipped from our fingers and slammed down against the top of the fence. A prickly feeling shot up my back as I heard the sound travel across the yard. I saw Hal dive to the ground and lie still. "Get down!" I told Kit. "Lay as flat as you can on the roof!"

Kit and I flattened ourselves against the roof and watched Mr. Gene's house. Not a second later, his kitchen light came on and his face pressed against the glass. I knew that he couldn't see the tin lying over the fence from where he was, but he could see us on the roof of the trailer if we weren't low enough.

"What are we going to do?" Kit whispered.

"Shhh! Suck in your stomach."

"Anybody comin'?" Hal asked.

"Shhh!"

We watched Mr. Gene's face. It was staring directly at us. Kit was breathing loudly, and his feet were shaking. It seemed like ten minutes passed before Mr. Gene stepped away from the window and turned off his kitchen light. We lay there quietly for several minutes until Hal called to us from below. "Anybody see you?"

"No," I said. "Mr. Gene looked out his window, but he didn't see us."

"Mr. Gene!"

"Shhh. He might not be asleep again."

"I'm gettin' out of here!"

"We need you, Hal. He'll be back in bed by now. Kit, go ahead and start out there."

Kit was still shaking from our close call. He nodded at me and began to crawl out onto the sheet tin. I knelt on the end so that it wouldn't slip. Sliding forward on his knees, Kit made his way to where the metal hung over the outside of the Pinson fence. When he stared down at the ground at the other end, he looked back at me.

"That's good," I whispered. "Now, remember what I said about the monkey-landin'?"

Kit nodded and looked back at the ground. I thought he might hesitate, but he got up to the edge and jumped off. He hit the ground almost like I showed him and rolled across the grass. I held my breath, hoping he wasn't hurt, until he stood up and brushed off his pant legs. He turned around and smiled. "Like that?"

I looked down at Hal. "I told you we'd bust out of here."

Hal smiled at me nervously. "Let's just hope you're right about the kitchen door. If you can't get it open, we ain't gonna be able to get him in here again."

I jumped down from the roof, and we ran across the play yard and slipped back into the bunk room.

"What are y'all doin'?" we heard a kid named Eddie say from his bed.

"Go to sleep, Eddie," Hal snapped.

"I've got to get somethin'," I said. "Wait here."

I hurried to the bathroom, stood on a chair, and carefully pulled a shower rod loose. After stripping it of the curtain, I tucked it under my arm and returned to Hal.

"Y'all are gonna get us in trouble," Eddie said.

"Eddie, if you don't want me to beat the crap out of you," Hal said, "then shut your little baby mouth."

We continued into the dining hall, where I stopped in front of the kitchen door. "Watch this," I said.

I took the shower rod and stuck it through the slot in the wire mesh where the dishes were returned. By working it sideways I was able to press against the deadbolt latch, and in a second the cage door popped loose and swung open.

"I ain't believin' this," Hal said. "All them nights I was hungry."

"Come on," I said.

By the time we made it to the back of the kitchen, we heard Kit tapping on the inside door of the supply room. I unlocked and opened it, and he stood there grinning. "I can't believe it," Hal said. "We're just gonna walk out of here."

I motioned through the open door with my hand. "Go find somethin' you can drive."

Hal went outside and disappeared into the parking lot around the corner. I turned to Kit. "You sure you wanna go?"

Kit nodded his head.

"Why are you so quiet?"

"I'm just a little scared is all."

"About what?"

"About getting caught," he said.

"Shoot, we'll get out again if they catch us. What about your medicine?"

"I don't need it."

"You sure?"

Kit hesitated for a second, then said, "I'm sure. I don't need it anymore."

"We won't need anything anymore, Kit. We can make everything we need."

"And we'll go to Alaska?"

"Yeah. And we'll go to Alaska, where there's all kinds of people that live in the forest and don't need the government."

Kit began to knead his hands together with excitement. "Tell me what kinds of things we'll eat, Moon."

"Anything we want. Deer, rabbit, coon, turkey, acorns, pine-needle tea, huckleberries, thistle, cattails, poke salad. There's everything you could want out there."

"That's what I want. I want to get my own food out of the forest."

"We'll hide for a while and I'll teach y'all some things about livin' out. Once everybody's stopped lookin' for us and we've got plenty of supplies, we can start for Alaska and find some more people that hate the government."

"Yeah," Kit said.

Both of us thought about all of that while we waited on Hal.

"I've gotta get a gun, too," I said. "Maybe we can find the way to my shelter and get Pap's rifle. You know anything about the roads around here?"

Kit shook his head.

"Hal prob'ly does," I said.

Suddenly, we heard something that sounded like a big truck coming around the corner. Kit and I looked at each other. "What'd he get that makes such a loud noise?" I said.

Kit's eyes grew wide. "I don't know."

Hal pulled up to the door and stopped. "Hey, Moon?" came his voice. I looked out and saw Hal standing in front of a bus.

"Why'd you get that?"

Hal shrugged. "It's the only thing that had keys in it. I found 'em under the seat."

"Mr. Gene's going to be mad now," Kit said. "He loves his school bus."

"How many does it hold?"

"It's got about twelve seats in it," Hal said. "It'll hold everybody with two people in a seat."

"All right, I'll go see who all wants to go. Whoever wants out of here might as well come on now."

"What!" Hal said. "After all this you're gonna go and get us busted?"

"I won't get us busted."

"Crap," Hal said. He shook his head and spit. "Suit yourself. I think you're crazy."

I started back towards the bunk room with Kit following me. "Moon, I don't think we should get everybody up. I think we should just go ahead and leave while we can."

"It doesn't seem fair," I said. "I'll bet everybody in here's about to go crazy thinkin' about gettin' out."

I flipped on the light to the bunk room. "Everybody stay quiet," I said. "We're bustin' out of here. Anybody that's comin', we've got a bus outside the kitchen."

# 17

All the other nineteen boys at Pinson got on the bus with their blankets and pillows.

"Should we get any of this food, Moon?"

"Naw, it'll be too much to carry and we'll already have everything we need in the forest."

Fifteen minutes after we pulled away from the boys' home, a sign said we were driving south on Highway 69. Hal sat straight in the driver's seat and squeezed the steering wheel. I stood beside him, looking out the windshield and hoping that I'd see Mr. Abroscotto's store. I didn't know the name of the highway that went from Tuscaloosa to Gainesville, and neither did Hal. All I knew was that it was somewhere between us and Livingston. I figured the police would find us if we tried to stay near the shelter, but I wanted to get Pap's rifle and the rest of the bullets before we found a place to live.

Kit sat behind me, while the other boys jumped on the seats and yelled and fought with their pillows.

"Where we goin'?" Eddie yelled.

"Forest," I said.

"What're we gonna do?"

"We're gonna go live out there. Catch our own food and stay away from the government."

Everyone cheered and I smiled back at them. "We're gonna make our own clothes out of animal skins and swing on vine swings."

Some of the younger boys began to bounce on the bus seats again. "We're not ever gonna go to school, and we can stay up as late as we want. We're gonna shoot guns and make traps and swim in creeks and catch animals for pets. I know how to do it all."

"Can we throw away our uniforms?"

"You don't have to wear anything. Everybody can be naked if they want."

"We'll make Moon president!" somebody yelled.

I held my hands up in the air. "And . . . and we'll whip up on anybody that tries to catch us and tell us what to do."

All of the boys cheered and shook the seats. I was so excited that my hands trembled. Kit was standing on the seat and yelling and jumping along with everyone else. Hal was still quiet with his eyes locked on the road. "You doin' okay, Hal?"

Hal nodded. "Yeah, but I ain't seen no signs for Gainesville. We're about to come to some place called Moundville."

"I don't wanna be president," I said. "You're still president."

Hal didn't answer me. He was concentrating too hard on the highway to care about what I said.

"Can't you get them to shut the hell up and stop rockin' the bus?" Hal said.

"They're goin' crazy back there."

"Jesus," Hal said. "Johnny, get 'em to shut up!" he yelled back to one of the older boys.

"What's after Moundville?" I asked him.

"I saw a sign that said Talladega National Forest. I think it's next."

"Let's just go there, then. That sounds like a good place."

"What about the rifle?"

"We can make it without a gun for a while. I can rig just about any kind of trap there is. Weapons, too."

Hal nodded. "Whatever. You better know what you're talkin' about. I'm sure as hell gonna be pissed about starvin' out in the forest with a bunch of crybabies."

The headlights of an approaching car came into view, and Hal straightened and gripped the wheel tightly. The car whooshed by and Hal sank back into the seat.

I reached into my pocket and pulled out the fastener I'd taken from the Ping-Pong table. "Open that door, Hal. I'm gonna make a knife for us."

Hal looked over at me and quickly back at the road ahead. "What you doin' now?"

"I can sharpen it on the road."

Hal shrugged and pulled on the handle that opened the folding doors. "If you fall out it's not my fault," he said.

I went down the steps and lay on the landing where the road rushed by my face. I looked up and saw Kit watching me nervously. "Gonna need a knife, Kit," I reassured him.

"Might have been easier takin' one from the kitchen," Hal said.

"We can make this work."

"His butt's gonna fall out, Kit."

"No it's not," Kit said.

I took the piece of metal and held it to the road. Orange sparks flew as I sharpened the edges and tip. In about five minutes I had a knife that would do to skin an animal. I came back up the steps with my new knife and showed it to Kit. "Here," I said. "You hold on to this. We'll need it later."

Kit took the knife like he'd never held one before. He felt the newly sharpened edges and studied it. I turned back to watch the road with Hal.

After an hour passed, the bus grew quiet. Some of the boys had gone to sleep in their seats and others had spread their blanket and pillows on the floor and slept there. I helped Hal watch for signs that told us where Talladega National Forest was. Sometimes I'd look over at Kit, and he'd straighten up and smile at me like he wasn't tired.

Eventually we passed a sign that told us we were entering the National Forest area.

"Where you wanna go from here?" Hal asked.

"Any road that goes into the forest is fine with me," I said.

Before long we came to a sign for Payne Lake that pointed up a paved road to our left. Hal glanced at me and I told him to take it. I turned around to announce that we were almost there, but everyone was still asleep. I looked down at Kit, and he was rubbing his eyes. "Don't go to sleep, Kit."

He sat up in his seat and looked out the window.

"Headed to a lake," I said. "Gonna set out from there."

Kit nodded, covered his mouth, and yawned.

We drove about a quarter of a mile until we came to a chain across the road. Hanging from the chain was a sign that said THIS ROAD CLOSED AFTER DARK.

Hal stopped the bus. "What now?"

"We'll have to walk the rest of the way."

"I'm tired," Hal said.

"You can't be tired! We've got food to trap and a shelter to build. We haven't even found a good place to live yet." I turned to Kit. "You're not tired, are you, Kit?" Kit shook his head. "Kit's not tired." I faced the back of the bus. "Hey, everybody!" I yelled. "We're here. It's all the forest you can get everywhere around us. Come on!"

Some of the boys moved about on the floor and sat up in their seats. One of the eight-year-olds began to cry. "I'm cold," he whimpered.

"I wanna go back," another boy said. "I don't wanna bust out anymore."

"Yeah, Hal," one of the older boys said. "Mr. Carter's gonna be all over us for this."

"But we can live in the forest without the government and get our own food and build our own shelter with nobody to tell us what to do!" I said.

Another boy began to cry, and someone from the back said he was scared. I held up my hands. "I thought everybody wanted to go."

"Johnny's right," another one of the older boys said. "We'll get in too much trouble."

"I'll whip up on anybody that tries to catch us."

"Let 'em stay if they want," Hal said. "I don't wanna listen to 'em."

I looked at Hal and then back at the others. "All right, anybody that wants to go back can stay here on the bus. The law'll prob'ly come for you when it gets daylight in a couple of hours. Anybody that wants to go with me and Kit and Hal can come. But you can't cry. Hal doesn't like crybabies. We've gotta get goin' because we don't have much time." I grabbed my blanket, opened the door to the bus, and walked onto the road. When I turned around, Hal and Kit had their blankets and pillows and were following behind me.

"Better leave those pillows," I said. "Just gonna get hung up on briars."

"What are we gonna use?"

"We can use our jackets or marsh grass."

Hal frowned doubtfully and threw his pillow back into the bus. Kit put his back, too.

"Let's go," I said.

"You sure we're gonna find some food before long?" Hal asked.

I nodded. "We've got some hikin' to do first, but I'll find somethin' for us right after daylight." I turned to Kit. "You okay?"

Kit nodded.

"I don't know what's wrong with everybody," I said. "I thought they were ready to go with us."

"I sure don't have anything to lose," Hal said. "They're gonna send me to Hellenweiler soon anyway."

"Hellenweiler's not good," Kit said. "They tell stories about that place."

"Well, y'all don't have to worry about Hellenweiler or Pinson or any of those places anymore. Come on."

## 18

The waking birds told me that daylight was less than an hour away. Hal and Kit fell behind as I made my way up a small hill that was matted in pine needles. The smell of sap and rotten logs came to my nose like warm soup in the chilly air, and I wanted to lie down and sleep and breathe it. But I knew that getting some distance between us and the bus was the most important thing. Afterwards, I would figure out how to get food.

At the top of the hill I came to a rusted fire tower. I waited until Hal and Kit came tromping up the hill, and then I told them my plan.

"Hal, you think you can get up that tower?"

Hal sat down and shrugged his shoulders.

"Then you climb it while Kit and I go find some food. You can keep watch. I'll bet you can see the bus from up there. But we won't be able to stay here for long because we've still gotta make some more distance."

Hal yawned. "Let's get some sleep first."

"We can't sleep yet. We'll have plenty of time to sleep later. The law's gonna be after us soon and we've gotta keep goin'."

Hal stood up slowly. "All right," he said. He turned and stared up at the tower. "You crazy?"

"You can do it."

Hal moaned and spit.

"We'll be back after a while," I said.

Kit and I continued down the other side of the hill, and we heard Hal panging around on the fire tower behind us. We hadn't gone far when the forest opened up into a hardwood bottom. A short distance beyond that we found a patch of foggy swamp with cattails. I took the knife from Kit, stripped to my underwear, and waded into the icy water. Kit watched me while I cut and gathered cattail roots.

After about thirty minutes I had enough for breakfast. The sun was just showing through the trees, and I zipped back into my uniform and we set out for the fire tower again. When we stood beneath it, I yelled up at Hal. "What do you see up there, Hal?"

There was no answer. "Hal!" After a second, I saw his face peer down at me. "Can you see the bus? What's everybody doin'?" I asked him.

Hal rubbed his eyes and looked out towards the bus and then back at me. "Just sittin' around."

I started up the tower ladder. As I moved upwards, the forest spread out below me with patches of chilled fog still caught between the small hills. The sun felt good on my back and the fresh air slipped through my teeth.

In a few minutes, I crawled into the tower box with Hal. I could see some of the boys playing in the road and others lying in the grass at the edge of the ditch. "Have you seen the law yet?"

Hal shook his head.

"You've been nappin', haven't you?"

"Maybe. What the hell?"

"That's all right. We got some food."

Hal's eyes grew wide. "What you got?"

"Cattails."

"What's that?"

"Come on down and try some. You'll like 'em. Taste like potatoes."

The three of us sat around the base of the tower and ate the cattail roots as the sun burned off the fog. Hal and Kit agreed the plant tasted better than they thought it would, although not as good as a Pinson breakfast.

"But there's no school today," I reminded them. "I figure we'll stay and watch that bus for a while. You two can nap while I go back up and keep a lookout. Once I see the law, we can get movin' again. That way, you two'll be rested and can keep up with me."

"What're we gonna eat for lunch?" Hal asked me.

"We'll take some of these roots with us, and I reckon I can find some yucca plants on the high ground. Maybe some thistle and acorns."

"What about meat?" Hal asked.

"We don't have time for meat yet. Once we make camp, we can get some meat. It's gonna be tough goin' on you two for a while."

Hal sat up. "I'm okay," he said. "Long as you can get us somethin' to eat."

"Yeah," Kit said. "We're fine."

"All right, then. Y'all take a nap and I'll keep an eye out for the law."

# 19

I sat in the fire tower and watched the jays complain and dart about the treetops below. I was eye level with two buzzards that glided by occasionally and got so close I could make out their wrinkled faces. From where the bus was, I followed the blacktop road with my eyes, back the way we had come until it joined the main highway.

I reasoned by looking at the sun that it was close to eight o'clock when I saw the green truck turn off the highway and head towards the bus. I watched it move slowly around the curves like whoever was in it was taking his time and looking out into the forest. When it came around the last bend and the bus was about fifty yards in front of it, the truck stopped. The boys lying in the grass stood up and watched it. Some of the others who had been playing in the road began to walk towards it. After a moment, the truck moved again until it was next to the bus. I waited until I saw a man in a brown uniform step out and begin to talk with them before I started down the tower.

On the ground, I shook Hal and Kit awake. "We'd best get goin'. The law's gotten here."

"Let's sleep a little longer," Hal said.

"You can't, they're gonna come lookin' for us and we've gotta get far away from here. You ready, Kit?"

Kit nodded. "I'm ready."

We went down the other side of the hill and circled

around the bottom where Kit and I had gathered the cattail roots earlier. The walking was easy as we strolled beneath giant pine trees that cast so much shade the forest floor lay free of brush. The skies were blue and the day was growing warmer.

After a while, the trees thinned and we came to a thicket. Our blankets were caught and pulled by the briars. I showed them how to stuff them inside their Pinson jackets so that we looked like three fat boys.

We fought and picked through the briar thicket until we came to a clear gravel-bottom creek. We found a tree that lay all the way over the water, and I began to walk across it.

"Do we still have to be fat?" Kit called to me.

I shook my head. "Just fat in the stickers."

"Good," Hal said. "We're hot."

"Take off your jackets and tie 'em around your waist. You'll have to carry those blankets again."

We all took off our jackets and tied them. I draped my blanket around my neck and they did the same. Then I held my arms out to keep my balance and moved slowly across the log to the other side. When we were all across, we got on our stomachs and drank from the clear water. Afterwards, we lay back against a giant live oak to rest for a few minutes. I looked at my bright orange uniform and then at their white ones. "We've got to make some new clothes. We stand out like deer tails in these things."

"Out of animal skins, right?" Kit said.

"That's right."

"That's when I get my hat?" Kit asked.

"Yep," I said.

"How much farther?" Hal asked.

I was about to tell Hal I didn't know, when I thought I heard something. I told them to get quiet while I stood up and turned my ear back down our trail. I held my breath and listened. After a second, I heard it again. "Dogs are after us already," I said.

Kit's eyes grew wide. Both of them jumped up from where they were sitting. "Dogs!" Kit said.

I was still listening. I nodded. "Just one, but he's comin' fast up our trail. He's still a mile or so back."

"What the hell we gonna do about that?" Hal said.

"I don't know yet."

Hal started to say something but didn't. A worried look spread across Kit's face. "What's it going to do when it gets to us, Moon?"

"You two don't worry about it. Gimme that knife, Kit. If its tail's not waggin', then I'll fight it."

"That's crap," Hal said. "You can't fight a dog off with a knife. Especially that one."

"We'll see," I replied.

"Perfect," Hal mumbled.

Kit gave me the knife and I started walking ahead. After a few seconds they ran to catch up with me. Pap had always told me that if you get in a fight with an animal, you have to get meaner than you ever thought you could. He said that if you have a knife, it's like a big tooth, and if your tooth is bigger than the animal's, you might have a chance. But I knew that chance was slim and I was scared.

For the next thirty minutes, we sloshed our way through a cane thicket where water came up over our ankles. All the while, the barking of the dog grew closer.

"This water will wash away our scent, won't it?" Kit asked me.

I shook my head. "It's still all over this cane we're brushin' against."

Kit moaned.

We broke out of the cane thicket and started up a long hill. When we topped the hill, we faced a steep ravine that was covered in kudzu. I looked back at my friends and they stared down the trail in the direction of the barking.

"We might as well wait here," I said. "We'll be tangled up down there by the time that dog reaches us."

"I'm gettin' up a tree," Hal said. "Gonna watch your butts get chewed up."

He dropped his blanket and walked over to a black oak that grew over the ravine. In a few seconds, he was climbing up the branches. Kit looked at me like I should tell him what to do. I swallowed nervously and nodded at him. "Go ahead and find one, too, Kit."

"Are you going to fight him?"

"I guess so."

"Have you ever fought a dog?"

"No, but I don't aim for us to be sent back to Pinson."

The barking grew louder. I imagined the dog loping through the thicket and our scent from the cane stems flowing into its nose. I told Kit to get going, and he dropped his things and began to climb the black oak after Hal. I pulled out the knife and turned and faced the trail. I got into my fighting stance and concentrated on where I thought the dog would leap out.

## 20

The bloodhound burst from the cane thicket and leaped into my chest before I had time to study his tail. I landed on my back with him on top of me. My arms were tangled somewhere beneath me and my legs were pinned down by the dog's weight. Kit and Hal yelled at me from up in the tree. All I thought about was what it would feel like when the bloodhound took his first bite of me.

I squeezed my eyes shut and waited, but the bite never came. The bloodhound licked me until I brought my hands up to shield my face. The tongue slapped me with slobber on my cheeks and forehead and I turned over on my stomach. "Stop!" I yelled at the ground, but I felt my hair getting wet and cowlicked. Eventually, I managed to draw my knees up and stand. The bloodhound looked at me like I should tell him what to do. When I began to wipe my face with the sleeve of the uniform, he put his nose into the air and woofed.

"He's nice," Kit yelled from the tree.

I studied the dog's tail as it whipped left and right. I breathed deeply and lowered the knife. "Yeah. Come on down."

In a moment, they were with me on the ground and Kit

began to pet the bloodhound on the back. I finished wiping my face and leaned over to read the dog's tag.

*Snapper*
*Davy Sanders*
*34 Big Pine Road*
*Gainesville, Alabama*

"It's Sanders's dog," I said. "Named Snapper."

"Who's Sanders?" Hal asked.

"He's the law. He's the constable that made me go to Pinson. I figure he's about hornet-mad I busted out of there."

"He doesn't train much of a dog," Hal said.

"I imagine this dog's about as happy to get away from Sanders as everybody else is."

Hal shook his head. "I think you're crazy, Moon."

"You haven't seen crazy until you've seen Sanders."

Kit hugged Snapper around the neck. The dog was so large that he didn't have to bend over far to do this. "Let's bring him with us."

"I don't care who comes," I said. "Dogs or people."

"I think it's almost lunch," Hal said.

"We've gotta make some more time. As soon as Sanders figures out we have his dog, he's gonna think of somethin' else. He's prob'ly been followin' Snapper and he's not too far away." I looked at Kit and he nodded at me.

"All right," Hal said, sighing. "Let's go."

We fought our way down the side of the ravine until we were at the bottom, where a creek ran through white sand.

Snapper came after us, drooling lines of foamy spit from his mouth and slapping us with his tongue when we weren't paying attention. He seemed to prefer Hal, who wanted to have the least to do with him.

"Stop it, Snapper," Hal kept repeating. I'd look over and Hal would be sidestepping away from the dog and the long lines of slobber that hung from its jowls.

"I hate this dog!" he said.

The sun was almost over our heads and the day had turned warm. High above us, the wind brushed the treetops, but the forest was still and quiet in the ravine. We trudged through the white sand, which squeaked under our shoes, and didn't say much to each other.

After we'd been walking awhile, I felt myself getting hungry, and I started making plans to get food for all of us. I hadn't been thinking long when we came up on a hickory tree that had covered the bottom of the ravine with its nuts. As soon as I explained to Hal and Kit what we'd found, we sat in the sand and began breaking the nuts open between rocks. We filled up on them and leftover cattail roots and afterwards even Hal agreed that he was feeling a little better. We eventually leaned back against the wall of kudzu, feeling full and listening to the rustle of hickory leaves.

"Well, that's nothin'," I said. "We're gonna have fresh deer meat soon."

Kit bent over and drank from the creek. He looked up at me after he took a swallow. "We can drink from here, right?"

"Wherever the water's runnin'," I said.

"Just not where it's sitting still?"

"That's right."

Kit smiled and seemed proud of himself. I lay back on the sand and put a magnolia leaf over my eyes.

"You nappin'?" Hal asked.

I nodded. "I figure we've got time to rest a little more. Sanders can't track us easy without his dog. Not this far. He prob'ly already turned back."

"Good. It's about time you slowed down."

Hal and Snapper and Kit lay on the sand next to me, and Snapper put his head across Hal's chest. "Stupid dog," Hal said. But he didn't make him move.

The creek trickling past and the breeze swishing the treetops far overhead and our full stomachs helped us drift off to sleep. When I woke, I could feel that the wind had shifted and the air had a touch of dampness to it. I pulled the leaf from over my eyes and wondered what it was that woke me. Then I heard a gunshot in the direction we'd come from, followed by a faint yell. "Snapper! C'mere, you sorry sumbitch!"

Snapper had his head up, looking in the direction of the yell. I could tell by the sound that the gunshot had been aimed into the air.

Kit and Hal woke after the second shot and sat up and looked at me.

"He ain't turned back yet!" Hal said.

"I guess we'd better get on," I said. "He sounds mad."

I had just gotten the words out when Sanders yelled again. "I know you're out there, boys! You're mine, you militia bastard. You hear me! I got another dog back at the house."

"Great," Hal said.

"I'm gonna whip him good," I said.

"No you're not," Hal snapped. "We're gonna get out of here."

"I think maybe you shouldn't try to whip him, Moon," Kit said.

"All right," I said. "Come on."

We gathered our blankets and hurried down the ravine. Snapper trotted beside Hal and kept getting in his way. Hal continually tripped over him and told him to move, but Snapper walked against his leg.

"I think that hound likes you, Hal."

Hal gave me a sour look and spit. "Well, there's some crazy fellow back there shootin' at us that don't."

## 21

Late in the afternoon the air became chilly again and we put our jackets on. I could tell that Hal and Kit were getting tired of walking, so I slowed and did a better job of clearing a trail for them.

They seemed to find new energy when we came to a creek that poured over a small waterfall into a pond. They followed me to the bottom of the waterfall and walked around the edge of the pond.

"You two can rest now, if you want. Sanders won't come back today."

Hal looked at me like he was about to say something, but didn't. Kit and Hal spread their blankets in the grass and lay down to rest. After taking a long drink, Snapper plopped down beside Hal and shut his eyes. I looked at the sun and judged there to be a little more than two hours before it would get too dark to see. The forest grew quiet as it usually does late in the day, and a few clouds moved over us and cast shadows on the trees.

The sides of the ravine sloped up to small embankments that edged a hardwood bottom. I took the knife and went in search of a hickory tree. I didn't have to travel far before I found hickory nuts on the ground and looked up into the trees until I saw hickory leaves. Wrapping my legs and arms around the tree, I ratcheted myself up until I could grab the lowest limb. I swung myself into the tree and balanced with one arm against the trunk. I cut a straight branch that was about as big around as my wrist and dropped it to the ground.

Back at the pond, I shaved the smaller growth from the hickory branch until I had a pole about six feet long. As I was whittling a barbed point on the end, Kit woke and watched me.

"Go find a piece of dry, dead wood, Kit."

Kit nodded and stood up. He began walking and then turned back. "How will I know the right kind?"

"Find a piece on the ground that's about as big around as your leg and two feet long. If you can break it against the tree, it's dead. Be quick. It's gonna get dark soon."

Kit nodded and hurried away. I set the hickory pole down and grabbed one of the small branches I'd shaved from it. Using a shoelace, I made a tiny bow. By the time I finished, Kit had returned with the dead wood.

"What are you making?"

"Fish spear."

Kit sat across from me and watched as I took another of the small branches and shaved a straight stick as long as my arm and as big around as my thumb. Wrapping the bowstring around my small stick, I made a drill to use against the dead wood Kit found. After I drilled a small dish into the wood, I told Kit to go pull some bark from a dead cedar tree I had seen up the hill. He stood once more and took a few steps in the direction I pointed. He turned and looked back at me.

"It's a furry-lookin' tree," I said.

"How can you not even know what a cedar tree looks like?" Hal said, disgusted. Kit and I watched him stand from where he'd been sleeping. "Come on," he said, sighing, "I'll show it to you."

I used the cedar bark they brought me to kindle the fire from the heat made at the tip of the bow drill. Kit and Hal watched quietly while I hardened the pointed tip of the spear in the flame.

"What about the smoke?" Kit asked. "Won't someone see it?"

"Look up there," I said, pointing at a place several feet over the fire where the smoke dissolved. "You don't get much smoke with dry wood."

Kit looked at Hal. "Bet you didn't know that."

Hal squinted his eyes at Kit. "You better watch your mouth," he said.

We both knew he didn't mean it, and smiled.

We rolled up our pants legs and thrashed through the shallow pond until all of the fish were corralled at one end. I speared six bass that together were enough to feed the three of us and have some left over for later. As I tried for the last fish, Hal tripped over something in the muddied water and fell. He went completely under and exploded back up yelling. He thought he'd been tripped, and I saw Kit's eyes grow wide when Hal charged towards him.

"No, Hal!" Kit yelled.

I hurried out of the way as both of them crashed beneath the surface. Snapper got excited, sprung to his feet, and launched himself into the water with them. Before long, the two of them stood and fell, tripped and laughed their way to the bank with Snapper leaping up at their faces.

As the forest grew dark the four of us watched the fish cooking on a spit I rigged from more of the green hickory branches. A breeze slipped through the trees at the top of the ravine. Kit and Hal sat wrapped in their blankets and stared at the food, their uniforms and jackets draped over a rack I made near the fire to dry them out. Snapper lay between them with his chin on the ground and jowls flayed out. He moved only his eyeballs to watch my hands tend the fish.

"How did fish that big get in that pond?" Kit asked.

"They swam, stupid," grumbled Hal.

"Come in when it floods," I said.

"Shut up, Hal."

Hal raised his hand from beneath the blanket and held it above Kit's head like he was going to hit him. But he didn't, and put his hand back down. Kit looked at me and his eyes burned with mischief.

"You like this, Kit?"

He nodded.

"How about you, Hal?"

Hal shrugged. "Better than goin' to Hellenweiler."

When the fish were done, I stabbed three fillets with sticks and gave one to each of them. The other fillets I wrapped in one of my socks for later.

Kit and Hal ate quickly. I could tell they were hungry and that the fish tasted good to them.

"Tomorrow we can boil water and make pine-needle or sassafras tea."

"Is it good?" Kit asked.

I nodded. "Real good. We can get some mint weed and make it taste even better."

We lay on our sides and watched the fire dying. A bobcat screamed in the distance. Snapper's ears twitched and a low moan came from his throat.

"What in hell . . ." Hal said.

"Bobcat," I replied. "Pap said it sounds like a screamin' woman."

Hal and Kit looked behind themselves into the shadows. "Hope you can whip that thing," Hal said.

"Won't mess with you," I said. "Nothin' out here will mess with you if you don't mess with it."

"How long until we go to Alaska?" Kit asked.

I shrugged my shoulders. "I guess we'll go when y'all learn about livin' in the forest."

"Alaska's a long way," Hal said.

"Yeah," Kit replied, "but there's more people like Moon up there. It's a place where they won't chase him. Isn't that right, Moon?"

"What Pap says."

"What you think they're gonna do to us if they catch us, Moon?" Hal asked.

"They're not gonna catch us."

"That Sanders fellow seems pretty mad at you. I ain't never seen somebody act like that over a couple of people runnin' away."

"He might be mad about me whippin' up on him."

"Well, he's plenty pissed for some reason."

"Anybody that doesn't know you can't just set a bloodhound loose to run after his nose can't be too smart."

"Why's that?"

"Bloodhounds aren't mean by nature like some other dogs. You've got to keep 'em on a leash and let 'em take you to whatever they're trackin', or else they run off."

"How you know about bloodhounds?"

"I know about all kinds of animals. I've got animal books back in the shelter. I've got tree books and plant books and trap books. Pap's got about a hundred wrapped in a garbage bag under the spice shelf."

"My daddy never did learn to read good," Hal said. "He was so drunk most of the time, he could barely see."

"Is that why they sent you to Pinson?" Kit asked.

Hal shook his head. "Naw, I lived with my momma. She ran off and took me with her when I was eleven. We lived in a place called Elrod for a while. I got in a lot of trouble, stealin' and stuff, so they took me away from her. Said she couldn't control me, but I never did like livin' with her. I didn't want anything else but to be back with Daddy."

"I thought you said he was drunk all the time?" Kit said.

"It didn't matter none to me. He was still the best daddy

you could have. We lived outside a little town called Union, and we'd hunt and fish and work on the truck together. Just hang around the clay pit. It wasn't his clay pit, but he looked after it for the owner and took the money from people comin' in to get truckloads of dirt. We had a trailer parked up on the edge of it, and when it rained for a couple of days, that pit got a little water in the bottom. Come dark, Daddy'd take me outside to where we had some chairs set up. He'd tell me how lucky we were to have waterfront property. It looked like a lake in the moonlight. After a while, he'd finish whatever he was drinkin' and throw it out there in the lake. It'd stab into the mud and seem like it was floatin'."

"Y'all sit out there and watch those bottles?"

"We'd watch for a while. Wouldn't be long before Daddy'd get to shootin'. He likes to shoot bottles. Sometimes we'd line a bunch of 'em on the edge of the pit and blow 'em to pieces."

"I'd like that," I said. "Shootin' bottles."

Hal stared into the fire. "He said I was his best friend. He cried when I left with Momma. I didn't like seein' him cry."

"My pap was my best friend, too," I said. "I cried when I knew he was dyin'."

We were all quiet for a few minutes. An owl called from down the ravine. "I just remember the hospitals I was in," Kit said into the fire. "I got to be friends with a couple of the nurses and doctors, but I'd always have to move on to another hospital or boys' home." Kit looked up at me. "I've been in a lot of places besides Pinson. I used to live at the Crichton Children's Hospital in Delaware until they found I had an aunt in Alabama. They sent me down here to live with her, but by the time the paperwork was done and I was on the bus, she was dead."

"She died while you were on the bus?" Hal said.

Kit nodded. "That's right. I got to Birmingham and stayed at the hospital there while they decided what to do with me. I got sick again and ended up staying for a year. They stuck me in the back with needles and gave me medicine that made my hair fall out. They said I almost died. When the doctors decided I was better, they sent me to the George Jenkins Boys' Home in Montgomery. It was the worst place I've ever stayed, but anything was better than the shots at the hospital. George Jenkins didn't have air-conditioning, and it was stuffed full of boys in a bunk room without windows. You could hear people breathing at night like they had honey in their throats and were about to choke. When you'd wake up in the mornings, sweat soaked your bed. After six months I got sick again and they sent me back to Birmingham. I stayed in the hospital another year before I was better and they sent me to Pinson."

"He's what they call 'property of the state,'" Hal said.

"Well, so are you," said Kit.

"Yeah, but you're the real thing."

Kit's face grew tight with frustration. "No more real than you, Hal!"

"You're not anybody's property now," I interrupted. "Neither one of you."

"That's right, Hal. I'm not anybody's property."

Hal leaned back on his elbows and spit to the side. "Whatever," he said.

Kit looked at me. "We're still going to Alaska, right? You haven't changed your mind, have you?"

"Course we're goin' to Alaska," I said. "Soon as we get you two trained and get supplies. I figure we've made close to five miles today. We'd have gone farther if there weren't so many hills. Tomorrow we'll walk some more to get far away from Sanders. We can start makin' camp tomorrow late afternoon."

"I wonder how big this forest is?" Kit said. "We haven't seen a road or heard a car since the fire tower."

"It's a national forest," Hal said. "They're about as much woods as you can find."

"Are we going to build a shelter like the one you lived in?" Kit asked.

"No, we'll do that when we get to Alaska. I've got another kind in mind for here."

Kit smiled to himself. He rolled into his blanket and stared at the sky like he was thinking of Alaska. Hal and I watched the fire for a while without speaking. I thought about what Kit had said about all of those places he'd lived and of Hal not getting to see his pap.

"Hal?" I said.

"Yeah?"

"You have any paper in your pockets?"

"What for?"

"Pap said I could write him letters and burn 'em and he'd read the smoke."

"That's the stupidest thing I ever heard of. No, I don't have any."

"You never heard of that?"

"No."

"Have you ever heard of that, Kit?"

Kit shook his head. "No, but that doesn't mean it won't work."

"You two are screwed up," Hal said. "I'm goin' to sleep."

I got up and put my blanket over the clothes so that they wouldn't collect more moisture from the air that night.

"What are you gonna sleep with?" Kit asked.

"I'll be okay with just my clothes."

Hal grunted disapprovingly.

I stretched out by the fire again and put my hands behind my head. "Hal?" I said.

"What."

"Maybe you could teach me some good cuss words sometime. I'll say 'em to Sanders."

"You ain't sayin' nothin' to Sanders while I'm around."

"I'll whip up on him, then."

"No you won't. Go to sleep."

# 22

I woke before sunup and climbed out of the ravine through thick fog. At the top of the hill, the land looked like islands of treetops between the clouds. I sat on a smooth stone and watched the sunlight slide up the trees and listened to the forest come alive. I thought about Hal and Kit still asleep. I was glad they were with me. Then I thought about Pap again. Using a piece of pine bark and a rock shard, I began to scratch a note to him. I soon discovered that it would take me all day to tell him everything that I wanted to say, so I settled for only a few words.

*Pap, I love you.*

From somewhere below I heard a dog barking, and it wasn't Snapper. It was too far away. It was another dog coming down the ravine. I shoved the pine bark into my pocket and began to run back down the hill to the pond. When I dropped into the fog again, the sound of the dog was faint and dulled.

Snapper rose as I stumbled into camp. He took Hal's blanket on his back with him, and Hal sat up suddenly. "Hey!" he said to the dog and then crossed his arms over his chest. "Damn, it's cold."

"Shhh!" I said. "Get up, Kit!"

Hal and Kit took their clothes from under the blanket on the drying rack and began to put them on.

"They're still wet!" Hal said.

"They'll dry out the rest of the way when you get to walkin'," I said. "Now, listen."

"What is it?" Kit asked.

"Sanders is back with another dog," I said quietly.

Hal snatched his blanket from Snapper's back. "Gimme that!" he said.

"There's a dog coming, Hal," Kit said.

Hal scratched his head. He threw the blanket to the ground, frustrated. "I heard. He'll just have to eat me, 'cause I can't run. I haven't had any decent sleep in two days. I'm half frozen. I got a crick in my neck. I smell like a bloodhound that's got ticks and mud and spit all over him . . . I just can't run. I can't climb a tree."

"Get quiet!" I said. I heard the dog's bark through the fog again. I went and stood beside Snapper and watched him while I listened. He whined and looked at me. "It's comin' too fast for it to be on a leash. I think Sanders got up early and turned another one loose on us."

"Maybe it's one of those that's naturally mean," Kit said.

I shook my head. "It's a bloodhound. Sounds just like Snapper."

We set out that morning with another dog added to our company:

*Sawbone*
*Davy Sanders*
*34 Big Pine Road*
*Gainesville, Alabama*

"What're we gonna do with all these damn dogs?" Hal asked me.

I shrugged my shoulders. "We don't have to do anything with 'em. They'll do what they wanna do on their own."

"How we gonna feed 'em if they keep followin' us?"

"Dogs are better at gettin' food than people are. They'll be all right."

We climbed from the ravine and started up out of the bottom. Along the way I showed Hal and Kit the difference between a red oak tree and a white oak tree, and we collected acorns until our pockets were bulging.

When we came to the top of the hill, we sat down to rest. The fog had evaporated out of the valleys and we saw the countryside rolling away to the south. Patches of green showed the pines and darker gray patches showed the hardwoods. The sky was clear and the forest flicked with life. A broadwing hawk sailed between the hills at eye level. I lay back in the leaves and the others did the same.

"I'd like to see this when the dogwoods bloom," I said.

"You got anything to drink?" Hal asked me.

"There's gonna be water at the bottom of this hill. There's water at the bottom of every hill."

"What about the dogwoods?" Kit asked.

"They're the prettiest trees out here. It's like white cotton in the air. Plays tricks on your eyes."

"Can you eat it?" Hal asked.

"No. But you can eat sparkleberries and you can eat honeysuckle. They'll be out at the same time in most of the same places as dogwoods. A little later we'll get blackberries and mulberries and all kinds of stuff."

Suddenly, Hal hollered and rolled over. I sat up quickly and looked at him. He was rubbing his arm and eyeing a thistle plant growing beside him. "That thing's good eatin', Hal," I said.

I got up and walked over to the plant. I used the knife to cut a stem and strip its outer layer. "See here," I said, holding it up.

"There's more over there," Kit said. He pointed to an open field to our left.

We spent close to a half hour picking and peeling thistle stems before setting off down the other side of the hill. That afternoon we stopped at a creek that flowed from a marsh with bay trees and cattails. After a lunch of acorns and thistle stems and our leftover fish, I took off my clothes and waded naked into the cattails to gather our supper. Blue herons rose from their nests high in the leafless tops of the cypress trees and squawked at me.

Hal and Kit were lying on their blankets when I returned. The sun and lunch had made them drowsy. When I told them to look at my armful of cattail roots, only Kit opened his eyes slightly and smiled. I let them rest for a few minutes more before we set out through the hills again. We tromped up from the bottom and across a field of dried clay and rock shards. Once we were in the trees, we walked east along the top of a ridge. It was unusually warm and all of us wore our jackets around our waists.

"Where you reckon that Sanders fellow is?" Hal asked.

"I don't know. You scared of him?"

"I don't take to anybody that wants to shoot me."

"He won't find us, Hal. Pap and I hid out for years and nobody found us."

Hal shook his head and didn't say anything.

"We can stop and set some traps if you want."

"No," Hal said. "Just keep goin' to wherever it is you're takin' us. God knows I don't know where in the hell we are."

## 23

Towards late afternoon we had traveled a few miles across hills and down several valleys and through their creeks. I came to the top of a ridge and knelt to examine a track. I'd only seen one such track ever before, but there was no mistaking it. Kit and Hal caught up to me and stood over my shoulder. "What is it?" Kit asked.

"It's a puma track," I said. "Pap told me that a puma needs thirty square miles of territory with no sign of people."

"That means we're far away from civilization?" Kit asked.

"That's right," I said.

"Great," Hal said. "In the middle of nowhere with a mountain lion."

"It won't hurt us. Pap said I was too big."

"That boy in *Old Yeller* was about your size," Hal said.

"That's just a made-up story. Pap knew about animals."

"All right, you fight it then," Hal said. "With that knife of yours."

Kit and I smiled at each other and started down the other side of the ridge. Just before the sun fell below the forest canopy, we stopped and sat on a log to rest. I looked around and studied the trees. "This is a good place," I said. "We'll camp here."

"Finally!" Hal said. "What's for supper?"

"Snake and dressin'."

Hal looked at me. "Snake!"

"Snakes are good," I said. "There may be some out since it was so warm today. I'll make some pine-needle tea to go with it."

Hal spit at the ground. "I ain't eatin' any damn snake. It was bad enough eatin' fish out of your old sock."

"I'll eat some," Kit said.

"Come on," I said to Kit. "You can help me. Hal, there's a white oak tree over there. You collect some acorns from under it while we're gone."

"More acorns . . . What about real meat?" Hal asked.

"We're gonna get some soon," I said. "We'll have all the good food we need once I rig some weapons."

Hal rolled his eyes and sighed. He got up and dragged his feet in the direction of the oak tree with the dogs following. Kit and I set out through an open stand of old pine trees. After a while, I found what I was looking for. I showed Kit a longleaf pine filled with holes starting about fifty feet from the ground. From each of the holes sap ran down the tree, making it look like a giant candlestick.

"Those holes were made by a red-cockaded woodpecker," I said, pointing at the top of the tree. Kit nodded and stared.

We walked around the tree. "Sometimes, there'll be a snake climbin' up to get the woodpeckers. He'll get to those sap runs, and they'll make him dizzy. He'll fall to the ground. If you catch him after he falls, he'll usually be stunned. You can just pick him up by the tail and knock him against a tree."

"I don't see any snakes," Kit said.

"Poke around in the grass and we might find one. Be a corn snake or a rat snake prob'ly."

After some kicking around, I found a black rat snake. I grabbed it by the tail and knocked it against a tree. Kit wanted to carry it, so I gave it to him, and he dragged it back with us.

Hal was sleeping against a log when we returned. He opened his eyes and winced at the snake. Kit swung it towards him, and Hal rolled over and shouted, "Hey!"

Kit and I began to laugh. "It's just a black rat snake," Kit said confidently.

Hal held up his fist and shook it at us with wide eyes. "I'll trade a black eye for a black snake! You keep that thing away from me."

I showed Kit how to make a slit down the belly and around the neck and peel the skin back like a sock. Afterwards, we removed the head and intestine and stuffed the stomach cavity with a paste made from white oak acorns, cattail roots, and thistle.

I found a piece of dead wood nearby and dropped it in front of Kit. "You remember how I started that fire?"

Kit nodded and took the bow drill from me.

"I need a bath," Hal complained.

"Sweat cleans as good as swimmin'," I said.

He looked at me and didn't say anything.

The sun set and the birds became quiet as the forest grew dark. I left Kit and Hal and the dogs and walked downhill to look for a creek. I hadn't gone far when I found one of the giant loblolly pines leaning over so I could walk up its trunk and stand high above the ground, which sloped away beneath me. I could hear water down below and the tops of the trees swishing to the breeze. I imagined that I would be able to see a long way with daylight.

When I returned, Kit was still drilling on the wood and faint curls of smoke drifted up from the bowl. I had brought some juniper bark back with me, and I shredded it and laid it in the bowl. I blew on it gently, and a tiny flame appeared.

"I found a creek down there," I said. "We'll call it Kit Creek. Got to have names for things."

Kit smiled and I could tell he liked having a creek named after him. We cooked the snake and dressing on a spit and ate it like sausage. Kit claimed that his was better than anything he'd had at Pinson. Hal didn't eat his share. He put his back to us and chewed on some of the leftover cattails.

After supper, I suggested we go drink from Kit Creek. Hal said he would go later, so Kit and I set out alone. I showed him the tree I found and we walked up into it. "This is where we'll live for a while," I told him.

"Up here?"

I nodded. "And underneath. We'll make a lookout up here and build our sleepin' room down below."

Gray clouds moved over us, and the forest grew even darker. Thunder rumbled in the distance. I looked up at the sky and felt a twang of worry. For the first time, it occurred to me that I might not be able to keep Kit and Hal comfortable. I tried not to think about the weather and continued to tell Kit about our new home. "We'll start tomorrow," I said. "We've got water below and plenty of forest to the east. Hardwood down below and pine forests up top. That'll give us all types of plants to eat."

Kit looked around like he was imagining us there. "I'll bet you can see a long ways from here with daylight," he said.

I nodded. "That's what I was thinkin'. We'll be able to tell better tomorrow mornin'."

"And you can whip up on anybody who climbs this tree trunk."

"You're right," I said. "Somebody comin' up here's gonna get a butt-whippin'."

Kit became excited and laughed. "Come on," I said. "Let's go get some water."

We came down the tree and walked to the creek. "I don't think Hal likes it out here," Kit said.

Kit only said something I already knew, but I hadn't let myself believe it. "He's just gettin' used to things," I said.

We bent and scooped our hands full of water and drank. "He was talking some more about his daddy while you were gone a while ago. He says he wants to see him again."

I took a deep breath. "You think he's gonna leave?"

"I don't know."

I drank the cool water and stared at my hands as I swallowed. "I don't want him to go," I said.

"Me neither."

"He's really not mean."

"I know."

I didn't want to talk about it anymore. I stood up and started back, and Kit followed. We passed Hal tromping down the slope to the creek in the dark with the dogs following him. I looked up at the sky again, and it was heavy with storm.

"It's right down there, Hal," I said. "It's not far."

"I'll find it," he grumbled.

"Just let the dogs show you where to go."

Back at the fire I told Kit my plans to build our shelter, then begin to make weapons and traps. I could start by making a bow out of the fish spear I made the night before. It was hard not to wonder about Hal, though, and if he was going to leave. I didn't want to bring it up when he returned for fear that it might make the idea come to his head if it hadn't already. Instead, I thought of everything I could to make him comfortable.

"Take some of these pine needles, Hal, and put 'em under your blanket. You can stuff your jacket with dry marsh grass and it'll make a better pillow."

Hal sprinkled the pine needles I handed him across the ground halfheartedly. Then he looked around like he might see more marsh grass nearby.

"We can go back down to Kit Creek, and I'll show you where the soft grass is," I said.

"I didn't have a soft pillow last night. I don't guess I'll be missin' one much tonight."

The thunder rumbled closer, and I looked up at the sky. *Don't rain now*, I said to myself. But I knew by the thickness of the air that a storm was closing on us. I looked over at Hal with a sinking feeling. He was spreading his blanket and didn't seem to notice the weather.

Kit and I watched the fire after Hal rolled up in his blanket to go to sleep. After a few minutes, Kit leaned over and whispered, "What do you think?"

"I don't know."

"It's going to rain tonight, isn't it?"

"Yeah."

"He's not going to like that," Kit said.

"We just need to get the shelter built. We've gotta get it built fast and get him comfortable. First thing in the mornin' . . . Then we've gotta get him some food he likes." I looked at Kit. "He'll stay then. Don't you think?"

Kit looked at me and nodded quickly, but I could tell he wasn't sure.

"He'll stay then," I repeated to myself.

Kit eventually lay on his side and watched the fire until he fell asleep. I stared at his closed eyes and felt myself getting lonely again. I reached into my pocket and pulled out the crumbled piece of pine bark I'd written to Pap on that morning and dumped it on the hot coals. I lay down and watched a little flame lick the edges of it, creating a thin line of smoke that curled up into the darkness.

## 24

The rain came hard that night, and red clay ran down the hillside into our hair and down our backs. The three of us sat shivering with wet blankets hanging over our shoulders. I realized I'd made a mistake. Pap had always told me that shelter was the most important thing in the forest. He said you could go for days without water and even weeks without food, but being caught out in a storm would get you sick and maybe dead.

The one thing I knew we had going for us was that it wouldn't get too cold as long as we had cloud cover to keep the heat down near the ground. The temperature was still well above freezing. We might not get sick if we made a shelter and dried our clothes and blankets before nightfall the next day.

"Let's go find a magnolia tree!" I yelled at them through the storm. "The leaves are big enough to keep the rain off." They looked up and nodded at me with chattering teeth. We walked stiffly through the darkness, trying to place our feet where they didn't slide from under us with the mud. The dogs followed like they didn't care and didn't feel the rain at all. I located a magnolia and pointed for them to get under its broad leaves. The three of us crawled beneath and sat with our backs against the trunk.

"Holly trees can keep you out of the rain, too," I said. They didn't respond. The dogs settled a few yards from us and watched with their chins on their paws.

The rain didn't come as hard under the tree but still dripped on us steadily. Hal was the first to put the wet blanket over his head for protection. Kit soon followed, and I was left staring at the two lumps beside me.

"We're gonna have shelter tomorrow," I said loudly. "And weapons. We'll be able to kill a deer and get meat."

Neither of them replied or moved from under their blankets.

"And no school," I reminded them. "And we'll—"

"Shut up, Moon!" Hal yelled.

I grew sick with worry as Hal's words echoed in my head. I wanted to ask Kit if he was mad at me, too, but I was afraid of what he might say. I lowered my chin to my chest and let my own teeth start to chatter. The rain poured around us and dripped from the leaves down onto my head and then off my bangs and into my lap. After a while, I pulled the blanket over my head and crossed my arms and shivered.

The storm slowed to a cold drizzle in the dark early-morning hours. No one else stirred when I got up and left for the leaning pine tree. Even the dogs nestled deeper into the leaves and seemed to want no part of moving about.

I found my way to the place where we'd made the fire and then walked downhill until I saw the black shadow of the leaning pine and heard the roiling of the swollen creek below. I worked until just after daylight placing long poles of shaved bay branches against the trunk and crossing them with fans of green pine needles to shed the rain. On the inside of the shelter, I cleared the ground of rocks and sticks so that it would make a smooth surface for the marsh grass I would put down later. When the lower shelter was complete, I dragged the soft boughs of bay trees up into the limbs and crisscrossed them to make a platform. On top of those, I laid a bed of dead pine needles that were dried of sap.

An hour after daylight, I had mostly completed a rough shelter that would keep the three of us dry. Above was the lookout platform where we could also sleep when the weather was warm. The drizzling rain had stopped, and the forest was overcast and dripping.

When I returned to the magnolia tree, Kit was there with his blanket wrapped around his shoulders. He smiled weakly.

"Where are Hal and the dogs?" I asked.

Kit hesitated for a moment. "Gone," he finally said.

"Gone?"

Kit looked worried. "A while ago he got up and left. The dogs followed him."

"Back to the fire? Lookin' for me? Where?"

"He said he was going home."

"Home?" I said.

Kit nodded.

"Already! Which way?"

Kit pointed up the hill. I spun around and ran. I broke from the trees and searched right and then left and saw Hal and the dogs sitting in the distance.

"Hal!" I yelled. The dogs looked back at me, but Hal stared away.

I ran after him, jumping fallen timber and ducking low branches. Once I tripped and fell on my face. When I got up, Hal was watching me. He made me walk the rest of the way until I was stooped before him with my hands on my knees and catching my breath.

"I thought . . . I thought you were leavin'?" I said to the ground.

"I am. Soon as I figure out which way to go."

"Don't leave, Hal!"

"I just can't do this anymore. I'm cold and wet and hungry. I got ticks in my hair—"

I stood up. "I can get ticks out. All you have—"

"I know you can do all that. I've never seen anybody that knew more about livin' out."

"The shelter's almost built. I'm gonna make my bow today. I got up early so I could get everything done," I pleaded.

"I wanna get home," he said.

"Hal, you know all that I said about not carin' who came? Dogs or people? Well, I like it that y'all came."

Hal looked down like he didn't know what to say.

"I cared who came," I said.

"Be honest with you, I could probably take all this for a while longer, but I wanna see my daddy. I got a few more years before I'm eighteen and the state releases me. If I've got to spend 'em hidin' out, I wanna hide out with him as long as possible."

I didn't want him to go and I felt like crying, but I knew he was right. "You go ahead, then," I said. "I wish you were gonna stay with us, but I know about paps and I'd wanna be with mine, too. I thought you just didn't like me."

Hal shook his head. "I just wanna see my daddy."

"Well, you best turn around and go back down the hill, where you can follow the creek. If you trace any water long enough, you'll get to roads and people. You takin' those dogs with you?"

"I don't seem to have much choice. I didn't ask 'em to come."

"I've never seen dogs take to anybody like that."

Hal spit. "Well, I ain't one to be mean to 'em," he said. "I'd better get on if I'm gonna find a road and hitch a ride to Daddy's place."

I nodded.

"Good luck with Alaska," he said.

"All right. Good luck hidin' out with your pap."

Hal smiled weakly and turned to go. I was sitting there watching them walk away when Hal turned and looked at me again. "Thanks for gettin' me out of Pinson, Moon."

## 25

It wasn't hard to lift Kit's spirits when he saw the shelter I'd started making. After we set our blankets out to dry, I moved the wall supports in closer since there would only be the two of us. Then we added another layer of magnolia branches and collected marsh grass to dry in the sun and then spread across the floor later. I explained to Kit the importance of building between two hills with a creek at the bottom. We would be sheltered from the hardest wind and rain of the storms and have plenty of clean water to drink. The leaning pine was green enough so that it wouldn't collapse, and the giant fan of its wrenched-up root structure diverted water as it came downhill. Since the forest was thick around us, we cleared some branches to the south where sunlight would provide the longest-lasting heat and light to warm and dry out the shelter. Our entrance was cut out of the southeast wall, where we would catch the most daytime sun.

The ceiling of the room was only a few feet from the ground and the walls just wide enough for us to sleep side by side. I explained to Kit that, unlike the shelter I lived in with Pap, this was aboveground and didn't insulate as well. But with such a small space, our body heat would help us keep each other warm. When the weather wasn't cold, we would sleep up on the lookout platform.

I was relieved to have our shelter finished. The sky had cleared to blue and the temperature was dropping. A breeze swayed the treetops in our little valley, and I could sense a cold front moving in. But I didn't want to tell Kit in case it worried him.

Before noon, we gathered rocks and made a cooking pit about fifteen feet away so that we wouldn't catch fire to our shelter. Kit found two logs that he rolled over to the pit for our seating and looked from the logs to me with pride. When the sun was directly over our heads we had a camp area that would have made Pap proud.

For lunch we boiled acorns in a soup can that Kit had found floating in the creek. While he was straining the acorns using a sock, I caught a snapping turtle. I cut the meat from its shell, and we boiled it in the same can with some sassafras root.

After lunch, the sun mostly dried our clothes. We were tired after our long morning and lay back in the sun with full stomachs and the treetops swishing gently overhead. I looked at Kit and he was smiling at the sky. "It's good, isn't it?" I said.

Kit nodded without looking at me.

"That storm washed away our trail," I said. "Sanders won't be able to get any more dogs after us now. We're gonna be okay, Kit."

"I know," he said.

I closed my eyes and napped.

Before the sun set, I finished making my bow and two arrows. The arrows were made from cattail stems I'd gathered earlier. An owl or a hawk had dropped the carcass of a dead squirrel nearby. I used the leg bones to shape tips for my arrows, which I tied with some intestine from the turtle. Holding the arrows high over the fire shrank the intestine until the points were secured tightly. My shoelaces didn't make the best bowstring, but they would have to do until I was able to kill a larger animal and make a string from its sinew. I told Kit we would be ready to hunt in the morning.

The temperature was dropping quickly and we put on our dry jackets. Looking at the blankets, still on their drying sticks, I knew they wouldn't be enough to keep Kit comfortable. I sent him to collect several large stones from the creek. When he got back, we let them heat in the coals of our fire until they were hot to the touch. Then we dug a small depression in our shelter floor and placed them in it. After covering the floor again with about four inches of dirt, we laid down a few inches of the dry marsh grass. The stones would remain hot into the next day and keep us warm from beneath that night.

We ate what was left of our acorns, turtle meat, and sassafras turtle broth for supper. I could tell Kit was ready to sleep and didn't want to admit it, so I told him there wasn't anything left to do. I spread the three blankets on the floor of the shelter. Kit's eyes were half closed as he crawled inside and pulled the top two over him. I walked down to the creek with stiff legs and a sore back. I washed the soup can and brought back water for putting out the coals. As the fire hissed and smoked, I sat and listened to the forest and felt proud of all we'd accomplished.

## 26

The warm stones beneath us and the thick walls of the shelter kept us warm that night as the icy front settled over the forest. When morning came, we lay on our backs between the blankets well after daylight, not wanting to face the cold.

"I hope Hal made it," Kit said.

"He made it if he followed the creek."

"What if he had to spend the night out there?"

"He had his jacket and those dogs to huddle up with."

Kit was quiet with his thoughts. "Bet he likes those dogs now," he finally said.

We laughed at Kit's joke.

"When do we have to get out from under here?" he said.

I lifted the edge of the blanket and exhaled into the air. My breath clouded out before me. I let the blanket back down over my face. "We'll let the sun warm things up for a little while."

"Good," Kit said.

I guessed it to be about eight o'clock when we crawled outside. It was just below freezing and the leaves were brittle and icy under my feet. We pulled the blankets out of the shelter and draped them over our shoulders for warmth. I gave Kit the extra one, but he still shivered and I knew that, as thin as he was, the cold probably passed right through him.

"Maybe we should make those deerskin clothes," he said to me.

I was determined to make sure that Kit didn't get uncomfortable and leave like Hal. "You stay here," I said. "I'll go huntin' and get a deer for us."

Kit nodded and started gathering wood to rekindle the fire.

It wasn't long before the sun warmed the forest into the low forties. I moved silently along the top of a ridge where I hoped to spot a deer feeding near a wide creek below. Even though I knew I would be able to find game, I was worried about my weapon. Pap and I had made plenty of spears and bows and arrows, but only for practicing in case there was ever a time when we wouldn't be able to get bullets. We had killed squirrels and rabbits with our homemade weapons, but never something as large as a deer. I wasn't sure that my hickory stick and shoelaces would shoot an arrow with enough force.

After I crept across the ridge for close to twenty minutes, I spotted a doe. I angled downhill, stopping whenever she lifted her head and looked about. I slipped quietly through the trees until I was about twenty yards from her. She didn't detect me because there was no breeze and the ground leaves were moist and silent from the melting frost.

I placed the tree between myself and the doe so that I had cover while I prepared my bow and arrow. Once I had the nock of the cattail shaft fitted to my taut shoelace string, I craned my head around the tree. The doe fed with her head down again. It seemed that the entire forest had become quiet, watching me and the deer. I lifted the bow, pulled back the arrow, and leveled it on the doe's neck. When I released, the bow *thwonged* noisily and the doe leaped into the air as the arrow caught her just above the shoulder. She crashed through a gallberry thicket at a full run, and I felt myself shaking uncontrollably. Pap had told me about buck fever, but I had never had it until then.

I found her a hundred yards down the ridge by following her blood trail. The arrow was broken off near the skin where she fell on it, and a faint trickle of blood came from the wound. Her glazed eyes told me she was dead. Just to make certain, I nudged her with my foot and she didn't move.

Even after I had field-dressed the deer, she felt over a hundred pounds, and I knew I wouldn't be able to get her back to camp alone. Taking a long piece of wisteria vine, I strung her up a tree. I made sure her head swung a few feet from the ground because I didn't want coyotes to get to my kill before I returned with Kit.

When I told Kit I'd killed a deer, he leaped up from shelling acorns and followed me to the ridge. We skinned and butchered the doe on the spot until all that was left was the carcass hanging from the tree. I explained that we'd return when the ants and sun had cleaned the bones, and we'd make tools from them.

"At the bottom of this hill is a big creek," I told Kit. "We'll call it Deer Creek. It'll be a good swimmin' place when we get some warm days."

We pulled the rest of the deer on one of the blankets. Back at the shelter, the first thing I did was make two drying racks. On one we placed the stomach, intestine, bladder, and sinew. These first three items could be cleaned and used for food storage, while the sinew could be pounded and separated for thread, fishing line, traps, and bowstrings. On the second rack I put the venison that I planned to build a fire under and smoke.

To save the pieces of the deer that we weren't going to smoke, I made a storage pit in a small shelter under the pine tree. I showed Kit how to line the inside of the pit with hot rocks so that the moisture was steamed out of the dirt. Leaving the rocks in place, we then lined the pit floor and walls with a thick layer of dried grass.

Into the pit we placed the deer's eyeballs, which could be used for paint and to make glue. We also saved the brain to treat the hide, and the hooves to crush and boil to make waterproofing oil.

I covered the pit with cedar bark to keep away insects and worms. To disguise the scent, I put on another layer of strong-smelling pine needles. Finally, I laid a slab of limestone over the top to protect against pawing animals. What little that was left of the deer I wrapped in a scrap of hide and hung from a branch to use as trap bait.

The cold front moved out and the weather became warm enough so that some days we didn't even need our jackets. Over the next week, we worked on scraping and drying the deer hide and smoking our jerky strips over hickory coals. It was pleasant work under clear skies, surrounded by the smells of hickory smoke and curing meat. We would work for a while and then have a meal of venison jerky and whatever vegetation we'd prepared for the day. With our stomachs full and our faces and hands streaked with soot and animal fat, we'd lie back and nap under the rustling leaves.

Sometimes we went for hours without talking, only smiling at each other and keeping our hands busy with shelling acorns or trimming jerky and rubbing the hide with the deer brains. Kit began to learn how things were done, and I had to show him less and less.

One morning we heard a plane and ducked into the shelter and watched as it passed overhead. It was the small, single-engine kind like Pap and I had sometimes seen flying over our shelter.

"You think it's looking for us?" Kit asked.

"I don't know," I said.

We heard it pass nearby two more times that day, and then we didn't hear it again.

The next day I told Kit I was going to check on the hanging deer carcass to make sure that the squirrels weren't eating the bones. I made my way back to the ridge, moving silently and watching for signs of game. When I came within a hundred yards of the place, I heard someone shout.

"Heyyy!"

I froze and held my breath. My eyes darted about and took notice of all the patterns that the branches and leaves made so that I could tell if anything was out of place. I knew the voice was Sanders's and it set my heart to pounding in my chest.

I wasn't going to move until I was sure that no one was watching me. I heard Sanders's voice again from across the ridge, although I couldn't make out the words. He seemed to be cursing loudly to himself. I slipped through the trees, careful to always have a large trunk between myself and the direction of Sanders's voice. After a while, I saw movement in the place where we left the carcass. By lying on my stomach, I was able to wiggle close enough to watch. Sanders had cut the carcass from the tree and was pacing around it in circles. His uniform was torn on the jacket sleeves, and the front of his shirt and pants were soaked with sweat. His hair had pieces of straw and leaves clinging to it, and dirt was smeared over his face and hands.

"Sum-bitch," he said while shaking his head. He kicked at the bones and finally flung the carcass off into the bushes, losing his balance and stumbling after it. I realized he was too tired to be very alert, so I stood and backed away until I was out of sight again. Then I turned around and ran to the top of the ridge, where I could watch him with little chance of being discovered.

Sanders sat near the carcass. After a while, he got up again and staggered down the ridge towards Deer Creek. He had not gone far when he stopped and leaned against a tree. He rested for a moment before yelling out over the valley.

"Hey! Anybody hear me?"

He was quiet for a few seconds, as if he was listening for something. Then he kicked at the ground and hung his head. I watched him for what seemed like five minutes before I wondered if he'd fallen asleep. I began to get up slowly, keeping an eye on him the whole time. Just as I straightened my legs, I saw him pitch forward and scream "Ahhh!" As he tumbled down the hill, I spun around and ran for the shelter.

Kit was collecting firewood when I got back to the campsite. He watched me wide-eyed as I caught my breath.

"Sanders," I said. "He's out there!"

"Where?"

I pointed back at the ridge. "Not far from where we left the deer."

"Did he see you?"

I shook my head. "No. He's mad and tired and yellin' for somebody to find him. Last I saw him, he was fallin' down the ridge."

"You think he's been out all night?"

"Yeah, I think he got lost. And if he finds us, he's so mad there's no tellin' what he'll do."

Kit's hands fidgeted at his sides. He sat down on the log across from me. "Policeman can't hurt you!"

"Pap says the government can do whatever they want to you if they get set on it. Sanders is a crazy constable. There's no tellin' what he can do."

"You have any ideas?"

"Yeah," I said.

"What?"

"Whip up on him."

"Moon!"

I stood up. "Whip up on him good!"

"No, Moon!"

"Come on. I need your help."

# 27

"What if he shoots us, Moon?"

"He won't shoot us. Even if we let him see us, he's too tired to hit anything he aims at."

"How are you going to whip up on a full-grown policeman?"

"We'll have to trap him."

Kit groaned to himself as we walked back to the ridge where I'd last seen Sanders. My mind raced with ideas as to how I would trap something so large. I imagined pits being dug, trees bent over with snare loops, logs made into deadfalls . . .

"You know you can't kill him, Moon."

"I won't kill him, Kit. I never killed anybody."

"I don't see why we have to do anything to him. I say we just run."

"I'm not runnin' from him anymore."

We reached the top of the hill, and I told Kit to crawl beside me on his stomach. We wiggled up to the edge so that we could see down into the valley where Sanders fell. We listened for a few minutes and didn't hear anything.

"You think he's hurt?"

"Maybe."

"What if he's hurt?"

"Then we'll hog-tie him and think of some way to get him out of here."

"You can't tie him up!"

"Shhh! Yes I can. Pap let me practice on him before."

Kit groaned again. I picked up a rock and lobbed it down into the trees below. We listened after it but heard nothing.

"If we just leave, then maybe he'll never find us."

I stood up. "Yeah, but we won't get his gun, either."

"What?"

"His gun."

Kit stood up and began to walk back the way we'd come.

"Hey," I said. "Where are you goin'?"

"I'm not taking a policeman's gun, Moon."

I ran after him and caught his shoulder. "We've got to have a gun, Kit. We can't make it in Alaska without a gun."

He kept walking.

"Kit, don't leave me," I pleaded.

Kit stopped and stared at the ground. "Why do you have to mess with him, Moon?"

"Because I need that pistol. He took my rifle from me."

"What about your bow?"

"That bow won't be near as good in Alaska, even with the deer sinew on it."

"What about your pap's rifle?"

"I don't know how to get back to our old shelter."

Kit sighed and looked at me. "It'll be all right?"

"Yeah," I assured him.

"I don't want to get shot."

"Don't worry, we'll trap him good. We won't get shot."

I told Kit to take off his shoes so we could walk quieter. We slipped through the forest until I heard Sanders moan. I looked back at Kit and raised my hand so he would hold still while I moved closer. He nodded, and I turned in my feet so that I stood on only the outside edges of them. After getting my bearings, I began to lift and place them slowly into the leaves, watching where each foot went. I ducked under branches and twisted around bushes like someone in slow motion.

When I had traveled about fifty yards, I saw movement ahead of me. I stepped sideways to put a large tree between myself and whatever it was. I looked back to check on Kit, but I couldn't see him through the brush. Sanders moaned again, and I felt my neck hairs rise.

I reached the tree and peered around it. Sanders was lying on his back next to Deer Creek. His eyes were closed and his stomach heaved up and down. His clothes were torn and muddy and grass-stained from where he'd been sliding and rolling down hills. He was covered with scrapes, and a T-shirt that he had been using to clean them was beside him, stained with blood. He still had his gun belt on, and the pistol was snapped into the holster.

I stayed behind the tree for a few minutes, listening to him breathe and trying to figure out how to get the pistol. Once again I imagined snares and pits and rope swings and giant crashing logs. It wasn't long before I had the perfect plan in my head. I turned around carefully and slowly made my way back.

Kit and I returned to the top of the ridge about two hundred yards down the valley. We then made our way to the creek again where it ran swift between steep banks. I found two long pieces of wisteria vine and worked with them for a while before Kit spoke. "What are you going to do?" he asked.

"Snare him."

"How?"

I pointed at a large log lying a few feet away. "Roll that over here," I told him.

Kit got behind the log and began pushing it towards me. I made a lasso out of one of the vines and placed it in a deer trail that ran the edge of the creek. I tied the other end of the lasso to one end of the log. Finally, I took the other vine and tied it to the log as well.

The two of us got under the log, and with all of our strength we stood it up against a tree near the creek edge, with the end I had tied the vines to in the air. I pointed to some bushes a few yards off the deer trail. "You get in those bushes," I told Kit. "When Sanders trips on that lasso loop, you jerk hard on the other vine."

Kit stared at me blankly.

"It'll work," I reassured him. "Just pull hard."

I grabbed the end of the pull vine and put it in his hand. "I'm goin' to get him. I'll be back in a minute."

Kit groaned and tightened his hands.

Sanders was still sound asleep.

I picked up a stick and poked him in the stomach. He didn't wake, but his hand came up and slapped at his side. I poked him again. This time, his eyes opened and he stared at the treetops.

"Sanders," I said.

"Hunh."

"It's Moon."

Suddenly his eyes flashed in my direction. His face shot flame red and veins stood like tent ropes under his skin. "Ahhh!" he yelled. He rolled over and began to run towards me on his knees with his hands out in front. I turned and ran down the deer trail.

"Boyyy—you better stop right there! You're dead, kid!"

I slowed after about a hundred yards and zigzagged and ducked easily along the deer trail. I heard Sanders crashing through the forest like a wild hog, and I imagined the stickers tearing into him. I jogged past Kit and looked at his wide eyes in the brush. "Get ready," I said. "Here he comes."

When Kit pulled the vine, I was crouched down the trail where I could see everything, but not so far that I couldn't stand and lead Sanders away from Kit if things went wrong. Sanders tripped over the raised lasso and fell heavily into the leaves, just as I had planned. The giant log slipped off the tree and went crashing into Deer Creek below, jerking the lasso tight around Sanders's ankles. His legs were yanked so hard that he spun around like a compass needle. He tore chunks of bushes and grass from the ground as the log pulled him towards the creek bank. Finally, he managed to grab a small clump of bushes that held, and he rolled over onto his stomach. The log bobbed and swayed in the creek, ready to pull him with it if he let go. I came running back up the trail until I was standing over him. He glanced at me briefly and then looked at his hands holding the bush.

"I whipped you good this time," I said.

All he could do was yell, "Ahhh!"

I bent over and unsnapped his holster. I took the pistol out and jabbed it in my pocket. "I'd be fine if you hadn't taken all my things," I said.

"Kill you," he gasped.

I stared at him. Suddenly, I felt myself getting angry again. "I'll kill *you*!" I screamed. "You took me away to Pinson! Leave us alone!"

"Moon!" Kit yelled.

I stood there breathing heavily.

"Moon!" he yelled again. I looked over at him. "Come on," he begged.

# 28

I told Kit that we had to wait a while before we shot the pistol just in case there were more people out in the woods looking for us.

"You think it's loud?" he asked me.

"It's gonna be loud. I've never seen a pistol this big."

"You don't think he drowned, do you?"

"No. Once those vines get some slack, they spring loose. I'll bet he went ridin' down that creek a ways, though. I don't want him messin' with me anymore, Kit."

"Do you think he found his way out yet?"

"If he walked that creek, he's bound to hit a road eventually."

"Or float down it."

"That too."

Kit sighed. "This is crazy, Moon. I'll bet he's going to have the whole police department after us."

"Obregon from jail said he didn't have any friends."

"Maybe we should start walking towards Alaska soon."

I shook my head. "It's too cold up there right now. We'd do best to wait until spring. Stay here in our shelter as long as we can. Teach you more stuff."

Over the next two weeks we made improvements to the walls of the shelter, piling on more pine boughs and anything we could find that kept off rain. Even though the venison seemed like it would last until spring, I made snares and deadfalls in the forest that brought us rabbits, possums, and a few raccoons.

The deer sinew was dry and cured. I twisted it into a thin cord and strung the bow with it. I finished it out by wrapping the handle with deer skin and carving a small channel for the arrow shaft.

Outside of patching our shelter, making weapons, and checking traps, there was still time to play. I made a vine swing across Kit Creek and stacked a mound of pine straw and magnolia leaves to land in. We made flutter mills out of twigs and leaves and had contests to see whose would last the longest. Kit liked these things, and it didn't take much of them to get his mind off Sanders.

On some nights we'd lie up on the lookout platform and stare at the stars. Kit smiled when I talked of the fun we would have when spring came. How the creeks warmed and we could make spears and swim down in the clear water looking for bass and bream.

"What about Alaska?"

"We'll load up on food and then we'll head out. We can't leave for Alaska without plenty of supplies."

I told him how we could boil blackberries in the can to make syrup to pour over acorn cakes. I told him of catching frogs as big as our feet and of lying on our backs in kudzu with a full vine of honeysuckle and fresh eggs from duck nests that I would cook with bacon from a wild hog I would kill.

The only night sounds that came to our ears were from owls and coyotes. Occasionally we heard a bobcat. Sometimes we heard sounds that I couldn't figure out, and I told

Kit about the time Pap had seen a Bigfoot in Montana. Kit got scared about the Bigfoot until I told him that there weren't any in Alabama.

I slept with the pistol beside me. Almost every night I would take it from under the marsh grass and turn it over in front of my face. The writing on it was the only thing I had to read, so I memorized the make and model and serial number.

> COLT'S PT. F. A. MFG. CO.
>
> HARTFORD CT. U.S.A
>
> UNITED STATES PROPERTY
>
> MODEL OF 1911 U.S. ARMY NO. 445309

One morning Kit asked me if he could hold the pistol, so I pulled it from under the marsh grass and gave it to him. He held it out carefully and studied it.

"You're gonna have to learn to shoot it, you know," I said.

"I will."

"I can set up some targets for you."

"What about bullets?"

"We'll have to buy some more when we get money from things we sell."

Kit gave me back the pistol. "We've been out here a long time, Moon."

"Yeah," I said, returning the pistol to its hiding place. "We've got everything we need."

"We should look for some medicine."

I looked over at him. "You sick?"

"I don't know. Sometimes I don't feel good. I think we should have some medicine ready just in case."

"We'll get some today."

I knew of a place on the hillside where black willow grew, and we spent the morning pulling bark and grinding it into aspirin. We stored the medicine with the meat in the ground, where it would stay dry.

"Nothin' to worry about now, Kit."

Kit smiled and it seemed like he wasn't worried anymore.

That afternoon we used the knife to scratch out patterns on the deer hide for two hats. Using twine I'd made from the inner bark of a cedar tree, I bound the pieces together and gave Kit the hat with the tail still attached. He wore it proudly, and we decided they were our symbols that we'd wear all the way to Alaska.

One afternoon, we lay in the treetop platform watching buzzards circle us. I told Kit that if we lay there long enough we might be able to get one to come down.

"Have you ever done it?"

"No . . . But I've thought about it a lot."

"How long do we have to lie like this?"

"We can do somethin' else. Let's go shoot the pistol."

"You think it's safe now?"

"It's been more than two weeks since we saw Sanders. I don't think he's comin' back."

I chose a rotten log as a target, and Kit followed me to a place about twenty yards back from the log and stood behind me while I inspected the gun.

"I thought you'd shot a gun before?" he said.

"I have."

"Why do you always look at it like that?"

"Because I haven't ever shot one like this. It's an automatic. And it's big."

After a minute, I discovered how to slide back the top of the pistol so that it loaded a bullet from the magazine. I held it out in front of me and aimed at the log. I sucked in my breath and squeezed the trigger. The explosion threw my arms over my head and left me deaf to all but a ringing in my ears. As I brought the pistol down, I saw that I'd hit the log where I was aiming. I turned to look at Kit. He had his hands over his ears and pulled them away slowly. "I've never shot anything like that," I said, barely hearing my own voice. I laughed. "I can't hear anything."

"Did you hit it?" Kit asked.

"Sure, I hit it."

I turned back around and Kit slammed his hands to his ears again. I aimed the gun with more confidence this time and squeezed the trigger. The pistol bucked into the air, and the explosion punched so deep my teeth hurt. Wood chips flew from the center of the log where I was aiming. When I turned to look at Kit, he smiled and nodded.

"We're gonna get somethin' big with this thing in Alaska, Kit!" I yelled.

# 29

Another ten days passed before the last cold front moved in. Although the temperatures dropped way down a couple of nights, our shelter stayed warm and dry because of the improvements we made and the hot rocks we slept on.

In spite of our warmer home, Kit developed a sniffle that wouldn't go away. After three days, he began coughing during the night and having headaches. I gave him the black willow aspirin and kept a supply of hot pine-needle tea ready whenever he wanted it.

"If this black willow and pine-needle tea doesn't work, I'll get some yellowroot. That's even better. And I'll get some pine sap for you to chew. That'll help for sore throat."

Kit nodded. "Okay."

On the fourth night we lay in the shelter as the rain drizzled from an icy sky. The wind tossed the treetops above our heads and hickory nuts fell against the shelter wall. Kit coughed more than usual and an uneasy feeling came over me. The rain had not let up for two days and we had spent most of the time holed up in our shelter. Not even yellowroot tea helped, and the forest was too soaked to get dry wood for a fire without whittling each piece of firewood to the core.

"It'll be dry tomorrow," I said. "I'll get a fire goin' and make more tea."

He didn't answer me.

"This ought to be the last of the cold weather. I can tell by the way the trees are changin'."

I looked towards Kit's face in the darkness, but I couldn't see anything. I reminded him of all the things we would do when spring arrived. I talked to the ceiling throughout the night, keeping Kit company while his coughing kept him awake. At daybreak, he crawled out into the rain and began puking. I went after him and watched helplessly as he clutched his stomach and drew his knees up. The rain was soaking us and my mind spun trying to remember all the medicines Pap had taught me about. But in the end I couldn't think of anything we hadn't tried.

"I don't know what do, Kit!" I cried. "My medicine won't work on what you have."

He didn't answer me.

"This yellowroot is the best thing I know about. Sometimes you can eat red clay and that helps. I can go find some of that. I don't know . . . What do I do, Kit?"

He rolled over on his back and lay there with his eyes closed and the rain falling on his face. I watched his stomach rise and fall to his breathing. "I'm cold," he said. It was the first time I'd ever heard him complain.

I ran to the fire pit and grabbed the knife. I picked up a piece of firewood and began to whittle it as fast as I could. It wasn't long before Kit called me. I walked over to him with the wood in one hand and the knife in the other.

"Don't worry about me, Moon. I'll be okay."

"I don't know how to make any more medicine!" I cried.

"It's okay," he muttered. He tried to get up, but he fell back and coughed at the sky.

"I'm goin' to get some help! My pap said to leave *him* alone, and I never should have done it."

I dropped the firewood and began to run downhill to the creek. I hadn't gone far when I turned and ran back. "I don't know where to go, Kit! I don't know how to find a doctor. It might take me too long."

Kit tried to say something but started coughing again.

"I'm not leavin' you, Kit!"

I dove into the shelter and grabbed the blankets. I rolled Kit onto one and placed the other two over him. I tied the two corners to the ends of a log about as big as my leg. By standing behind the log, I was able to walk with it against my waist and sled Kit behind me.

The wind came cold up the creek bed and thrashed the treetops. I plodded my way through the blowing rain, my head spinning with fear that my first real friend in the world was about to die.

"I don't want you to die, Kit," I said back to him.

"I'll be okay," he mumbled.

"Don't talk," I said. "You go to sleep. I'm gonna find a road and some help."

The air was so icy and damp it seemed to lick my bones. My mind was blank as I placed one foot in front of the other. I hadn't gone far before my legs were weary and my waist felt bruised and raw where the log pressed into it. I collapsed to my knees and began to cry. Kit was silent beside me, and I didn't turn to look at him.

"I don't care about Alaska, Kit. I'm not goin' without you. I'm not goin' at all. Pap said there were more people like him up there. But I don't wanna be like those people! I don't wanna be by myself, Kit!" I staggered to my feet again and heaved against the sled. "I don't wanna be anywhere by myself anymore!"

I had been dragging Kit for almost two hours when we came to a swamp where a beaver dam had backed up the creek. I leaned into the log and started uphill to the ridge above. With all of the tree roots and fallen timber, I felt like crying out with frustration every few feet.

At the top of the ridge, I dropped the log, fell to my knees, and rested.

"Kit," I said.

He mumbled something I didn't understand, but it was enough to get me to my feet again. I pulled the log up to my waist and looked across the top of the ridge. At first, I didn't notice the gap in the trees. But after I started pulling, I realized that we were on an overgrown trail of some sort. Then I saw that the trail was raised on a bed of gravel and it reminded me of the old logging railroads that Pap had told me about. We had found a tram road.

I figured the tram road would take us out of the forest eventually and would certainly be easier going than the creek bottom. I began pulling again. "We're gonna make it, Kit," I said.

When we came to the blacktop that afternoon, I stood at the edge of it for a while before I knew it was there. I was so tired that everything was blurry. I let the log drop from my waist and stared across the highway. After a moment, I looked up and down the empty two-lane road. The sounds of the forest returned to my ears, and I felt a strong thirst in my mouth.

I turned around slowly and knelt beside Kit. I put my hand gently on the top of the blankets that covered him. "Kit," I said.

He moved slightly and mumbled. I pulled the blankets back to see his face. It was sickly pale. He kept his eyes closed and clutched his stomach.

"I found a road," I said. "We've just gotta wait."

He nodded without opening his eyes.

"A car's gonna be along soon. I'll get them to take you to get medicine . . . I'm not gonna go to Alaska. I don't know what I'll do, but I won't live up there without any friends. I'll wait for you to get better and let you decide where we're gonna go."

I heard a noise and looked up. A white car was coming our way. I stood and ran to the middle of the road. I waved my arms until I was sure the driver saw me, and then I ran back and stood over Kit. "I'll stay out here until you're better and you can come find me. You just follow this tram road and I'll be watchin' for you. If you get somewhere they won't let you out of, I'll come break you out. I'll whip up on everybody in there. Kit?"

The car began to slow as it approached us. I took a few steps towards the forest. "I'll get you out of anywhere, Kit. You hear?"

The car crossed the bridge and pulled onto the roadside and the passenger window rolled down. An old woman peered out at me. "You okay, child?"

I pointed at Kit. She looked down at him and gasped. She turned and said something to the driver. A man stepped from the other side of the car. "What's happened here, son?"

I turned and ran for the trees.

# 30

I walked far enough into the forest to hide myself and collapsed at the base of a pine tree. The cold slipped through my thin wet Pinson uniform and I hugged my arms to my chest tightly and concentrated on keeping my teeth from chattering.

The clouds eventually slid away, and the sun began to warm me. I fell asleep against the tree and didn't wake until I heard a car stop on the road. My heart began pounding in my chest. Fortunately, my Pinson uniform was so dirty that it no longer showed such a bright orange. I lay close to the ground and crawled through the damp leaves to get a look.

Sanders stared at the blankets that lay near the road. I saw his jaw clenched tight with anger. He put his hands on his hips and scanned the forest. Finally, he kicked the blankets and spit on them. "It ain't over, boy!" he yelled. "It ain't even close to over! You're gonna come out of there, and I'll get you when you do!"

Sanders had been gone for over an hour and it was getting on towards evening. Kit Creek went under the blacktop not far from where the tram road came out. I walked to the bridge and drank until I was out of breath. Then I dipped in the soles of my shoes to strip away the mud that was caked to them.

I didn't want to return to the campsite. The thought of

being there without Kit made me sick with loneliness. But my mind didn't give me any direction to go. I walked to the road, collected the blankets, and slipped back into the forest. Not far from where I'd watched Sanders earlier, I found a large cedar tree and climbed up it. The trunk split into three parts to make a bowl about ten feet from the ground. I curled up in the bowl and laid my head so that I saw the road through the treetops. I wanted to be there if Kit returned.

When the sun set I still wasn't hungry. Only a few cars had passed on the road since I'd been there. I couldn't remember feeling so empty inside since Pap died. All of the night sounds and the gurgling of the creek and the stars above my head—all of the things that used to make me feel safe and happy—just reminded me of how alone I was. I thought about Hal and rolled over and pulled my knees up. I thought about Kit and felt my throat tighten and swell. Then I thought about Pap, and I began to cough and cry in the bowl of the cedar tree. I'd counted on his memory to make me feel safe. But he was completely gone, not only in body but in spirit as well. And what bothered me most of all was that I was doubting all the things he told me were right.

The next morning, I watched a van stop where Kit and I had waited near the road. A man and a woman with a television camera got out and set up on the roadside. The man pointed the camera at the woman while she stood near the trees and talked into a microphone.

"Yesterday, the boy they call Alabama Moon brought one of two other escapees from the Pinson Boys' Home to this place for medical attention. Mr. and Mrs. Clayton Jones were out for an afternoon drive when they saw Alabama Moon waving them down. When they stopped to help, he fled into the forest and has not been seen since.

"The sick boy has been identified as ten-year-old Kit Slip. He is currently being treated in a Tuscaloosa hospital. It is believed that the third Pinson escapee, Hal Mitchell, is still at large with Alabama Moon in this forest behind us.

"The three boys escaped six weeks ago. They stole a school bus and drove all of the residents to a point near Payne Lake, about eight miles from here. From there, Alabama Moon and the two other boys fled into the forest.

"His father, Oliver Blake, presumed to have died in January, had raised the boy to live off the land. It is therefore believed that Alabama Moon can remain in the wild indefinitely. After burying his own father, the last of his known kin, he is presently considered a ward of the state. He is wanted for evasion of the law and the attempted murder of a law enforcement official. Efforts have been made to locate the fugitives by search plane and on foot with dogs. However, the boys are believed to be hiding in the most remote and inaccessible parts of the Talladega National Forest, and efforts to find them thus far have been unsuccessful.

"Constable Davy Sanders has traveled here from Livingston to make four expeditions into the forest trying to bring the boys to justice. On the last mission, Alabama Moon attempted to shoot him and left him for dead. Constable Sanders denies that they can remain in the wild much longer. He claims that the boys will have to come out sooner or later, and when they do, he'll be waiting . . . And until then, so will we.

"This is Nancy Centers, TV News 10."

I didn't care when I heard the part about attempted murder. It didn't seem like it mattered what people thought of me anymore. They were going to be after me no matter what. They just wanted me locked up somewhere.

After the television crew left, I spent another hour watching carpenter ants climb around near my face. The sound of the creek grew fainter as the water drained out of the forest. Robins fluttered in, settled, pecked at the leaves, and left again. Squirrels darted about the forest floor and chased each other up the trees, making bark and leaves rain down.

When the truck came, I hadn't heard any cars for almost an hour. It pulled up next to the bridge and stopped. A creaky door opened, and I could just make out someone—a boy—walking around to the rear. He climbed up into the bed and yelled, "Moon!"

I felt my nerves jump. I lifted my head to get a better look. When the boy yelled my name again, I recognized the voice and was flooded with excitement. I stood up in the cedar tree and waved my arms. "Hal, I'm over here!"

Hal brought his hand up to shield his eyes from the sun. "What you doin' up there?"

I shrugged my shoulders. "Sleepin'. Waitin'."

"Well, come on down. My daddy's with me."

I tossed the blankets to the ground and leaped on top of them. I got so excited that I tripped twice getting out to the truck. Hal looked happier than I ever remembered seeing him. He jumped down from the back of the truck. "Heard they got Kit. Heard they found him sick. I told you he needs that medicine."

I nodded while I caught my breath.

"I heard it on the radio last night," Hal continued. "They got him at the hospital in Tuscaloosa."

"He all right?"

Hal nodded. "The news said he was pretty sick, but they got him hooked up to some stuff."

"How'd you find me?"

"Hell, they gonna have you all over the TV again. When they said they found Kit on the road, I figured you might still be nearby. I can't believe you dragged him all the way by yourself. I had a hard enough time makin' it out alone."

"You comin' to live with me again?"

"No, I was comin' to see did you wanna stay with us for a while. I was gonna walk back for you if I had to. They're prob'ly after you hard, considerin' all the stuff Sanders been sayin'. And now they got this old trail to go on. Come meet my daddy."

I nodded at Mr. Mitchell through the passenger-side window. He was big like Hal, but with red hair and a red beard. His nose was so pink and swollen it looked like you could wring water from it. He looked me over and shook his head. "I ain't never seen such a critter." I could tell he liked me, and I smiled at Hal.

"You should have seen him when his hair was long," Hal told his pap.

"Moon, you livin' in a hole out there?" Mr. Mitchell asked.

"Close to it. I've been livin' in a tree since yesterday."

"How'd you like to come stay in the clay pit for a little while? We been needin' some company."

"You know Sanders is stalkin' me like a wildcat. He finds me there, he's likely to try and whip up on all of us."

"Hell, I know how to take care of lawmen like Davy Sanders. He don't amount to more'n a little ol' sand snake to me."

"Daddy played Little League baseball with him," Hal said. "Says he's mean, but dumb as a skillet."

Mr. Mitchell leaned out of the window and spat a long line of tobacco juice. He turned to look at me. "He thinks just 'cause his daddy's the judge down in Sumter County that he can run around and do whatever he wants. Not even his jurisdiction."

"He might think it," I said.

"Yeah, well, he was on TV a few weeks ago. Said you ate his dogs and shot at him."

"I didn't do that!"

"I know. I been drawin' down my savin's tryin' to feed a couple of bloodhounds and a little wiener dog."

I turned to Hal. "You still got 'em?"

He nodded. "Yeah, you didn't know about the sausage dog, though. I found her while I was walkin' out. She was lost as hell, chasin' squirrels. I think Sanders came after you with his momma's dog after those bloodhounds ran out on him."

"Did he tell the TV about me draggin' him into a creek and takin' his pistol from him?"

Mr. Mitchell laughed. "Naw, he didn't say nothin' about that. Why don't you climb in and tell us all about it."

"I might get sick if you don't keep the windows down."

"Son, these windows ain't down, they're gone."

Mr. Mitchell's truck was beat up all over. It had dents from the tailgate to the headlights. So many parts had been replaced on it that it was six different colors. It was piled full of cans and empty five-gallon oil buckets and magazines and sacks of garbage. The cab was crammed with just a little bit less of what was in the back.

Hal leaned into the truck and scooped up an armload of cans and magazines and empty chewing tobacco pouches. He backed out with his load and went to drop it in the truck bed. When he came back, he climbed in and slid to the middle, kicking more trash around with his feet.

"Slide on in here, Moon," Mr. Mitchell said.

I got in and pulled the door shut.

As we drove towards the Mitchells' place, some of the new trash that Hal put in the truck bed fluttered out onto the highway. At one point, I heard a clatter and turned to see a five-gallon bucket bouncing down the road behind us.

"You're losin' buckets back there, Hal."

"Let 'em go," Mr. Mitchell said.

I heard a paint can clatter off the truck. "You're losin' all kinds of stuff."

Mr. Mitchell shrugged and spit out the window. "Yeah, well, this old boy don't get out on the road much."

Mr. Mitchell began to tell me about Sanders coming on television and talking about how dangerous I was. He said that everybody that lived around the Talladega National Forest was on the lookout for me.

"I oughta whip him good," I said.

"You might get your chance if he finds you."

Mr. Mitchell pulled a bottle of whiskey from under the truck seat and took a swallow. He screwed the cap back on and shoved it under. "Hal says you gonna head to Alaska pretty soon."

"Not until I hear from Kit. I'm not gonna go up there by myself."

"What if he's too sick?" Hal asked.

I shrugged my shoulders. "I don't know."

Mr. Mitchell spit again, coughed, and wiped his mouth. "I'll tell you, Davy Sanders might be a fool, but he's a dangerous fool. I suggest you stay holed up with us until you get you a plan made."

"We can stay holed up and shoot bottles," I said.

Mr. Mitchell smiled. "Damn straight we can shoot bottles." He pulled out the whiskey and took another drink. He let down the bottle and looked at it. "I 'bout got this'n ready to set up soon as we get back."

"I wish I had Sanders's gun. Y'all should have seen that thing I took off him. It'd blow out your eardrums."

"Where is it now?" Hal asked.

"Back in the forest gettin' rusty."

Mr. Mitchell smiled and shook his head. "Moon, I'll do what I can, but you better hope he don't get his hands on you. That's all I got to say."

## 31

I told Hal and his daddy what Kit and I had been doing. Mr. Mitchell drove along and smiled at my stories and drank from his whiskey bottle. After a while he pulled off the road and got out of the truck and walked around the passenger side. Hal slid over and got behind the wheel.

"Hal gonna drive us?" I asked.

"Boy can drive a bus, he can sure 'nough drive my truck for me," Mr. Mitchell said as he climbed back in.

We crossed the Black Warrior River, and I stared down at the muddy water below. It reminded me of the cedar bluff overlooking the Noxubee River where Momma and Pap were buried.

"You make it out before it got cold on you, Hal?"

"Barely. I followed the creek like you said and come out on the road about dark. Some old fellow came along and let me ride with him. He was pretty jumpy about all those dogs crammed in his car and he was eyein' me like he knew I was up to somethin'. I finally got him to drop me off at a place I recognized and I walked the rest of the way. I don't think he figured out anything about who I was 'cause ain't nobody been to Daddy's lookin' for me."

We parked near a clear-water creek just outside a town called Clinton. Mr. Mitchell dug around in his toolbox until he found a can of Spam. Hal pulled a loaf of bread from behind the seat and we made lunch on the tailgate. It had been a long time since I'd had any meat with fat in it, and I was sorry there wasn't a whole can just for me.

Mr. Mitchell's place outside of Union was just how I pictured it would be from Hal's description. His trailer was old and yellowed and had tires on top to keep the wind from blowing the roof off. The bloodhounds came running around the corner and jumped up and scraped at the truck.

"I don't guess you'll be needin' a place to put your things, will you, Moon?"

"Nossir. I don't have any things."

They showed me a mattress I could sleep on in Hal's room and said it was the best they had to give me. The little wiener dog was already lying on it, and she looked at me like she wasn't giving up her spot.

"She gonna get mad at me?"

"Naw," Hal said. "Just scoot her over. She'll get under the covers with you at night. She likes gettin' under things and crawlin' in holes. Daddy had to dig her out of an armadillo hole last week. She was down there for two days."

"She get it?"

"Hell yeah, she got it," Mr. Mitchell said. "Them dogs is crazy. She got dead squirrels lyin' all over the yard like dish-rags."

"What's her name?"

"Says Daisy on the tag."

I lay down on the mattress beside Daisy. "Next to lyin' on leaves and red bugs, this feels pretty good."

Mr. Mitchell nodded at me and walked towards the room at the end of the hall. "I'll see you boys later," he said.

Hal told me his daddy usually took a long nap in the afternoon and we'd see him for supper and bottle-shooting later. He showed me where the bathroom was and gave me everything I needed for a shower. "How many bugs you think you got in your hair?"

"Prob'ly a bunch," I said.

"Daddy ain't gonna like bugs gettin' in the mattress. He already got onto the wiener dog about fleas."

"Well then, I reckon we oughta shave it all off after I take a shower. Spring's about here anyway."

I used some soap they had for cleaning grease off your hands and scrubbed the dirt off me. My fingernails and toenails had pine sap under them and we used gasoline to soften it and then scraped it out with a pocketknife. After that, Hal gave me some of his old clothes to wear in place of my Pinson uniform. I pulled on the blue jeans and a T-shirt that said "Moe Bandy" on it and looked at Hal.

"Fit pretty good," I told him.

"Yeah. Last time I used 'em I was about your size."

Mr. Mitchell had mashed some wooden crates into the mud and covered them with plywood for a front porch. Hal set some chairs up for us and ran an extension cord out of the trailer to plug his daddy's electric razor into. As he shaved my head, I looked out over the clay pit and let the hair fall over my shoulders and into my lap. "I can see why he likes this place," I said. "You can shoot guns all day long out here. Not too many places you can shoot guns all day long."

"Daddy'll be awake in a while and we can set up some bottles."

I nodded. "Sounds good. You know, Sanders still has my rifle."

"Not much way to get it now."

"Your daddy let you take his truck by yourself?"

Hal stopped shaving me. "Yeah, but I ain't takin' you to get your gun from Sanders."

"How about you takin' me to get Pap's gun?"

"At your old home?"

"Yeah."

"Hell with that. We're gonna let the law cool off a little bit. Daddy said even if you didn't wanna come back with us, we should come warn you to stay hidden for a while."

"Okay," I said. "We can wait a while. But I'm glad you came and got me. I don't wanna be out there by myself anymore. Once Kit gets better, we'll figure somethin' out. You know how I can talk to him?"

"He's prob'ly too sick to talk to."

"When he gets better, though."

"The radio said what hospital he's at. We can go up to the Laundromat and use the pay phone to call in a few days."

"I thought he was gonna die out there. I've never felt so bad about anything in my whole life. I should have told him to bring some medicine."

"You didn't know."

"Pap was wrong about a lot of things. You can't make every kind of medicine in the forest. I can't make everything Kit needs."

## 32

After my haircut, Hal got some black garbage bags and started taping them over the side truck windows with duct tape.

"What's all that for?"

"You just hold on, skinhead."

When he was finished, we got in the truck and went riding

down into the clay pit with the bloodhounds chasing behind. Once we were at the bottom, Hal mashed the gas pedal as far as it would go. The back tires threw mud fifty feet behind us and we fishtailed until I had to clutch the seat to keep from sliding across the cab. Finally, he straightened the truck and we sped towards the opposite side.

"What're you doin'!" I yelled.

"Muddin'!"

There was a long strip of mud in the middle of the clay pit that we hit next, and a wall of rust-colored water shot up over us. The truck slowed and Hal gritted his teeth and floored it again. Clumps of mud clopped against the truck and covered us inch by inch until we could only see through what the windshield wipers scraped clean.

"Daddy made some heavy-duty wipers for us," Hal yelled. I was so excited I couldn't answer. I gripped the seat and held on. The tires slowly caught the ground, and the wall of water fell, and I saw we were still headed straight for the high clay wall of the opposite side. Just as I was about to ball up for the crash, Hal yelled, "Hold on!" and whipped the steering wheel with one hand. We slid sideways for about thirty feet until we slammed into the clay bank. I saw cans and buckets and trash bags fly into the air through the rear window. Hal grabbed the steering wheel with both hands and I saw his knuckles go white. "Hammer down!" he shouted, and jabbed his right foot to the floor.

We scraped the side of the bank for a few yards and then tore away from it.

"You're crazy!" I yelled.

"Fun, wasn't it?"

"You're gonna bend up your truck!"

"Daddy don't need no Sunday car."

"Well then, let's go again."

Hal's eyes twinkled and he straightened his right leg, and we tore off for the other side. The bloodhounds had almost caught up with us and made a wide circle to give chase again. They were so covered with clay mud all you could see were their eyes, like they'd been dipped in tomato juice.

We made three runs through the clay pit before Hal said we were low on gas. We drove back up to the trailer and washed the dogs and truck down with a hose. The afternoon was growing late and my stomach hurt from laughing so hard. After Hal finished washing everything, he gathered up the hose and threw it under the porch. "What you think about that?"

"Most fun I ever had," I said.

Hal nodded and ripped one of the garbage bags from a window. "You ain't the only one that knows about stuff."

"What else you got?"

"We'll get Daddy up. He's got a machine gun from Vietnam we can shoot those bottles with."

"Machine gun!"

"Yeah. Real one."

"Let's go get him, then!"

Hal woke his daddy while I waited outside. Mr. Mitchell came out in his underwear with the machine gun Hal told me about. He had scars across his stomach and tattoos on his shoulder. His underwear was split and so thin that it was little more than yellowed cheesecloth.

Hal went around to the back of the trailer and got some

empty bottles from a trash pile and stood them at the edge of the clay pit. I sat beside Mr. Mitchell on the porch and watched him load his gun. I had heard and read about machine guns, but I'd never seen one.

"Where can you get one of those?"

Mr. Mitchell rubbed his eyes like he was still tired. He scratched under his arms and took a while before he answered me. "You just kinda ask around."

"Pretty loud?"

Mr. Mitchell nodded. "Yep. Especially for a man with a headache."

Hal came back and stood behind us on the porch. Mr. Mitchell looked at us. "Ready?"

"Ready," I said.

Mr. Mitchell jerked the machine gun up to his shoulders, and I slammed my hands over my ears as it shot fire from its barrel. All of the bottles seemed to blow apart at once and rain down into the clay pit as he swept the barrel once right and then once left. I was so excited my ears started to itch. I let my hands down and yelled out, "Wahooo!"

Hal ran around the back of the trailer, and I heard him picking through the trash pile for more bottles. Mr. Mitchell laid the gun across his legs and looked over at me. "Wanna try it?"

"Heck, yeah!"

After Hal set up the new bottles and returned, I took the gun from Mr. Mitchell and brought it to my shoulders. I lined up the iron sights and put my cheek against the stock. "Now?" I asked.

"Make 'em pay, Moon."

I squeezed back on the trigger and the gun exploded. I let off the trigger and watched the one bottle I'd aimed for fall away into the clay pit. Mr. Mitchell told me to move my barrel along the line of bottles when I pulled the trigger and I could get them all. I sucked in my breath, took aim, and turned every bottle in the line to glass splinters.

"You a damn good shot, boy."

"I told you he would be," Hal said.

When it was his turn, Hal walked to the edge of the pit and fired the gun from his hip at the far side. Puffs of dust spit from the clay bank. Before he was done, a giant wall of dirt fell away and slid to the bottom.

It was well after dark when Hal and I stopped shooting. Mr. Mitchell had made a seat for himself on the tailgate of the truck and drank whiskey and scratched and chuckled at us. "You boys would have been hell in 'Nam," he said. "I reckon you two gonna be icin' them shoulders tonight."

Hal made hamburgers for supper, and I'd never tasted anything better. I ate two before I sat on the sofa and held my stomach. Mr. Mitchell watched me. "Touch easier than killin' your own food, ain't it?"

"Yessir," I said.

"Don't hurt yourself over it. You gonna blow up, you don't slow down a little bit."

"He always eats too much when you give him regular food."

Mr. Mitchell played country music on his record player and lay back in a big chair across from me. He took a pouch of tobacco from a table beside him and stuffed some in his cheek. Hal sat on the kitchen counter and pulled his shirt off. He licked his finger and began to clean his belly button.

"What's today?" I asked.

"Saturday," Hal replied.

"You get a lot of people comin' by here to get dirt?"

Mr. Mitchell spit in an empty whiskey bottle beside him. "Sometimes," he said. "Depends on what they got goin' on construction-wise."

"I'll bet you can make a bunch of money sellin' dirt. You don't ever run out, do you?"

Mr. Mitchell seemed to think for a few seconds. "Guess you don't."

"We gonna go see Kit, Hal?"

"How we gonna do that? They catch me or you both, they gonna take us away."

"We could sneak into the hospital."

"He's prob'ly not feelin' better yet."

"Well, I hope he doesn't think I forgot about him. Hope he doesn't think I'm mad at him."

"I told you we'd call him in a few days."

"You think he'll still wanna go to Alaska?"

"Moon, what you gonna go to Alaska for?" Mr. Mitchell asked me.

I was about to tell him what Pap had told me, but I didn't. It didn't seem right anymore. "I've just been plannin' on goin' there for a while. I told Kit I'd take him."

"You'd freeze up there."

"I don't really care where we go. I just don't wanna go by myself."

"I'd rather live out there in that clay pit than Alaska," Mr. Mitchell said.

"Clay pits don't bother me."

“Any place you don’t wanna live?”

“Pinson. Jail. Most any place where you get locked up. It makes my insides tighten up like somebody poured bad water down my throat.”

The wiener dog jumped into my lap, and Mr. Mitchell watched it. He spit into the bottle again and said, “I’ll bet you Sanders’s momma raised hell on him for losin’ that dog.”

“I’ll bet he got lost lookin’.”

“For you or for the dog?”

We lay in Hal’s room that night with the window open because the weather was pleasant. The wiener dog nosed under the blanket with me and lay throbbing against my side. I trained my ears to listen for the night sounds, but all I heard was the rustling of pecan trees.

“What else do you have around here?”

“Got a chainsaw. Bet you ain’t never used one of them.”

“Let’s go get it.”

“Not now.”

“Is it loud?”

“Yeah.”

“Loud as that machine gun?”

“No.”

“Bet you don’t have many wild animals around here with all that shootin’.”

“Daddy don’t shoot it much. Just when he’s got company.”

“You’re lucky,” I said.

“I know.”

“I could ride in clay pits and shoot machine guns and eat hamburgers for a long time before I’d get tired of it.”

"Yeah. And it's good to be back with Daddy again."

"Yeah," I replied. One of the bloodhounds moaned outside the window. "Hal?"

"What?"

"I don't miss my pap as much anymore."

"How come?"

"I don't know. You think that's bad?"

"No."

"I think he might have been wrong about a lot of things."

"About wantin' you to live out there in the forest?"

"I like livin' in the forest. I don't know where else I'd live, but I don't wanna be by myself. We were always by ourselves. We didn't ever see anybody except Mr. Abroscotto."

"Why don't you stop thinkin' about everything so much?"

"You reckon Kit's all right?"

"He's fine."

"You know how he hates those hospitals."

"I'm sure he hates dead a lot more."

"You know, my pap didn't seem like he cared if he died. I don't wanna die for a long time."

"Moon, I'm tired."

"I'm not. This is the best bed I've ever slept in, but I'm not tired. Stay up and talk to me."

"Tell you what. Let's go to sleep and I'll show you that chainsaw tomorrow."

"That sounds good to me. I'll stop talkin' now."

# 33

The next morning, I lay in bed an hour before daylight watching Hal's eyes and waiting for them to open. He was still asleep when the sun slipped over the trees, and I felt that I couldn't lie there much longer. I saw the lump of the wiener dog near his stomach. I picked a toothpick off the floor and tossed it at the lump. The dog rose under the covers and stuck her head out and looked around. Hal opened his eyes and stared at me. "What are you lookin' at?"

"Waitin' for you to get up."

"What time is it?"

"Thirty minutes after daylight."

Hal moaned and rolled over.

"We're gonna do the chainsaw today," I reminded him.

"Why don't you go outside and help Daddy while I sleep."

"He up?"

"Yeah. He's prob'ly out in the clay pit."

The wiener dog watched me for a few more seconds and then sighed and nosed her way back under the blanket. I pulled on my clothes and left to find Mr. Mitchell.

I walked down the road to the clay pit as the sun rose over the pines, which were powdered orange thirty feet up from the clay dust. A hawk soared overhead and a rabbit darted into the brush at the edge of the road. I hadn't gone far when I heard the clanking of someone working on a piece of equipment. I rounded a bend in the road and saw Mr. Mitchell leaning under the hood of a front-end loader. He wore greasy khaki trousers and was barefoot and shirtless. I walked up behind him and watched him for a few seconds. "Hey," I said.

Mr. Mitchell jumped up and bonged his head on the underside of the hood.

"I didn't mean to scare you," I said. "I can sneak up on just about anything without even meanin' to."

He climbed down from where he stood on the loader shovel, sat on the ground, and held the top of his head with both hands. I watched him rock back and forth, taking deep breaths. Finally, he looked up at me. "Damn, Moon," he said.

"You need some help?"

He took one hand from the top of his head and studied it, then pushed himself up to stand again. He winced and went to lean against the front-end loader. "All right," he said. "Why don't you go over to that shed and get me some oil. You know what that looks like?"

"Nossir, but I can read."

He nodded. "Good. Go get me some that says '400.' "

When I returned with the oil, he was leaning under the hood again. He reached back and I climbed up and put the oil into his hand. "I've never seen an engine up close," I said.

"You're lucky."

"Looks like a bunch of parts."

"It is."

"How do you know what it all is?"

" 'Cause I been runnin' these for close to twenty-five years."

I nodded. "You gonna wash it?"

"Don't gotta wash this thing."

"You gonna put some dirt in some people's trucks?"

Mr. Mitchell began pouring the oil into the engine. He looked at me while the can drained. "Maybe," he said. "It's Sunday, so might not be anybody until tomorrow. Where's that boy of mine?"

"He's bedded down with the wiener dog."

Mr. Mitchell spit to the side and shook his head. "You got to twitchin' in there, didn't you?"

"Yessir. I can't sleep much past daybreak unless I'm in jail where there aren't any windows."

He looked at the oil can and shook the last of it out. He tossed it into the weeds and shut the hood. I climbed down after him and followed him to the shed, where we sat on five-gallon buckets. Mr. Mitchell pulled some chewing tobacco from his pocket and packed his cheek full. I watched him work the wad around and spit out a long line of juice. "You know what I can't figure?" he said.

I was watching the brown spit bead in the dust. I shook my head.

"Why your pappy wanted to live out in the woods like he did."

"He hated the government."

"What started all that business?"

"I don't know."

"Your pappy have any friends?"

I shook my head. "Only person we ever talked to after Momma died was Mr. Abroscotto. He had the store up the road."

"He know your pappy for a long time?"

"Yessir," I nodded. "Ever since he went to live in the forest."

"Maybe he knows."

"I don't think he'd tell me anything. I whipped up on him pretty good."

"You ain't gonna whip up on me, are you?"

"Nossir. I hope I'm done whippin' up on people."

Mr. Mitchell spit and chuckled to himself. I heard the dogs barking up the road and turned to see Hal coming towards us with the bloodhounds jumping up at him. When Hal stood before us, Mr. Mitchell suddenly leaped up and put him in a playful headlock. Hal began punching him in the stomach. Mr. Mitchell looked at me and smiled. "It ain't nothin for me to find somebody to whip up on."

"Crap, Daddy!" came Hal's muffled cry. "Your underarm smells like horse piss."

Mr. Mitchell let him go. Hal stumbled backwards, wiped at his face with his shirt, and spit at the ground. Then he looked up at me and laughed. "Kick his butt, Moon."

"You boys go have some fun," Mr. Mitchell said. "I'm gonna get me a six-pack and sit up in that loader until I got buzzards roostin' on me."

"It won't work," I said.

"Well, we'll see."

"We're gonna get a chainsaw and go cut on some of those big trees that fell in a storm," Hal said. "Moon ain't never used a chainsaw."

By noon we'd stacked up a giant pile of tree parts. Hal sat in the branches of a large top and chewed tobacco while I busied myself inspecting an abandoned squirrel nest.

Hal spit and asked me, "Anything in there?"

"No. Baby squirrels make good pets, though."

"I got enough pets already."

I walked up the trunk to where Hal was and sat across from him. He held out a bag of Red Man chewing tobacco. "You want some?"

"Why would I want some of that?"

"'Cause it's good, dumbass."

I shook my head.

"Fine, then," he said. "Daddy left it in the truck."

"Your daddy lets you live just about any way you want, doesn't he?"

Hal shut his eyes and worked the tobacco in his cheek. "Just about."

"Hal?"

"What?"

"Why you think my pap made me live like he did?"

"I don't know."

"Your daddy said he can't figure it out, either."

"Maybe some people were after him?"

"He always thought the government was after him."

"Well, there you go."

"Why were they after him, though?"

"Hell, Moon, I don't know. You ain't out there no more, so no sense in worryin' about it."

I could tell Hal didn't have any answers for me, so I lay back and we both napped under the pine needles.

That night I got a pencil and paper from Hal and wrote Pap a letter on the kitchen counter.

Dear Pap,

I know it's been a long time since I've written anything more than a couple of words to you. If you can see me, then you know where all I've been. You know I haven't had anything but pine bark to write on and that doesn't make for an easy letter. Sometimes I wonder if you really get these words in the smoke. Seeing as how I don't ever hear from you, I've made decisions that I don't know if you'll like. I decided not to go to Alaska at all if I've got to be alone. I don't think I can live like you wanted me to live. I think I'd be too lonely. Why did we have to live out there like we did, Pap? Why couldn't I have any friends? I'm going to talk to Mr. Abroscotto again. I don't know what to do. I'm not mad at you, Pap.

Love, Moon

"You got some matches, Hal?"

"You can burn it on the stove."

"All right."

# 34

A couple of days later, Hal and I took the truck to get my things at the old shelter. Mr. Mitchell told us to drive into Union and head south to get to Gainesville. We'd pass through town and then I'd start recognizing things.

"Your daddy doesn't mind you takin' his truck out of here by yourself?"

"I'm goin' to Hellenweiler just as fast I get caught drivin' as walkin'."

"You're not gonna get caught."

"That's what you always say . . . and you been caught at least once."

"They can't keep me, though."

Hal laughed. "We got laundry to do, too."

"Where are we gonna do that?"

"Laundromat."

"I've never been to a Laundromat."

"You ain't never been lots of places."

"That's the place you told me they have a phone?"

"Yeah. And they got good-lookin' girls."

"I don't care about girls. I wanna use that phone."

"We're gonna call him soon. He hasn't been there that long."

"But they said he was okay, right?"

"Yeah, I told you that already. He's okay."

"Good."

I could tell we were getting close to where I used to live by the smell of the forest and the types of trees I was seeing. "We're almost there," I said.

"You recognize all this?"

"Yeah."

It wasn't long before we came to the bridge over the Noxubee River. "Stop right here," I said.

Hal pulled over and stared at me. I got out and scooted on my rear down the hill to the swamp. When I got to the bottom, I heard Hal yell at me from above.

"What you want an old wheelbarrow for?" Hal asked.

"It's mine. Sanders threw it down here."

"That the one you been talkin' about?"

"Yeah. The one I hauled my pap around in."

"Jesus. You need some help?"

"No, I've got it. It's just jabbed down in this mud pretty good."

I finally managed to get the wheelbarrow out of the mud and drag it back up to the truck. Hal helped me put it in the bed and then we set out again.

A few miles down the road I told him to pull over once more. "This is it," I said. "You wait here and I'll be back in a little while."

"There ain't nothin' here."

"I've got trails out there that I can take to the shelter."

"All right. How long's a little while to you?"

I shrugged my shoulders.

"That's what I figured. How about I go to the Laundromat and come back?"

"All right," I said. "You can find me later." I bent over

and picked up a stick. I stabbed it in the ground. "Right here."

My feet fell quickly on the old footpaths like I'd just left the day before. I pictured what lay before me all the way to the shelter—every crook in the path, low branch, rise and fall, gurgling creek. The patterns and sounds of the patch of forest where I had lived for so long came back to me. I had run the trails so many times that I knew how firm the ground was before every step. I knew enough about what lived in the bushes and trees around me to tell the time of day by their movement and sounds.

After an hour and a half I was close to the shelter, yet I got the feeling that something was wrong. Somehow things were different, but I didn't know how. I slowed to a trot, and finally I took off my shoes and walked on the outsides of my feet. I approached the clearing and suddenly I knew that it was the forest noises that weren't right. A disturbance had passed through and left silence behind it.

Scattered about the clearing were our tools and the few items of furniture Pap and I had in the shelter. The curing barrel was knocked over. Parts of the roof were pulled away.

I walked slowly into the shelter and found it unusually bright inside from sunlight that beamed through the holes in the roof. The hide pile was thrown about the room and a jar of nails lay shattered and spilled where the cupboard had been. Pap's books were in a soggy pile on the floor.

I wasn't sure what I was feeling. I wasn't mad. I wasn't unhappy. I was confused.

Remembering what I had come for, I felt around in the

ceiling supports and my hand touched Pap's rifle. I pulled it from its hiding place and looked it over. It was in good shape except for a little rust on the barrel. I found our tube of grease on the floor and squeezed some onto a rag. I gave the rifle a rubdown and then stepped back out of the shelter.

"Wasn't anything I could have done about this, Pap," I said out loud. "I guess I'm not supposed to be here anyway. Supposed to be in Alaska by now."

All I wanted was the rifle. I turned my back to the shelter and stepped into the forest once more. This time, I took a path down through a cane thicket and across a stream where I used to run traps. I crossed a rusted barbed-wire fence that Pap once said looked to be a hundred years old by the way it was grown into the sides of the trees. I moved quickly through the hills and valleys and across Mr. Wellington's dirt road and back into the forest. After a while, I heard cars on the blacktop. I came out of the trees and continued the half mile to Mr. Abroscotto's store. I saw him through the window that looked over the gas pumps. His back was to me, and I knew that he was watching the television above the tobacco shelf.

He didn't turn when I walked in and the little bell jingled on the door. I stood there watching him and feeling nervous about how he would act. My hands were tired of holding the rifle, so I set the butt of it on the floor and held it at the end of the barrel. "Hey," I said.

He turned and glanced at me briefly, then looked at me again and stood up. "Moon?"

I nodded at him.

"That you?"

"Yessir."

He leaned over the counter and stared at me like he couldn't see very well. "Hardly recognized you without your hair."

I rubbed my head and nodded. Mr. Abroscotto looked like he didn't know what to do. "Why don't you put up that gun," he said.

"You might take it from me."

"Why are you standin' there and holdin' it like that?"

" 'Cause I was carryin' it."

"Have you got it loaded?"

"It's always loaded."

"I'm not comfortable with you standin' there with a loaded rifle in my store."

"You think I'm gonna shoot you?"

"No . . . You're not, are you?"

"I've never shot anybody. I wouldn't shoot you, Mr. Abroscotto."

He walked around the counter and came to stand before me. He was still watching me in a way that made me nervous. "Set it over there by the door, anyway."

I glanced behind me, careful to keep him in sight, and saw a place near the door where I could lean the rifle and still be able to grab it quickly if I had to run out. I leaned it against the wall and faced Mr. Abroscotto again.

"I wanted to ask about my pap."

"You know how many people are lookin' for you?"

"I know Sanders is after me."

Mr. Abroscotto nodded. "He's in here at least twice a week askin' if I've seen you."

"I think he tore up our old shelter. I just came from there."

"I'd hate to think what he's gonna do when he gets his hands on you. You shouldn't mess with people like him."

"Maybe he won't catch me."

"After everything he says you did to him, he's gonna give it all he's got. You know, you could get me in trouble bein' here. I don't need any of his kind of trouble."

"That's why I'm standin' by this door. You tried to turn me in once already."

Mr. Abroscotto shook his head and stepped behind the counter. "So you wanna know about your father, do you?"

"That's right. Why'd he bring me out here?"

He turned and looked at me and leaned against the tobacco shelf. "Okay. Why don't you sit down and I'll tell you what I know."

I slipped down the wall to the floor.

"Moon, I didn't meet your father until you were about two years old. He'd just moved out into this forest, and he had you and your mother, Caroline, with him. They carried you around in a burlap sack with a piece of hemp rope—some kind of papoose setup. Neither one of 'em talked much. They'd tell me what they wanted, trade a few things, and be gone."

"With me in the sack?"

"That's right. Nobody knew where y'all went out in that forest. You'd think that after knowin' your father all those years, I'd have some idea where it was you lived. But he was careful to cover his tracks, and I don't make a habit of gettin' in another man's business."

Mr. Abroscotto reached down and took a sip of cola that

was on the counter. "Anyhow, your father and I talked once after your mother died. He came in here with you late one afternoon as I was closin' and sat down on the floor just like you're doin' now. He told me that she was dead, that he'd buried her in the woods. I asked him if there was anything I could do, and he just shook his head. He was quiet for a long time. You never could tell what he wanted. That was the only time I thought maybe he was gonna tell me somethin' about himself. Finally, he asked me if I'd ever been in a war and I said no. He said once you've been in a war, you don't need much to live. I took that to mean he'd gone to Vietnam, and somethin' that happened to him over there made him want to live like he did."

"What happened in Vietnam?"

"What happens in most wars—people get killed. However, a lot of people didn't think we should have been over there."

"They made Pap go, and he didn't want to?"

"Somethin' like that."

"Is Sanders mad at Pap about Vietnam?"

"No . . . I don't think—"

"Why won't he leave me alone?"

"You're startin' to learn that life's not as simple as you thought it was, Moon. There's mean people out there. Sanders just has a bad streak in him."

"I told him a bunch of times I wasn't scared of him, and he's still after me."

"I know you're not scared of him. You're not scared of anything. You're screwed up, Moon. You're all messed up.

You have no sense of reality. You've got to get some help."

I stood and grabbed my rifle. Mr. Abroscotto ducked behind the counter. "Hey, now!" he yelled.

I stood there with the rifle in my hands, watching the counter. "Moon?" he called out.

"What?"

"What are you doin'?"

"Leavin'."

Mr. Abroscotto peered slowly over the counter.

"I can tell you're not my friend," I said.

"I am your friend, Moon. I just know you need help, and I'm tryin' to talk sense into your hard little head."

"You don't know anything about me, and I've known you longer than anybody except my pap. You know I wouldn't shoot at you."

Mr. Abroscotto shook his head. "I'm sorry," he said. "It's just that the news—"

I turned and left.

I sat inside the edge of the forest for about fifteen minutes before Hal pulled up near the stake I'd used as a marker. I stood and walked to the road holding Pap's rifle. Hal watched me out of the truck window.

"What kind is it?"

".22."

"That all you wanted?"

I climbed into the truck and put the rifle between my legs. "No. You'd best mash that gas pedal."

"What'd you do now?"

"I went to that store. Mr. Abroscotto's likely to have Sanders around here lookin' for me."

"Crap," Hal said. He slammed down on the gas pedal and the tires threw dirt until they caught the asphalt and squalled.

"I wanted to ask him about Pap."

"I should've seen that comin'."

"He said Vietnam made him want to live in the forest."

"You happy now?"

"No. What happened in Vietnam?"

"I don't know. Ask Daddy."

"I will. You know what else?"

"What?"

"Someone's been to my old shelter and torn it up."

"You mad about it?"

I shook my head. "I don't care now. Nothin' else there I needed."

Hal turned the truck around and we headed back towards Union. He kept looking in the rearview mirror for a while, then relaxed. "You hungry?" he asked me.

"Yeah. You?"

"We'll stop up here at the lock and dam. I got some Vienna sausages and crackers. You okay?"

"Yeah."

Hal looked at me sideways. "All right."

We stopped at a point along the river where we could see the lock and sat on the tailgate. I pulled a sausage from the can and put it between two crackers and took a bite. "Pretty good sausage," I said with my mouth full.

"Yeah. They're pretty good . . . What you wanna do this afternoon?"

"You know what I wanna do."

"All right, all right, we'll go call him! I swear I ain't takin' you to visit everybody in the whole damn state!"

## 35

We stopped at a store not far from the clay pit. Hal looked up the number for the hospital in Tuscaloosa, put some money in a slot, dialed the phone, and handed it to me. I felt my stomach become jittery as I waited for someone to pick up. After a few seconds a woman answered.

"Bryant Memorial," she said.

"Is Kit there?" I asked her.

Hal shook his head like I'd done something wrong. He took the phone from me and spoke to the woman. "The boy they found on the road who's been in the news. Kit Slip . . . Yeah. He's a friend of ours . . . Yeah." Hal nodded with the phone squeezed between his chin and shoulder.

"He there?" I asked.

Hal shrugged. Close to a minute went by before Hal spoke again into the phone. "Okay. We'll call back later."

He hung up the phone. "They said he's restin' and he can't talk right now."

I felt my stomach grow calm again. "So he's prob'ly okay, then?"

"Sounds like he's fine. We'll try again in a few days. Give him time to rest."

Hal said he knew of a place to get parts for the truck. We drove through the countryside until we came to a field of wrecked cars. I walked with him as he looked under their hoods and inside of them. After a while, we came to an old police car with the blue light still attached. Hal climbed onto the roof and sat with the light between his legs. He pulled and rocked until it popped loose. Then he stood and lifted it up until the wires snapped and he had it free. "What you think about this?" he said to me.

"I think it'd look good on top of your truck," I said.

"You damn right it would."

We took the blue light back to the clay pit and worked under the shade of the equipment shed installing it. It was close to dark by the time the unit was glued to the roof and the wires were taped along the side of the truck and under the hood to the battery. Mr. Mitchell came up from the clay pit and parked the front-end loader. He was watching us when Hal got the light to work for the first time. He shook his head and took a swig from a whiskey bottle.

"How you like that, Daddy?"

"You boys gonna get us all throwed in jail."

"Hell," Hal said.

"I went and talked to that store owner today," I said to Mr. Mitchell.

"Oh yeah?" he replied.

"Yeah," Hal said. He pointed at me. "He's about to have the law down on us."

"What'd he say to you?" Mr. Mitchell asked.

"Said Pap got messed up by Vietnam."

Mr. Mitchell nodded. "I can see that. I didn't take to it much myself."

"What was it like?"

"It was a lot of people dyin' is what it was like. But all wars are that way. I think the difference with Vietnam was you had a lot of people that the government made go over there that didn't wanna go."

"Pap must not have wanted to go. He always said he didn't like people tellin' him what to do. Especially the government."

"I wish I knew more to say to you, Moon."

I stared across the clay pit at the tops of the pines, gauging the breeze. "It doesn't matter much now."

"Maybe one of these days, when you decide to get back to civilization, you can find some more people that knew him. Might be they'll give you the answers you need."

"Come on, Moon," Hal said. "Let's go up to the house and get somethin' to eat. We got some Spam and Doritos up there."

I looked over at Hal. "I've never had Doritos."

"I know. It'll make you forget about your pap. Come on."

We went mud-riding that night with the blue light on. Whenever the water and mud slid off our windshield, we saw the clay pit walls glowing an eerie blue.

"Need some noise to go with this," Hal said.

"I like it all right."

Back at the trailer, we lay in bed and listened to rain pouring down outside. Images of the flickering blue clay pit stayed in my head.

"Hal?"

"What?"

"Your truck gonna fill up with water?"

"No. Got holes in the floorboards."

I thought of the shelter Kit and I had made, far away through the darkness, and wondered how it was holding up. I imagined that some animal had crawled into it and found it a snug home. When I thought of myself lying in that cramped space with leaves and pine straw hanging close to my nose, I felt my soft mattress and the blanket and I was glad to be where I was.

"Hal?"

"What?"

"I don't know what I'm gonna do."

"About what?"

"About everything."

"I thought you were gonna go live in the forest with Kit when he got better."

"What if he doesn't get better? I won't have anybody to go with, then."

"Well, most people would rather sleep in a house and buy things at the store."

"Kit liked it out there."

"Kit likes anything you tell him to like. You're the only guy I know that ever made friends with him."

"How come?"

"I don't know. I guess most people at Pinson thought he was a wuss."

"What's a wuss?"

"Like a crybaby."

"He's not a crybaby."

"I know. I just didn't know him before. Nobody else knew him, either. He was always goin' to the doctor."

"But I think he really liked it out in the forest."

"I know he did. I was just kiddin' with you."

One of the bloodhounds whined outside the window, where it huddled under a woodpile roof. "You know," I said, "I don't see anything wrong with havin' a real house . . . Long as it's in the forest or next to a clay pit."

Hal yawned. "Ain't nothin' wrong with stayin' warm and dry."

"That's what I want one day, Hal. I want a house trailer drug off into the forest with no roads goin' to it."

"How you gonna get it out there?"

"I'll plant trees in the road after they roll it in."

"Crap."

"Maybe you could come live out there with me since I'd have that house trailer. It'd be fancy livin'. Cover it up with leaves. We'd never get caught."

"What in hell would we do all day?"

I sat up and looked at him. "What do you mean! We'd—"

"Shhh!" Hal said to me. "Gonna wake up Daddy."

I lowered my voice. "Rope swings and guns and traps and trees. Fishin'. All kinds of stuff."

"What about livin' with Daddy?"

Suddenly, the perfect world I'd imagined was gone and everything was gloomy. "Oh yeah," I said. "You've already got a house right here. Clay pit and all."

Hal rolled over and looked at me. "Moon, I don't expect to be out here runnin' around for too long. Sooner or later,

I'm gonna have to hit the road or go to Hellenweiler. I ain't leavin' Daddy, so I guess I'll let 'em take me away when they come."

I stared at him.

"What I'm sayin' is, I ain't tryin' to figure out what I'm gonna do, 'cause I already know, and I ain't really got much of a choice about it."

I nodded.

"I'd rather be in Hellenweiler than livin' out in that forest or walkin' down some road somewhere," he said.

I lay back down and stared at the ceiling. Then I spoke words that I never thought I'd hear coming from my mouth. "If I have to be all by myself, maybe I'd rather go to Hellenweiler with you."

## 36

I spent the next three days helping Hal and his daddy in the clay pit. If Hal's daddy didn't need the front-end loader to fill a truck, we made trails through the forest with it, using the giant shovel to push a path ten feet wide. Afterwards we'd get in the truck, and Hal would see how fast we could run the new track.

On Saturday morning Mr. Mitchell brought us football helmets to wear while we were racing in the woods. The helmets made Hal want to drive faster. I'd never thought about wrecking before, but we went riding after lunch and hit a gum tree head-on. The battery flew out of the front grill and jerked the police light from the top of the truck and flew it like a kite tail for twenty-five yards until it whipped into a tree and shattered into splinters. Both of us hit our heads on the windshield and knocked the spiderwebbed glass onto the truck hood. We rocked back into our seats and looked at each other.

"Whoa, horsey!" Hal yelled.

I pulled off my helmet and shouted, "What else you got!"

The truck was still running, and Hal racked it into gear and backed away from the tree. The windshield fell off into the weeds. We drove up the track to where the battery lay in the pine needles. Hal got out and followed the wire that led to the police light. When he saw the mangled piece of aluminum, he looked back at me and spit. "Damn tree."

After getting the battery under the hood again, we made another trip to the field of wrecked cars. We found a windshield, a new grill, some headlights, a hood, and a horn off the top of a Peterbilt truck. We put all of these in the bed and started back.

That afternoon and night, we worked at the equipment shed installing the new parts. We put the windshield on first since so much dust and so many bugs had gotten all over us driving without it. After that, Hal screwed the horn to his roof.

"Hey, Moon!"

I looked up. "What?"

"I'll show you what else I got."

Hal pressed the button for the horn. It was so loud I covered my ears as the sound echoed across the bottom of the clay pit and went skyward. The bloodhounds howled from up at the trailer, and the forest creatures ducked away and fell silent. Before long, Mr. Mitchell was shuffling down the road towards us without any clothes on.

"What!" he yelled.

"I ain't callin' you," Hal yelled back at him.

Mr. Mitchell made a motion like he was waving flies from his face and continued towards us.

"He gonna care that you mashed up the front of the truck?" I asked Hal.

"Hell no. He knows I'll fix it up better'n new."

When Mr. Mitchell got to the truck, he stopped and stared at it. He was swaying so much I thought he might fall over. His cheek bulged with tobacco so that when he spoke I could barely understand him. "You boys," he said. He looked away and spit. He was quiet for a minute and seemed to have forgotten what he was going to say. Finally, he looked at Hal again. "Damn," was all he said. He turned and began to walk up the hill.

The next morning we went into town to get oil for Mr. Mitchell.

"We gonna pass by the Laundromat?"

"Yeah. You wanna try and call Kit again?"

"Yeah."

We pulled into the Laundromat and went inside. I sat on a table next to the pay phone while Hal put in the money and dialed the number. He listened for a few seconds and then handed me the phone. "You know how to do it this time?"

I nodded and pressed it to my ear. When the woman answered, I looked at Hal while I spoke. "Can I have Kit Slip's room?"

"Hold please," she said.

I felt my hands shaking while I listened to music play over the telephone. "Got music playin'," I told Hal.

"Shhh," he said. "They're gettin' him."

After almost a minute, she picked up the telephone again. "May I have your name and telephone number and have him call you back?"

"I can't. This isn't my phone."

"May I have your name, please?"

"What for?"

"Constable Sanders requested—"

"Sanders!" I said.

"Excuse me?"

"I'm not fallin' for Sanders's tricks."

"I'm sorry, I'll have to—"

I hung up.

"What about Sanders?" Hal asked me.

"He's gettin' names and numbers of people who call."

"He's lookin' for us," Hal said.

"I've got to go check on Kit."

"The hell!"

"What if Sanders is hurtin' him?"

"Sanders can't do anything to him in the hospital!"

"The law can do whatever they want."

Hal began walking back towards the truck. "I ain't ready to go to Hellenweiler yet."

"Where are you goin'?" I yelled at him.

"Get back in the truck, Moon. Let's go home."

I started walking up the road away from him.

"Fine!" Hal yelled at me. "Just great! Go ahead and walk to Tuscaloosa."

I decided I would. I heard Hal drive the truck off in the other direction. Looking at the sun, I figured the time of day and the direction I was headed. Only a few minutes passed before I heard Hal coming back.

He drove along beside me and talked out of the window. "You know where you're goin'?"

"Tuscaloosa."

"You know how far it is?"

"It's prob'ly fifty miles, I reckon. At least."

Hal shook his head. "I oughta let you walk. You don't even know what road to take."

"I don't need—"

"I know you don't need any damn roads," Hal said. "Get in."

"You takin' me to Tuscaloosa?"

"Yeah, I'll take you, but I ain't goin' in."

I smiled. Hal stopped the truck, and I got in. "And you ain't gonna wear those clothes I gave you. You'll stand out for sure."

"You have somethin' else for me?"

"Yeah. We'll get you fixed up at the trailer and go to Tuscaloosa after lunch."

"Thanks, Hal."

"You're stubborn as hell."

# 37

Hal's daddy was down in the clay pit loading a dump truck when we got back to the trailer. Hal gave me new blue jeans and a plaid shirt instead of the Moe Bandy T-shirt I'd been wearing.

"Hospital's fancy," he said. "They'll throw you out in a second if you ain't fixed up."

Neither of us said much as we drove to Tuscaloosa. I was excited about finally seeing Kit again, but I could tell that Hal was worried about getting caught. He dropped me off at the entrance to the hospital and pointed to the parking lot where he would wait.

"Don't stay there too long. People start askin' you questions, get the hell out of there."

I nodded.

"I ain't stayin' around if cops start pourin' in here," Hal added.

"I don't want you to."

"Good, 'cause I ain't."

I saw a woman at the front desk talking on the phone. As I got close to her, I recognized her voice and knew she was the person who asked for my name and number earlier. I avoided the woman and followed some people down a hallway until I saw a man with a mop and bucket. "You know where I can find Kit Slip?" I asked him.

He looked at me blankly.

"The boy they found in the forest?"

I watched his eyes grow wide. "Oh, him," he said. "He's up on the fourth floor. Room 432."

"How do I get up there?"

The man pointed to the elevator, and I thanked him. I crowded into the box with some people and stood there for what must have been fifteen minutes as it went up and down and the doors opened and closed. Finally, a woman asked me where I was going, and I told her room 432. When the elevator stopped again, she told me to get out and walk past the nurses' station to the hall on my left.

The nurses all watched me as I passed them. One of them asked me if I needed help, and I shook my head and kept walking down the hall.

When I stood outside room 432, I heard a television. I only had to knock once before I heard Kit's voice tell me to come in. He was sitting up in bed, and his eyes grew wide with surprise when he saw me. "Moon! How did you get here?"

It felt so good to see my friend that my scalp tingled and my hands shook. "Hal dropped me off. I've been livin' with him."

Kit looked confused. I walked over to his bed and stared at a clear tube that went into his arm. "How did you find Hal?" he asked.

"He came lookin' for me. I was sleepin' up in a tree by the road waitin' for you to come back."

"I couldn't."

"What's that hooked up to you?"

"Medicine."

"Hurt?"

"No. I'm feeling a lot better today."

"You about ready for me to bust you out of here?"

Kit didn't say anything for a few seconds. "I don't know if I can leave yet."

"You said you felt better."

"I do. But I can't walk. I'm too weak."

The emptiness seemed to rush back into me.

"I want to leave," he said. "I hate it here."

I climbed up on Kit's bed. I lay next to him and stared at the television.

"What are you going to do, Moon?"

I shrugged. I fought back the knot rising in my throat.

"What are you so quiet about?" he asked me.

I felt that if I tried to say anything, I'd cry.

"I thought you were going to Alaska, Moon."

"I'm not goin'. Didn't you hear anything I said when you were sick?"

Kit shook his head. "I don't remember anything after you covered me up with those blankets."

"I got lonely out there. I wanted you to come back. I said I wasn't goin' anywhere without you."

Kit didn't say anything.

"I thought we'd be like brothers. We'd live out there together." I felt the tears start rolling down my face. "You're my best friend, Kit. I've never had a best friend except for Pap."

Kit rolled over and stared at the side of my face. "You're my best friend, too. I don't want you to be sad."

"I don't wanna be out there by myself anymore. It's not right out there."

"Where are you going to go?"

I shrugged. "Pinson makes me feel bad. Bein' out in the forest by myself makes me feel bad. Hal says he's goin' to Hellenweiler after a while. I don't have anywhere."

"I've never had so much fun in my whole life as when I was in the forest."

I wiped my eyes. "You really liked it out there?"

"I'd give anything to go back."

"I wish I knew how to make the kind of medicine you need."

"Me too," he said. "You can make just about anything else."

I nodded and wiped my eyes again. "I haven't cried but about three times in my whole life."

"It doesn't matter."

"Yeah, well . . ."

"You'd better not stay long," Kit said.

"How come?"

"Sanders has been coming around here."

I sat up and looked at Kit. "He do anything to you?"

"No, he's plenty mad, though. He wanted to know how to get to where we lived. I said I didn't remember, but he didn't believe me."

"He'd prob'ly kill me if he could."

"He says we shot at him and ate his dogs. I told the TV people that we didn't do any of it, but they don't believe me. They keep asking me if you told me to lie about it all."

"Well, I'm not scared of any of 'em. Sanders is makin' stuff up to get me in trouble."

"I know."

I lay back down and we didn't say anything for a while.

"Hal's out there waitin' for me," I finally said.

"I wish you didn't have to go."

"I'm just goin' back to Hal's trailer. I haven't made any plans yet."

"They're going to send me back to Pinson, you know. When I get out of here."

I didn't reply. I climbed out of the bed.

"Maybe you could come see me there sometime?" Kit said to my back.

I walked to the door and turned around. "I don't feel too good about all of this, Kit. I'm feelin' lonely. If it weren't for Hal, I think I'd be as crazy as Sanders by now."

"I want to be out there with you as soon as they let me."

"Hal says the law leaves you alone once you turn eighteen. That means we've got less than eight years."

"Until I come live with you?"

I smiled. "That's right. I'll have a place already fixed up somewhere. A trailer pulled off in the forest with leaves over it. No roads."

Kit nodded eagerly. I walked back to the bed and leaned over him. "We'll still kill our own food. We'll grow a garden and trade our vegetables for your medicine."

"And eat all of the things that grow wild in the spring."

"That's right. And make some more deerskin hats."

"Eight more years."

"But I'll see you before then. I don't know how, but I will. Maybe I'll climb up in the trees outside of Pinson and wave at you sometime. We can talk through the fence at night. I'll call you on a telephone and let you know."

Kit held out his hand, and I grabbed it. We shook on the deal like I saw some boys do at Pinson. I imagined the two of us, eighteen years old and living in our trailer, just like we'd been there a week already. I felt all right when I walked out of the room, but as soon as I faced down the hall and saw the nurses' station with all of the nurses staring at me, I felt sick again. I wanted to curl up on the floor until the pain and loneliness went away. I started to go back into Kit's room, but I only turned and looked at the door. I knew it wouldn't do any good. Suddenly, eight years seemed an impossible time to wait in the forest alone. Once again, I thought of Hal telling me that he was going to Hellenweiler eventually and that we weren't safe at his daddy's place for long. My future and the hall in front of me were a long, dark tunnel. I couldn't imagine that things could get worse.

I walked down the hall and up to the nurses' station. As soon as I turned the corner for the elevator, I felt an arm go around my neck and force me into a headlock. I stared at black shoes and black trousers. I didn't know that I'd ever picked up Sanders's scent, but the forearm flesh pressed into my nose brought back memories of him squeezing me against his chest on the side of the road. He squeezed tighter and tighter until I drooled on the floor.

"You think that hurts? I'm just gettin' started with you, boy."

# 38

Sanders put handcuffs on my wrists and ankles and hog-tied me. He thanked the women at the reception desk for calling him and picked me up. He carried me down the stairwell like an upside-down possum and took each step hard so that my wrists and ankles jerked painfully.

"What's the matter, boy? Looks like you lost the fight you had in you."

"You can't do anything to me that matters. I don't have anywhere to go anymore."

"We'll see about that."

"I'm not scared of you."

"Well, there's a lot of things you're about to learn, and scared's one of 'em."

People were already gathered outside and taking pictures of me when Sanders carried me out of the hospital doors. Before we got to his car, he stopped and answered the reporters while I hung there.

"Yes ma'am, this is him."

"Did he give you any trouble?"

"He's a wild boy, ma'am. As you can see," he said, jostling me around, "we've got techniques for his kind of trouble."

"Where will he go now?"

"He'll be in the Livingston jail waitin' to see the judge."

Sanders opened the back door of his police car and tossed me in. I landed facedown and turned my head so that my cheek pressed the seat. I could still hear the crowd following and see the flashes of cameras.

As we pulled away, Sanders got out his Copenhagen and put a pinch in his mouth. "You know where we're headed, boy?"

"Jail?"

"There too, but we got business to take care of first. Where's that third boy at?"

I didn't respond.

"That's all right. We can get to him later. Right now you're gonna show me where my pistol is."

"You lied about me shootin' at you. You said I ate your dogs. I wouldn't eat anybody's dog. I'm not showin' you anything."

Sanders spit into his cup. "You ain't showin' me anything, huh?" he said calmly.

"That's right."

"Well, we'll just have to see about that."

I felt myself getting carsick, so I took a deep breath and let it out slowly. "You can't do anything to me I care about."

"Maybe not . . . But I been thinkin'. That sickly little friend of yours'd prob'ly tell me what I need to know if I spent more time with him."

I felt my face growing hot. "You better not touch him!"

"You know, he'll be gettin' out of that hospital before too long. He'll need a police escort back to Pinson, seein' as how he's been in so much trouble. It'd be a shame if I had to give him that ride myself and work some answers out of him. He don't look to me like he'd hold out too long."

"You lied about us!" I yelled.

Sanders chuckled and spit into his cup again. "Boy, you think you can get around me? You think I'm just gonna go away?"

"I don't care what you do to me—just leave Kit alone."

"Well then, let's start again. Where's that pistol?"

Breathing deeply through my nose seemed to help the car sickness. As I lay on the backseat, I took deep breaths and thought about my situation. I realized that I would have to get Sanders out into the forest and get him lost and trap him. Then I'd have to go break Kit out of the hospital and take him somewhere safe. Maybe to Hal's, where we could all be together again. My mind raced with ideas of where I would tell Sanders the pistol was. I'd have to know the place to pull off my plan. I finally reasoned that there was nowhere I was more familiar with than the forest I was raised in.

"It's in my old shelter," I lied.

Sanders was silent for a moment. "How'd it get all the way back there?"

"I got a ride with somebody."

"When was the last time you were there?"

"I know someone tore it up, if that's what you wanna find out."

"Yeah, I got those surveyors to take me out there to your rabbit hole. I didn't see no pistol, either. Just a bunch of junk."

"I had the pistol with me. Then I left it there."

"For that sickly kid's sake, you better hope you ain't lyin'."

# 39

Sanders turned off the highway at Mr. Wellington's road, drove into the forest, and stopped. He got out and went around to the back of the car, and I heard him open and close the trunk. When he opened my door, he held a dog collar on a chain. He grabbed my ear, and I gritted my teeth as he pulled me across the seat.

"Just like a dog, boy," he mumbled as he fastened the collar around my neck. "That too tight?"

I didn't answer. He pulled the collar a notch tighter and pinched my skin in the buckle. "I'll hang you three feet off the ground with this thing if you try somethin' funny."

Sanders removed my ankle cuffs and jerked me to my feet. He draped a canteen of water around my neck, then shoved me forward. "Get on," he said.

We followed a trail of new orange flagging tape, tied to trees about every twenty yards. I walked slowly in front, my mind imagining my escape and building traps and weapons. I went through all the tools at the shelter and tried to remember where I had last seen them. I listened to Sanders behind me and gauged his energy by the sound of his footsteps and his breathing. He was tired after we climbed the first hill, but he got his energy back when we started through the flat pine forest. Once we came to Shomo Creek, he rested against a tree for a few minutes. When he jerked my leash, I knew it was time to move on again.

After we had traveled about a mile, Sanders yanked the leash so hard that I coughed against it. A sharp pain shot up into my head, and I gritted my teeth again. "Gimme some water," he said.

Usually, the forest worked with me. The sounds of the animals and the light patterns and the breezes carrying smell told me what it knew. That day, though, it seemed the forest had forgotten about me. It did nothing to help me. The animal sounds were distant and muffled. The sunlight lay in large, still blocks. There was no breeze. All that lay before me were endless hills of pine and swampy cane bottoms. As I realized this, my head grew dizzy and my thoughts wouldn't get straight. I couldn't remember what I had decided to do about Sanders. All I put together from my memory of the old shelter was a ruin of strewn logs and scattered cooking utensils . . . Suddenly, I felt that Sanders was going to kill me and leave me to rot. I thought of Kit. I thought of what Sanders would do to him after I was dead. I thought of dying and remembered what Pap said about not feeling pain when you died. I thought of Kit again. I thought of Hal. I had not said goodbye to either one of them. My only friends.

I rushed against the leash and felt it jerk me backwards until I lay flat in the leaves. Sanders laughed over me. He said something I couldn't make out, and I was lifted up by the collar. Even though I coughed and gagged, it didn't hurt. He draped the canteen over me again and I began to walk.

I trudged on through more hills and valleys, stopping for Sanders to rest every time the leash was jerked. Eventually, sunlight fell over me, and I was standing in the clearing with the ruined shelter before me. I had no plan. I couldn't even think of what to tell Sanders. I turned around slowly to face him. He was putting Copenhagen into his lip and breathing hard. He packed the tobacco with his tongue while his mouth hung open and gasped for air. Then he flicked the excess from his fingers and looked at me. "Gimme that water again."

I pulled the canteen off my neck and held it out to him. He snatched it, swirled off the top, and took a long drink. When he let it down, he said, "Ahhh . . . Bet you'd like some of this, wouldn't you?"

I didn't answer. My throat was dry, but bigger problems worried me.

He dropped the canteen to the ground and wiped his hand across his forehead. "Well, let's see it," he said.

"I don't have it."

"You don't have what?"

I shook my head slowly. "I don't have it."

"You don't have what?" he yelled.

I felt my body sag like it was waiting to fall to the ground with whatever Sanders was about to bring down on me. Suddenly, I heard a voice.

"What's going on here?"

Mr. Wellington had come up the trail behind us.

Sanders immediately loosened his grip on the chain and spun around to face the lawyer. "You just mind your own business and go back to your fancy lodge."

"What are you doing to that child?"

"Police business. We'll be done shortly."

Mr. Wellington looked at me and then back at Sanders. "What kind of police business requires a dog leash?"

Sanders's face was turning red. "Mister, I suggest you take your lawyerin' back down that trail before I write you up for obstructin' justice."

Mr. Wellington stared at Sanders. "Obstructing justice, you say?"

"That's right."

Mr. Wellington studied the ground and shook his head. He looked up slowly and his face became calm. "Constable, do you have any idea who you're talking to?"

Sanders's hands began to twitch with anger. He dropped the leash and took a step towards the lawyer. "You wanna play that game, old man? You wanna play who's who in Sumter County? That what you want?"

The chain was on the ground a few seconds before my senses came rushing back to me. I shut out the rest of their conversation and focused on the limp chain lying in the leaves. With a quick yank, I had it flying through the air and gathered at my stomach. Clutching it about my chest with my hands still in handcuffs, I sprinted for the edge of the clearing. I heard yelling and footfalls behind me as I sprang into the forest.

I ran until it seemed that everything around me was quiet. It might have been two hundred yards or it might have been a mile. I didn't know where I was anymore. When I lay down and let the chain fall back into the leaves, I didn't feel tired. All I heard was my breathing and my heart beating. The treetops overhead were still and the sky was overcast. The forest was endless in all directions. It seemed to stretch out forever with no people. It seemed full of animals that turned their heads away from me and spoke about me in whispers. All I thought about was the fact that I was still alive, and it no longer seemed to matter. Everybody I cared about was in trouble because of me.

## 40

The clouds slid over my upturned eyes the rest of the afternoon. Just before sunset, the sky cleared and buzzards circled me.

"You might just want me this time," I said.

As the forest grayed, a coon waddled up to the leash chain and pawed it. When I stood, it scampered away in surprise. I took off the leash and felt my neck where there was a ring of swollen skin. Looking at my wrists, I saw where the handcuffs had worn me raw enough to bleed in places. I rolled over a nearby log and gathered some slugs. By rubbing their slime on my wrists, I made them slippery enough to pull out of the handcuffs.

Using the stars, I got my bearings and set out through the forest. In forty-five minutes I was staring at the windows of Mr. Wellington's lodge. I watched until I saw him get up from a chair and walk into the kitchen. He came back shortly with a drink and sat down. I stepped from the forest and approached his door.

He opened the door before I could knock and stared down at me like he'd been expecting me a long time before. "What do you plan on doing now?" he asked me.

"I'm ready for the law to come get me and take me back to jail."

"The last I saw of the law, he was chasing you through the forest."

I stared at Mr. Wellington blankly.

"Come on," he said, motioning for me to step inside.

Mr. Wellington pointed for me to sit on the sofa, and he sat across from me in the chair. The clock ticked over his fireplace and moths thumped against the window screens. "I'll take you in the morning," he said.

I nodded and looked down at my knees.

"That constable's got problems. I've encountered men like him before. You don't need to be around him."

"He won't let me alone."

Mr. Wellington picked up the drink he'd left on the table and took a sip. He set it back down, and I felt him studying me. "Did you do all the things he said you did?"

"I didn't do the part about eatin' the dogs and shootin' at him."

"Why would he make up things like that?"

"I whipped up on him a couple of times. Maybe that's why."

"What does that mean?"

"Means I licked him."

Mr. Wellington scratched his chin. "You licked him, huh?"

"He wouldn't let me alone."

"But you didn't shoot at him or eat his dogs?"

"Nossir."

"Where are the dogs?"

"At my friend's house. He lives near a place called Union at a clay pit."

"Is this the other boy who escaped with you?"

"Yessir."

"How about the gun?"

"Which one?"

"Whichever one he thinks you shot at him with?"

"I left it in the forest."

"Out there where he had you today?"

"No. That's where I told him it was. I lied."

Mr. Wellington sat forward in his chair. "He wanted you to get it for him?"

I nodded.

"Why would he want it so bad?"

"'Cause it's his, I guess. I wish he'd give me back the gun he took from me."

Mr. Wellington sat back and chuckled to himself. "First of all, kid, they can't put you in jail, at least not for long. You're too young. I don't know what Sanders has planned for you, but he's been getting the general public riled up about you for some time now."

"I've got a feelin' I know what he's got planned for me."

"Well, I've been a lawyer long enough to know that his legal options are limited. However, this is not your typical situation. His father happens to be the judge. That can complicate things. This Sanders fellow is a bully and a bigot. He's got a chip on his shoulder that's probably been there since he was a child. He's unintelligent, and he's mean, and he's in a position of power. That's a bad combination to be facing."

I didn't reply.

"Not to mention that you seem to have caused irreparable damage to his pride."

"What's that mean?"

"It means you're going to need some help."

"I don't need help from anybody. He can't do anything to me that I care about. He's gonna go after Kit if he doesn't get his hands on me."

Mr. Wellington sighed and stood up. He walked into the kitchen, and I heard him turn on the faucet. When he returned he held out a glass of water to me. I took it and he sat back down in his chair. "You know why I came after you today?"

"Nossir."

"I feel responsible for a lot of what's gone on with you. I'm not going to stand for that constable and his ways, especially on my property. I never thought it would turn out like this."

"How'd you know I was out there?"

"The chime sounded that lets me know somebody's coming up my road. When no one showed, I drove out and found Sanders's car. I figured he was up to no good when I saw your footprints with his."

I was quiet for a minute. Finally I said, "You lied to me. Every grown person I know has lied to me except Mr. Mitchell and Obregon and Mr. Carter."

"You're right. Even though it wasn't a technical lie, I lied to you all the same. I'm sorry about that."

"I was lonely. I'd have gone away if you'd wanted."

"I know. The first thing that came to my mind wasn't the right choice. I could have talked to you, and I could have been your friend."

"Yessir."

"I've got too much money. I thought I could buy my way above the general human condition, but when you get old and retire and live alone, you realize you're not any different. Sometimes you're worse off."

"I don't know about any of that."

Mr. Wellington nodded to himself. "That's all right . . . You know, I've been following your story on the television and in the papers. I've defended enough criminals to know a little about character. I had my doubts all along that you were all they said you were. I'll give them 'feisty' and 'hard to hold,' but not the other things Davy Sanders is putting on you."

"I already told you he lied."

"I'm going to help you, Moon, and it's not just for your sake, but for my own as well. You might just go along with me, because I don't see that you've got anything to lose."

"I don't care what you do," I said.

"Then why don't you go into the bathroom and clean up while I fix you a sandwich. Then you can get some sleep in the guest bedroom. We've got a big day ahead of us."

## 41

Mr. Wellington came into my bedroom just after daylight, dressed in his robe. I had been awake since the birds sounded almost an hour before, enjoying the large, comfortable bed in one of his T-shirts. He had washed my clothes for me and set them at the foot of the bed.

"Get dressed," he said. "We've got to get an early start."

He walked out, and I heard him in the kitchen pouring a cup of coffee. I put on the clean clothes and went into the living room to wait. Mr. Wellington came in with his coffee in one hand and a newspaper in the other. He held the paper out to me and nodded towards the pictures in it. They were pictures of the place along the road where I'd left Kit when he was sick. "This where we need to go to get that gun?"

"Yessir."

"Let me get dressed, and we'll be on our way."

A half hour later we were in Mr. Wellington's truck and headed for the Talladega National Forest. After a few minutes, he leaned over the seat and rolled down my window. The morning was cool and humid, and the wind felt good on my face. He took a cigar out of the glove box and stuck it in his mouth. As he chewed it, I realized where the pleasant smell of the truck came from.

"You've got a fancy new truck."

"I'd rather have an old one."

"Why don't you get one? You're rich."

"Maybe I will."

I looked over at him. He continued to stare at the road ahead. "It's a long way in there to get that gun, you know, " I said.

"How old do you think I am?" he asked.

"Pretty old."

Mr. Wellington laughed. "I think we need to teach you some tact before we put you in front of a judge."

"All I asked for was to go to jail."

"Because you don't know any better."

I studied his face. "Pap never did like the law."

"I've gathered that."

"All you do for a livin' is the law."

"That's right. However, what I do is a lot different from what policemen and constables do. They enforce the law; I just explain it to people."

"How about explainin' it to me? How come Pap hated it?"

"Well, the law is just the rules that most of the people in the country decide that everyone has to obey. There are people like your father who don't like being told what to do. They don't like to obey the rules."

"How come?"

"I don't know. People have got different reasons."

"How do you learn what the rules are? I haven't meant to do anything wrong ever since Pap died, and people are chasin' me all over."

Mr. Wellington chuckled. "I guess that's why you're so famous, Moon. Everybody wants to hear about how a child can be raised out there in that forest with no sense of the rules."

We pulled over and got six sausage biscuits at a drive-through restaurant. I ate two of them before I spoke another word.

"Save some for lunch," Mr. Wellington said.

He reached over and took the biscuit wrappers from me and stuffed them into a bag. He pulled a black box from under the seat and pressed a button on it and set it on the dashboard. "I need you to tell me everything about what happened to you out there, Moon. I need you to start from the night you broke out of Pinson."

"You wanna know how Kit got over the fence and how we got the bus?"

"Everything. This is not going to be an easy case to make."

"What's that thing?"

"It's a tape recorder. You can talk to it and it remembers what you say."

"Talk to it?"

"That's right."

I started telling the tape recorder everything I could remember. Mr. Wellington kept his eyes on the highway and sometimes he'd nod and sometimes he'd smile, but he never interrupted me. One time he pulled over to the side of the road to look at a map.

"You lost?"

"No. Keep talking."

When I finally got to the part where he found me on the leash with Sanders, I stopped. Mr. Wellington reached in front of me and pressed another button. "That's quite a story," he said.

"It gonna remember all that?"

"It'll remember it."

We pulled over next to where the tram road met the blacktop, and Mr. Wellington looked past me and out the window. "This it?"

"Yessir. About five miles or so up into those hills."

Mr. Wellington got a small backpack out of the truck and put a camera, the rest of the biscuits, and two water bottles into it.

"We've got a good drinkin' creek at the shelter," I said.

He zipped the pack and put it on. "Just in case," he replied.

I shrugged and the two of us started up the tram road. Mr. Wellington didn't walk fast, but he didn't need to stop and rest much, either. Sometimes I'd get too far ahead of him and have to sit down and wait. Only once did he catch up to me and lean against a tree and take a sip of water.

He screwed the top of the water bottle back on and wiped his eye with one finger and said, "I can't believe you dragged your friend Kit all this way."

"I was scared. You get stronger and quicker when you're scared."

"Adrenaline," he said.

"That's what Pap called it. Said if I had enough adrenaline I could whip anybody."

He put the water bottle back in the pack and walked past me. "I wish you'd stop relying on that advice so much," he said. "Come on."

It was noon by the time we made it to the shelter. I looked around and saw our fire pit, cold and rain-spattered in the center. Several strips of jerky were still hanging on my meat racks. A breeze licked at the treetops and made the place seem quiet and strange. Once again, I felt that the forest had forgotten about me. It seemed distant and untouchable.

Mr. Wellington stood for a moment, his hands at his sides and his eyes looking over what Kit and I had lived in. "Not much room in that thing," he said.

"Stays warm that way."

He shook his head. "How many ticks and red bugs did you bring out with you?"

"Everybody sure does hate ticks and red bugs."

"I'm no exception."

"They don't bother me much."

I climbed into the shelter and found the pistol in its hiding place under the marsh grass. I also saw the two deerskin hats we'd made, and I got those as well. When I crawled back out, I gave Mr. Wellington the pistol and put one of the hats on my head. He stared at me as I adjusted it. "They're going to convict you for sure with that thing on."

"I made 'em."

"I assumed you did." He looked at the pistol. "And this is what you took from Sanders?"

"Yessir."

He took off the backpack and unzipped it. Then he put the pistol inside and removed one of the water bottles. He straightened up and took two large gulps before handing the water over to me. "Let's eat those biscuits," he said.

After lunch, Mr. Wellington stood and stuffed the trash into his pockets.

"Okay," he said. "Where is the log you shot?"

We walked to where I had shot the pistol at the rotten log, and Mr. Wellington took pictures of it. After he was done, he picked it up and broke off the ends so that he was left with only the middle section that I'd shot. He put this under his arm and tucked the camera away. "Now," he said, "take me to where you met with Sanders."

I nodded and set out for the place on Deer Creek where Kit and I had trapped him. I had to keep stopping and waiting for Mr. Wellington to catch up as I ducked my way through the forest. Eventually, we came to the spot. The ground had aged and showed no sign of a struggle, but Mr. Wellington took pictures anyway.

"So this is where you trapped him?"

"Yessir."

"And you hooked a log up to his feet, and it dragged him into the water down there?"

"That's right. He held on for a while, and that's when I took his pistol. Then he got pulled into the creek and floated away."

"You're sure that's what happened?"

"Yessir."

"I just find it hard to believe that you could pull off such a stunt. Someone as big as Sanders, and all."

"It doesn't matter how big they are, as long as you get the right trap rigged."

"Very well," he said. "We'll go with what you told me."

Mr. Wellington took more pictures and studied the surrounding forest. Finally, he put up his camera, and asked me if there was anything else I'd forgotten to tell him.

"Nossir. I told you everything."

"Okay, then, I'll see what I can do with this."

It was late afternoon when we made it back to the highway. Mr. Wellington said he would turn me in at the Tuscaloosa County courthouse so that we wouldn't have Sanders's father for a judge.

"You think Sanders's pap is like Sanders?"

"I don't know, and we won't take any chances. I'll drop you off and get these pictures developed and start working on the case. I imagine it won't be long before Sanders finds out where you are and all hell breaks loose."

"What are you gonna do with those pictures?"

"I don't know yet. I'll have to see how they come out, and I'll need some time to study them. But I'll think of something."

"What are you gonna try and do for me?"

Mr. Wellington looked at me and raised his eyebrows. "I'm going to try to clear you of attempted murder."

I shrugged. "All right. It doesn't make a difference to me. Law's gonna be after me no matter what. One place is as good as another if you've gotta be locked away."

"Well, maybe we can keep you from getting locked away."

"Nowhere else for me to go."

Mr. Wellington put the cigar back into his mouth and chewed it. "We'll just have to see about that," he said.

We got to the courthouse right before it closed. The clerk took me from Mr. Wellington and sent me with a policeman to jail. The policeman put me on the backseat of his car without handcuffs. After we pulled out of the parking lot, he looked at me in the rearview mirror. "You been hidin' out in the forest?"

"Little bit. I've been all over."

He looked back at the road. "What's that on your head?"

"Deerskin hat."

"Where'd you get that?"

"Made it."

"Yeah?"

"Yeah. I've got another one right here with the tail still on it," and I held it up for him to see. "It's all I've got left."

The policeman looked in the rearview mirror and studied the hat. He shook his head and turned to the road again. "You've got a fancy lawyer now, huh?"

"Mr. Wellington says he wants to help me, but I don't know what he can do."

"That constable down in Sumter County says you've been out shootin' at him and killin' his dogs. Judge Mackin won't cut you slack for that. I'd be glad that lawyer wants to help you out."

I shrugged.

"You're not gonna bite me or nothin', are you?"

"Nossir. I'm not aimin' to try and whip up on anybody anymore. I don't aim to bust out of anywhere, either."

"That's good." He nodded to himself. "That's good . . . I hear you've got a mean bite."

I was about to tell him I'd only bitten one person in my life, but I didn't. It seemed like it wouldn't do any good.

The Tuscaloosa jail was a lot bigger than the one in Livingston. There were prisoners across from me and on either side. Everybody started asking me questions right after the policeman left the room.

"Shot any people lately, kid?"

"You speak English?"

"Got any good recipe for dog?"

"What the hell's that thing on your head?"

I didn't answer them. I went to the back of my cage and lay on the cot. Before long I was asleep to it all.

That evening, the policeman who delivered me earlier brought everyone a food tray. I heard one of the other prisoners call him Officer Pete. We had pork chops and lima beans for supper. Even though it was prison food, I didn't feel like eating anything and picked through the beans with my spoon. When Officer Pete returned, I asked him if he'd heard anything from Mr. Wellington.

"Nothin', kid."

"You think he's gonna come back?"

"I've never heard of a lawyer turnin' down a chance to make money."

"I don't have any money."

"Then you prob'ly won't see him again."

Earlier, I thought I didn't care whether he helped me or not. But I was getting lonely in the jail. I wanted to see someone who didn't hate me. "How about the judge? When's he gonna talk to me?"

Officer Pete shrugged as he picked up the trays from the other prisoners. "I don't know anything about what they're gonna do to you, kid."

"Gonna put you in a zoo!" somebody yelled.

"I'd whip your wild little ass," said somebody else. "Screwed-up kid."

I figured these prisoners didn't like me since I hadn't talked to them. I lay back down on my cot and stared at the ceiling. Three prisoners began playing cards down the hall from me, and another started singing. I wondered what Hal and Kit were doing. I felt like I'd never see either one of them again.

"What you doin' down there, wild boy?"

I thought about never seeing Mr. Wellington again.

"You dreamin' about dog cobbler?"

I grew queasy with loneliness, and I rolled onto my side and pulled up my knees. I lay this way long into the night, taking deep breaths and listening to the other prisoners snoring and tossing in their sleep. Somewhere at the end of the hall, a clock ticked. I heard the phone ring a couple of times in the office outside, and someone whose voice I didn't recognize answered it. Even though I couldn't have felt any worse where I was, I knew there was no other place for me to go.

## 42

The next morning, I was on my back staring at the ceiling when the hall door was suddenly kicked in and slammed against the wall.

"Hey!" one of the irritated prisoners yelled.

I looked over at the doorway and saw Sanders standing there, his eyes searching each of the jail cages. His face was so swollen with oily poison ivy blisters that he squinted like the sun was in his eyes. His ears, ripped from briars, had orange medicine painted on them that made him look like he wore earmuffs. His hands trembled at his sides. I might not have recognized him had I not been expecting him.

Eventually, his eyes came around to my bed and rested on me. He didn't say a word, but walked over to the bars of my cage and stood there.

I sat up and stared at him. "You got lost out there again, didn't you?" I said.

I watched his jaw tighten until I was sure his teeth would shatter. Even through the swollen face, I could see veins popping out on his forehead. He swallowed and said calmly, "Come here, kid. I wanna tell you somethin'."

I shook my head. "You'll pop me across the face like you did that other fellow."

"Come here."

"No."

"You want me to get the keys and come in there?"

"Go get what you want."

Sanders looked around and saw the other prisoners watching him. He spit a brown gob of tobacco juice between the bars of my cage. "Damnit, kid," he hissed. "I said get over here."

"I said no. You come in here if you want."

Sanders clutched the bars tightly. "*Com'ere!*" he yelled.

I shook my head.

"Hey!" one of the prisoners yelled. "Why don't you keep it down. You crazy or what?"

Sanders pointed at him and spoke through clenched teeth. "You best keep your mouth shut, if you know what's good for you."

The prisoner chuckled. "Mister, you ain't got no authority here. You're just a constable."

Sanders took a step in the prisoner's direction. "Don't you—"

Officer Pete came through the door and looked around. "What's goin' on in here?"

Sanders stopped, and I saw his sides bulging in and out with heavy breathing.

"Mr. Sanders, I think it's time for you to leave," Officer Pete said.

"Yeah, get out of here, you idiot!" someone said.

Sanders turned and looked at me. "Let me in there with him. I need to discuss some things with that boy."

Officer Pete shook his head and grabbed for Sanders's arm. "I don't think—"

Sanders jerked his arm away. "Don't handle me," he snarled.

Officer Pete straightened and stared at Sanders. "Let's go. Now!"

After Sanders was led away, the prisoners began asking me questions. "Who the hell was that, kid?"

"Sanders," I said.

"I seen him on television," another prisoner said. "He's the one the kid shot at. Ain't that right, kid?"

"I didn't shoot at anybody," I said, tired of saying it.

"He don't act like it."

"He's always been mad at me. He's just extra mad because he caught poison ivy out there."

"I think that man's gone crazy," the prisoner next to me said.

I shrugged.

"You're lucky you're in this jail cell."

"There's nothin' lucky about me," I said.

A policeman I didn't know brought me breakfast. I managed to eat some of it and then lay back down to see if I could sleep. By lunchtime I was still staring at the ceiling. I was so tired that I felt sick, but sleep wouldn't come. When the new policeman brought lunch, I didn't get up for it. I let it lie on the floor until he came and picked it up again.

Officer Pete brought supper around five o'clock. I asked him again if he'd heard anything about what they were going to do to me. He got irritated with me as he moved to the next cage. "Look, kid, I told you I don't know anything. I'm not a news service for prisoners."

"But I've been here since yesterday."

"Yeah, and you've been a pain in the butt, too. We about had to handcuff that crazy fellow from Sumter County."

"But Mr. Wellington said he was gonna help me."

He turned and looked at me. "Consider yourself lucky. Some of these people have been in here a month."

I lay back down on my cot. Officer Pete came back. "You gonna eat anything?"

"He ain't had nothin' all day except a bite or two of breakfast," somebody said.

"I'm not hungry," I said.

Officer Pete picked up the supper tray. "Suit yourself."

## 43

That night I dreamed of being holed up by myself in the old shelter where I lived with Pap. Bigfoots came out of the forest and tore at the walls. I sat on the hide pile and clutched my rifle, even though I knew it wouldn't do any good against something as large as a Bigfoot. Eventually I crawled into the stage-two box through the muddy hole at the back of the shelter. I heard the Bigfoots digging at the ground. Before long, they were banging on the top of the box with their fists and scratching the door with their fingernails. I felt them rolling it out of the ground like a piece of culvert pipe and working themselves into a howling frenzy. Then, suddenly, I couldn't hear them anymore. I saw the doorknob to the little steel door at the end of the pipe begin to jiggle. I waited while my heart thumped loudly in my chest.

When I woke, Officer Pete was opening the door to my cage.

"Let's go, kid."

I sat up and looked about, getting my bearings. I rubbed my eyes while he waited with hands on his hips.

"Let's go," he said again. "I don't have all day."

I put on my hat and grabbed Kit's. "You wanna put some handcuffs on me?" I asked.

"We don't put handcuffs on kids," he said. "You're no threat to me."

I followed him into the office. As we approached the outside door, he turned to me. "Stay close and don't stop to answer any questions. Just get in the car."

I didn't know why he told me that, but I got up next to him. When he opened the door, I understood what he was talking about. Cameras were flashing and people were everywhere.

"Hey, Moon!" they shouted at me. "Say somethin' for us, Moon!"

"Who's your lawyer, Alabama Moon? We hear you've got a lawyer."

"Why'd you turn yourself in?"

I grabbed Officer Pete's belt loop and he pulled me along to the squad car. He opened the back door and I jumped in. I sat up on the seat and watched the people gathering around and flashbulbs going off near the window.

"Wave for me, Moon!"

"Bare your teeth for us!"

I looked at Officer Pete in the rearview mirror as he pulled away from the crowd. He glanced back at me and shook his head. "You're a real pain in the ass, you know?"

"I didn't do anything to those people out there."

"For somebody that hasn't ever done anything, you sure do have a bunch of folks stirred up."

"We goin' to see the judge?"

"That's right. That's what you wanted, isn't it?"

"I was just wonderin'."

"I'd be more than just wonderin' if I were you. He's pretty pissed off over all of this. He wants to know just what he's gonna do with a ten-year-old who's shot at a law enforcement officer."

"I told you—"

"I know what you said, but you've got a half-crazed constable from Sumter County that says he'll swear on the Bible otherwise."

"He'll be lyin'."

"Why would he lie about somethin' like that?"

"I don't know."

Officer Pete shook his head. "I don't know, either," he said.

Officer Pete took me into the courthouse through a back entrance where there weren't any reporters. He put me into another cage and left me alone. I sat there for an hour before he came back again. "All right," he said. "Judge Mackin's ready for you. He said if you get to actin' crazy on him, he's gonna put you in a straitjacket."

"What's that?"

"Somethin' you won't like. Now, come on."

When I walked into the courtroom, the first person I saw was Sanders. He sat in the front row and stared at me with his swollen face. He wore no expression and seemed to look right through me. My heart started beating faster when I saw Mr. Wellington in front on the other side of the courtroom. He was dressed in a three-piece suit, and his hair was slicked back behind a face that was scrubbed shiny.

Except for a guard at the entrance, the only other person in the room was Judge Mackin. He sat behind his desk on a raised platform in the front of the room with one elbow on the desk and his cheek pressed into his palm. He had white curly hair, a pink face, and droopy eyes that reminded me of a wild hog. Glasses sat perched at the end of his nose, and I heard him breathing heavily. When he spoke, he sounded tired.

"What's that on his head, Officer Pete?"

"It's his squirrel hat, Your Honor."

"Well, get him to take it off," the judge mumbled.

"Yes, Your Honor."

"You know better than that. I don't care how old he is."

"Take off the hat, Moon."

I took it off and put it under my arm with Kit's hat. The judge moved his eyes to watch me as I followed behind Officer Pete over to where Mr. Wellington stood.

"Why does he have two?" the judge asked.

"It's all I've got left," I replied.

The judge squinted at me. "Was I talking to you?"

"Nossir."

"Then stay quiet until somebody asks you a question."

"Yessir."

Officer Pete dropped me off next to Mr. Wellington, and I felt proud to have him on my side. I smiled up at him. "Thought you'd left me," I said.

Mr. Wellington put his finger to his lips and motioned for me to watch the judge. I felt him pull my hats from beneath my arm and saw him set them on the table in front of us. I looked at the judge and then over at Sanders. His eyes danced like the inside of his head was on fire.

"Now," Judge Mackin said as he removed his glasses and began to clean them with a handkerchief. "We've got an unusual situation here. Because of that, I'm closin' this hearin' to the public. Another reason for that is I've got a bad headache and all those people out there are drivin' me crazy." He set his glasses on the desk.

"Moon Blake," he said, "you've stirred up quite a commotion out there. I don't like commotion. I don't like people who shoot at our law enforcement officers. I don't like people who eat other people's dogs."

"Sanders is a liar," I said.

"Hey!" the judge snapped. "Did I ask you a question?"

I looked at Mr. Wellington. He put his finger to his lips again. The judge licked his mouth and turned to Sanders. "Okay, then, let's get started. Mr. Sanders, why don't you come up here and give your side of the story."

"I'm a constable, Your Honor."

"Whatever. Get up here."

Sanders acted like he was about to say something, but twisted his mouth around and stood up. He walked to the front of the room and stood before the judge. The judge winced and shook his head slowly. "What did you get into?"

"Poison ivy," I said. "He got—"

The judge jerked his head up and pointed his finger at me as his eyes grew wide. Mr. Wellington bent over and whispered in my ear. "Moon, you can't speak in here unless you get permission."

The judge continued to watch me as he held a book sideways towards Sanders. "You're not gonna tell a lie are you?"

Sanders put his hand on the book and shook his head. "No," he said.

"Good," the judge replied. He put the book on his desk. "Go on, then."

Sanders took a deep breath and sat down. "I'm gonna tell this one more time. I—"

"You'll tell it as many times as I want you to tell it. Just because your daddy's a small-time judge over there in Sumter County doesn't mean you're gettin' any kind of special treatment."

I saw the veins on Sanders's forehead stand up as he clenched his teeth. He stared at the back of the room, at some place on the wall behind us. After a second, his veins relaxed and he continued. "This boy's the son of an outlaw. He's—"

Mr. Wellington stood up. "Irrelevant, Your Honor."

The judge sighed. "Mr. Sanders, it seems we've got a fancy, big-city lawyer to deal with today. And he's right. Sustained. Did this boy attempt to shoot you or not?"

"He did."

"With what?"

"A pistol."

"What kind?"

".45."

"Where'd he get it?"

"He stole it from me."

The judge leaned back in his chair and watched Sanders. "He stole it from you?"

Sanders's veins rose again and relaxed. "Yes, Your Honor."

The judge looked at me. I nodded to him and his eyes grew wide. "Are you agreein' that you stole it from him or that you shot at him?"

"I stole it from him," I said, "but I never shot at anybody."

He turned back to Sanders. "Well, the kid admits he stole your gun. How did you let that happen?"

I leaned forward, but Mr. Wellington pulled me back. I saw Sanders kneading his hands together. He was still staring at someplace on the rear wall. "I was asleep," he said.

"He's lyin'," I whispered to Mr. Wellington. The judge cocked his eyes at me.

"It's all right," Mr. Wellington said quietly. "We can tell the judge when it's our turn to talk."

The judge continued to watch me out of the corner of his eyes while he talked to Sanders. "So he got your gun while you were asleep. What next?"

"He just backed up and pointed it at me and shot at my stomach and missed. Then he turned and ran off."

"And took your pistol with him."

"That's right."

Judge Mackin wrote something down. After a second he said, "Okay, tell me about the dogs."

"I sent three trackin' dogs after him and the two other boys that broke out of Pinson Boys' Home. I heard the dogs yelpin'. Later on I found their carcasses hangin' from a tree. Guts layin' everywhere. Meat cleaned to the bone."

"And you say the boy bit you, too?"

"Yes, Your Honor, he did."

"What else?"

"That's it."

The judge sat back in his chair and looked at Mr. Wellington. "Okay, lawyer, your turn."

Mr. Wellington stood calmly and made his way to the front of the courtroom. He faced Sanders. "Mr. Sanders, where were you when Moon supposedly shot at you with your pistol?"

Sanders looked straight at Mr. Wellington's eyes. "I was in the Talladega National Forest."

"Describe your surroundings."

"I don't remember."

"You mean you were lost out in the forest and then shot at, and you don't remember anything about your surroundings?"

"Who said I was lost!"

"Just an assumption. Perhaps I'm wrong."

"Listen here, you slick old sum-bitch, I was—"

The judge slammed his gavel on the desk without lifting his cheek from his palm. I jumped in my chair from surprise. Sanders paused for a moment and then spoke calmly. "I was near a creek, I think."

"You think?"

"Yeah, I was beside a creek."

"And Moon Blake shot at you once."

"That's right."

"Once?"

"That's right."

"How far away was he when he shot?"

"About ten yards, I guess. Close."

"And you saw the remains of your dogs not far from there?"

"That's right."

"I see," Mr. Wellington said. "Can I remind you, Mr. Sanders, that you're under—"

"He knows he's under oath, Mr. Wellington," the judge said wearily. "Stop fancy-pantsin' around and get on with it."

Sanders looked over at the judge. "Your Honor, I thought this was gonna be an informal hearin'. How come I got this lawyer in my face?"

"I can't keep the boy from havin' his own counsel, Mr. Sanders."

Sanders shook his head and looked back at Mr. Wellington. "Well, ask what you gotta ask, slick."

Mr. Wellington nodded politely. "You say you saw the carcasses of your dogs not far from where the shooting took place?"

"That's right."

"Are you sure it wasn't a single deer carcass that Moon had left not far from there?"

"You don't think I know a deer carcass from a dog carcass? And I said there were three."

"Very well," Mr. Wellington nodded. He walked to the table where I sat. He reached beside me and pulled a plastic bag from his briefcase. Inside the bag was Sanders's pistol. He held it up. "Is this your pistol, Mr. Sanders?"

Sanders's forehead veins popped up again and his eyes grew wide. He stood and held out his hand for it. Mr. Wellington walked over to him and held it in front of him, just out of reach. "Well," Sanders said, "lemme see the thing."

"You can see it fine," the judge said. "Sit down."

"Yeah, it looks like mine. Gimme that."

Mr. Wellington swung the pistol away and laid it on the judge's desk. The judge stared at it for a second and then looked at Mr. Wellington. "Go on."

"That's my pistol he stole!" Sanders said as he reached for it.

"Get your hand away from my desk!" the judge snapped. "I said sit down!"

Sanders clenched his teeth, sat, and stared at the back wall.

Mr. Wellington waited a few seconds, then continued. "Mr. Sanders?"

"What!"

"Did you shoot the pistol at all that day before Moon supposedly took it from you and fired at you?"

"No."

"And he only fired at you once?"

"That's what I said."

"How many shells does that pistol hold?"

"Nine in the clip and one in the chamber."

Mr. Wellington turned to the judge. "Your Honor, if you examine the clip, you'll see that there are eight bullets in it. The bullets are oxidized against the clip, evidence that they've been in there and positioned in such a way for some time and have not been tampered with."

Sanders smiled and shook his head. "Maybe he shot it again, slick."

Mr. Wellington nodded. "Yes, he did. Moon shot the pistol twice."

Sanders shrugged his shoulders and looked at the judge. "Can I go, Your Honor?"

The judge looked at Mr. Wellington. The lawyer held up his finger and walked to his briefcase. He pulled out some pictures and another small plastic bag with two bullets in it. He took these to the judge and set them on his desk. Again, the judge looked down and eyed them. "What is all that?"

"It's a picture of a log with two bullets in it. In that bag are the only two bullets that were shot out of the pistol. As you know, there are tests that can prove the bore markings on those bullets match Mr. Sanders's pistol. If you examine this picture and others I have taken of the log—and I even have the log itself if that becomes necessary—you will see these bullets are the same ones that were embedded in the log."

Sanders stood up. "So maybe he fired twice at me! Hell, when you're gettin' shot at, you lose track of things."

This time, the judge lifted his cheek from his palm and stared at Sanders. "If I have to tell you to sit down one more time, I'm gonna throw some rope around you and that chair."

Sanders sat with his hands shaking on top of the armrests. Mr. Wellington turned to me and winked. "Moon," he said, "how is it that we know this log was nowhere near Mr. Sanders at the creek?"

All of a sudden, I knew what he was doing. The answer to his question shot into my head and seemed like it was ringing a bell inside me. " 'Cause there aren't any pine logs by creeks! They're all up at the top of the hill!"

Sanders started to get up, but sat down again and leaned forward in his seat. "That's the craziest damned—"

"Hey!" the judge said.

"Craziest damned defense," Sanders mumbled. The judge shot him a look and Sanders settled into his chair. Mr. Wellington turned and began walking to our table. When his back was to the judge, he looked up and smiled at me.

After Mr. Wellington sat down, the courtroom was quiet and everyone watched the judge. He rubbed his temples and stared at the top of his desk. "I'm not sure what's been accomplished here," he said to the desk. "Bullets in a log. Bore markings. Inconsistencies in the number of shots. This is pretty shaky, Wellington. Maybe that log rolled down the hill. Maybe it washed up on the creek bank."

Mr. Wellington nodded. "I've thought of that, Your Honor. With your permission, I'd like to make a few more points."

The judge looked up and sighed. "Good. That would be helpful."

"I'd like to introduce my second piece of evidence, my client here, Moon Blake."

"Bring him up, then."

"Actually, with your permission, I'd like to demonstrate something outside the courtroom. I believe your police department has a shooting range not far outside of town. I'd like to go there for my demonstration."

Sanders twisted in his chair and threw up his hands.

The judge stared at Mr. Wellington for what seemed like a

long time. Finally he said, "Wellington, I think this is going to be a waste of my time. You and your fancy talk may work with a jury, but I can cut it down to what it is. You're not in the big city anymore . . . However, this is your lucky day. I don't feel good at all. You give me a nap and I'll take your country drive with you." He tapped the gavel on his desk. "Reconvene in two hours. Meet me in the garage so we don't start a parade with all those reporters out there."

## 44

Mr. Wellington said he'd see me later, and Officer Pete took me back to the cage to wait while the judge took his nap. I was there for what seemed like a lot longer than two hours before Officer Pete came again to get me. "Let's go, kid."

He took me down some stairs into the basement, where the judge was already in the front passenger side of a police car, staring straight ahead.

"He feelin' better?" I asked.

"I don't know," Officer Pete said. He opened the back door and I climbed inside.

We drove up from the basement and out into the sunshine. I turned to see all of the people still gathered around the courthouse steps. Some of them had grown tired and were sitting down. A couple were lying on the park benches out front with their cameras on the ground beside them. No one seemed to notice we were leaving.

The judge rolled his window down and I was relieved to

feel the cool air brush across the backseat. We hadn't gone far when I saw Mr. Wellington pull out behind us in a shiny car I'd never seen before. Then we saw Sanders in his car and the judge turned in his seat as we passed by. "Pete, where do you think he drives to get a car that scratched up and muddy?"

"He's been all over lookin' for me," I said.

The judge glanced at Officer Pete and then back at me. He started to say something but then didn't and faced the road again. After a few seconds he started shaking his head. "Stop up here and get me a hamburger, Pete. This boy had lunch?"

"No, sir."

"Get us all somethin', then."

"What you want?" Officer Pete asked me.

"Sausage biscuit."

"They don't have sausage biscuits right now. I'll get you a hamburger."

"Okay."

We pulled up to a drive-through restaurant and Officer Pete told the sign that he wanted three hamburgers and three Cokes. After the woman at the window gave us our food, Officer Pete handed mine to me through the sliding window between us, and we pulled onto the highway again. Mr. Wellington and Sanders were pulled over to the side of the road waiting. After we passed Sanders, I turned and watched him. His face was blood red, and he was holding his hands up in the air and cursing the traffic. "Sanders is mad back there," I said.

"What?"

"Sanders is mad again."

Officer Pete didn't reply. The judge chewed his hamburger slowly and swallowed. "What's wrong with that man, Pete?"

Officer Pete shook his head. "I don't know."

We turned onto a dirt road a few miles outside of town. I'd finished my hamburger and even though my tongue still burned from the Coke, I wished I had two more of each. We didn't go far before we pulled over near a long, narrow cement slab with a roof over it. On the other side of the slab was a field with a dirt mound at the other end.

Officer Pete opened my door for me as Mr. Wellington pulled up beside us. I got out and saw the judge strolling a few feet away from the car. With his back to us, he stopped and unzipped his pants and began to pee. Mr. Wellington got out of the car and walked up to us.

"You mind if I get a rifle out of my trunk, Officer? It's for my demonstration."

"Your Honor?"

"That's fine with me."

Mr. Wellington retrieved a rifle from his trunk and reached into his pocket and pulled out some cartridges. He began walking towards the shooting block and loading the rifle. When he passed me, I noticed that it was Pap's .22.

"Where'd you get that?" I said.

"Moon, you stay quiet," he told me.

"Where's Sanders?" the judge said.

Just as he said it, I saw Sanders's car rounding a bend in the dirt road. "He's comin'," I said. "He prob'ly got lost again."

"Moon, come over here," Mr. Wellington said.

Sanders's car came to a stop behind us. I noticed wet grass and mud hung from the front bumper. He got out and slammed his door and the judge stopped midstride and looked over at him. "You got a problem, Constable?"

Sanders started to say something, but then set his jaw and shook his head and stomped around the front of his car. He got to his knees and reached under and felt around for a few seconds. I didn't think his face could get any redder, but it did. He yanked and tugged until something bloody and furry came loose and he stood with it and slung it out into the weeds.

"You're a dangerous man to be in front of," the judge said.

Officer Pete nudged me forward. "Let's see what your lawyer's gonna do."

Mr. Wellington was waiting with his back towards us. When the four of us were standing behind him, he turned and held up the rifle. "This is a .22. Iron sights, no scope. How much would you say you weigh, Constable Sanders?"

"I haven't weighed myself lately. Judge, this is crazy."

"Guess your weight, Sanders," the judge said.

Sanders breathed heavily out of his nose. "Two twenty-five."

"How tall?" Mr. Wellington asked him.

"About six foot two."

"Big target for someone ten yards away."

Sanders began to shake his head. "Okay, lawyer. I know where you're goin' with this. You wanna show me this kid can hit somethin' ten yards away. Is that right?"

"That's right."

Sanders turned to the judge and raised his hands palm up.

"Didn't you ask him not to waste your time? What's this gonna show? For one, the kid's not nervous like he was out there in the woods with me. Second of all, that's not a pistol, judge. You know as well as I do that a pistol's a lot harder to shoot than that rifle."

"Wellington," the judge said, "I agree. I hope you have more to show me than this boy shootin' a ten-yard target."

"I'd gladly have Moon use the exact pistol he's accused of shooting at Constable Sanders with; however, it's evidence."

"And I don't think that kid's ever been nervous a day in his life," Officer Pete said.

Mr. Wellington reached into his pocket and pulled out a small aspirin bottle. He held it up briefly for us to see. Then he turned and began walking across the field. After he'd walked close to seventy-five yards, he turned and shouted back to us. "This far enough, Moon?"

I shrugged my shoulders. Mr. Wellington turned and kept walking another twenty-five yards. Finally, he stopped and pulled a pen from his shirt pocket. He knelt and stabbed the pen into the ground and stuck the aspirin bottle over it.

"There's no way he can hit that," Officer Pete said. "That's three hundred feet out."

"Give him your pistol, Officer Pete," Sanders said.

"Quiet, Constable," the judge said. "I don't know anybody who can hit somethin' that far away with a pistol."

I heard Sanders shuffle his feet behind me. "This ain't provin' nothin'," he said under his breath.

"Quiet."

Mr. Wellington walked back to us, picked up the rifle, and gave it to me. "Shoot it, Moon."

"Want me to make 'em pay?"

"Just shoot the bottle."

It was nothing to me. I'd done it more than a thousand times with Pap, practicing for the war he always said would come. I brought the rifle up to my shoulder and lined up the iron sights on the bottle. I held my breath and squeezed the trigger. The gun exploded and the aspirin bottle was gone.

I let the rifle down and handed it over to Mr. Wellington. It was a few seconds before anyone said anything. Finally, Sanders spun around and started towards the cars.

"Where you think you're goin'?" Officer Pete said.

"This ain't no way to run a trial! Bunch of tricks and nonsense!" Sanders shouted.

I saw the judge's face go red. "You turn around right now!"

Sanders stopped but didn't turn around. The judge took a few steps in his direction. "I'm gonna tell you this one more time, mister. This ain't your daddy's Sumter County, and I ain't your daddy. This is my county and my trial. Turn around!"

Sanders slowly turned and stared at the ground and clenched his teeth.

"Look at me!" the judge snapped.

Sanders lifted his chin. I thought the judge was about to say something, but just then we heard a vehicle approaching. Everyone except Sanders looked out at the dirt road. I hung my mouth open when I saw Hal driving towards us in his daddy's truck. Just above the passenger-seat window, the little wiener dog's head watched us curiously. In the bed, curled up on sacks of garbage, were the bloodhounds. "Hey, Hal!" I yelled.

Hal waved at us, and the bloodhounds heard me and tripped around in the garbage trying to stand up. "Recognize those dogs, Sanders?" Mr. Wellington said.

The judge looked back at Mr. Wellington and then at the truck again. The bloodhounds finally made it to their feet and began woofing at me. Sanders spun around and I couldn't see his face. After a second, he mumbled, "Sumbitch," and took out running towards the truck.

"Are those his dogs?" the judge said.

"Yes," Mr. Wellington replied.

"Hold it right there, Sanders!" Officer Pete yelled.

Sanders kept on. Hal mashed the gas pedal and spun the steering wheel so that the truck leaned into a hard turn. The dogs crashed and stumbled around in the garbage, and newspapers and trash flew out into the weeds. Hal straightened up the wheel and sped out the way he'd come. Sanders kept after him for a second, but finally stopped in the road and stared at the dust trail.

"Put him in your car," the judge said to Officer Pete.

"Which one?"

"That crazy fool out in the road, that's which one. Book him for perjury and I'll think of some more stuff before we get back to town."

# 45

The judge rode back from the shooting range with Mr. Wellington and me. "What about Sanders's car?" I said.

"Hell with his car, son. That thing's a disgrace to law enforcement."

"Am I goin' back to jail?"

The judge didn't answer me. "Wellington, was that the other missin' boy drivin' that truck?"

Mr. Wellington nodded.

"I guess he knows he just turned himself in."

"He does."

"And maybe got himself into trouble for bein' on the road without a license."

"He's a good driver," I said.

For the first time, I saw Judge Mackin almost smile. He looked at me with one corner of his mouth turned up. "Wellington, if I didn't know better, I'd say your client still hasn't learned a thing about the way the rest of the world operates."

Mr. Wellington smiled but didn't reply.

"Don't look so smug over there," the judge said. "If that constable had been half sane, all your fancy show business wouldn't have helped this boy."

"I'm not trying to fool you, Your Honor. I'm just glad things worked out the way they did."

"I'll tell you now, somethin's bothered me about this case from the start. I really couldn't put my finger on it until I got that bit settled with the constable." The judge rubbed his eyes and took a deep breath. "You see, there's this boy who's raised out in the woods and doesn't know a thing about the world but what he's seen within a couple of miles of his stick hut. One day this kid pops out of the woods, ten years old, and starts walkin' down the blacktop. We automatically think we got to put him in the system. Get him in the boys' home. Make him property of the state. Well, everybody can't fit that slot. Why can't you just put the kid on your sofa and help him out a little? Hell, put him on your floor. This kid would've been fine in somebody's barn. You'll kill a boy like this in an institution."

"I'm guilty, too," Mr. Wellington said.

"We all are. Damn system. This kid needs somethin' different." The judge turned around and looked at me again like he was trying to figure out what I needed. "Boy, what're we gonna do with you now?"

"I don't care anymore."

"You don't care, huh?"

"Nossir."

"Your Honor, I've got it worked out where Moon will go," said Mr. Wellington.

"Okay."

"I've located his uncle. He says he'll adopt him."

"Uncle?" I said.

"Where's this uncle while wild boy's raisin' Joe Cain all over central Alabama?"

"He's been in Mobile, Your Honor. He didn't know anything of the situation."

# 46

We dropped the judge off on the steps of the courthouse. All of the reporters were gone and the place seemed empty. He got out of the car and stretched his arms over his head like he'd had a long day. After a second, he turned around. "Looks like we gave the press the slip. You two wait here a minute while I get somethin'."

I climbed onto the front seat and began studying all the dashboard controls. "Where'd you get this car?"

"This is what I use when I'm trying to be fancy, Moon."

"Lots of lights and buttons."

It wasn't long before the judge returned with my hats in his hand. He leaned into the window and dropped them into Mr. Wellington's lap. "Moon, you write me a letter and let me know what it's like in Mobile."

"Okay."

"Wellington, he's under your care until his uncle comes for him."

"Thank you, Your Honor."

"Thank you for not wastin' my time today." The judge stood up, tapped the top of the car, and then turned away.

Neither of us said anything as we drove out of town. I found a button that made my seat lean back and another that made the window go down. I stretched out and watched the tops of the trees go by and the clear blue sky beyond. It was good to know Sanders was locked up and that Kit would be okay. It seemed like all of a sudden my mind was working easier and I felt better all over.

"What's my uncle look like?" I finally asked.

"You've seen the picture."

"I didn't pay attention to it then."

"It's in that envelope under the seat if you want to see it again."

I sat up and reached under the seat and pulled out a brown envelope. "Where's Pap's personal box?"

"It's in the trunk with your other stuff."

"How'd you get it all?"

"What do you think I've been doing for the past two days? Mr. Gene over there at Pinson's not real eager to help you, you know."

"Did you get my rifle, too?"

"Well, that's still at the Livingston police station, but I think I can get them to release it to me after the paperwork's complete."

I leaned back and dumped the contents of the envelope into my lap. Pap's watch and the money and the pictures were all there. The man in the photo was much shorter and skinnier than Pap but had the same face in a more boyish version. He seemed excited and energetic.

"He looks like he's gotta pee."

Mr. Wellington smiled. "I imagine if he's related to you, he might have a little twitch in him."

"You know what he's like?"

"I haven't met him, but I've talked to him on the phone. He sounds like a nice man."

"What's he do?"

"He's in the tree-trimming business."

"I've never heard of anybody doin' that."

"Well, it's done all the time. A man can make a decent living at it."

"How'd you find him?"

Mr. Wellington reached into his pocket and pulled out a penknife and gave it to me. "Pry open the back of that watch."

"The back of it?"

"That's right."

I opened the knife and inserted the tip of the blade into a small depression in the gear cover. It popped off and fell into my lap. I picked it up and studied the writing on the inside. It said "Zundel's Jewelers."

"That's the name of a jewelry company in Mobile that I happen to know about. I called them, and they told me the Blakes they knew. Eventually, I ran across the right one."

I folded the knife and gave it to him. After I put the watch back together, I put everything into the envelope again and looked out the window. "I oughta whip Hal good for doin' what he did today."

"I told him he didn't have to come. Once I got your pap's rifle from him, I said we already had enough evidence. However, he said it's what he wanted to do. He said that his time was up anyway and that you'd had a rough go with the world. He wanted to do all he could to get Sanders off your back."

I looked at Mr. Wellington. "I haven't had it so bad. Kit's the one that's had it bad."

Mr. Wellington nodded.

I pulled my legs up and put my feet on the glove box.

"Well, Hal ought not have done that. He could have hid out for a while longer."

"It'll be a couple of days before they get around to taking him to Hellenweiler. I'll drive you to see both of your friends tomorrow."

I nodded. "Good. I was wantin' to do that . . . How long have I got?"

"It'll be a few days before the paperwork's done. You're still property of the state, technically."

"Then I go to Mobile?"

"That's right."

"You been there before?"

"Sure. Plenty of times."

"What's it like?"

"It's a nice place to live. You've got Mobile Bay and the Gulf of Mexico out front. Stays warm most of the year."

"Got some forest?"

"Yes. It's got plenty of forest."

"Got a lot of people?"

"Yes. More than Tuscaloosa."

"That's a lot. I've never seen more than that."

Mr. Wellington reached over and patted my leg. I looked at the hand and realized it was the first time a grown person had touched me with kindness since my pap. "You'll like it," he said.

I stayed in Mr. Wellington's guest room again. I got up around midnight and took the picture from the envelope and studied my uncle's face under the lamp. Somewhere in the back of my mind, little black-and-white images of him flipped around. I thought I saw him standing beside a church. I thought I saw his face hovering over my own and smiling at me. As soon as I tried to hold on to one of these images, though, it fell away and left me with only the face in the photo. Then, a strange thought came to me. I walked across the hall to Mr. Wellington's door. I knocked lightly until he answered me.

"Moon?"

"Yessir?" I opened the door.

"Are you all right?"

"Yessir."

"What is it, then?"

"Will I have a brother?"

He sat up in his bed in the dark. He rubbed his eyes. "Yes," he said. "And a sister. You have two first cousins."

"I never thought about it before."

"Try to get some sleep. You'll have plenty of time to think about it later."

## 47

Mr. Wellington took me to see my friends the next morning. We stopped at Hal's place first, since it was on the way back to Tuscaloosa. I saw dust rising from the clay pit, and I guessed Mr. Mitchell was down there loading a customer. Hal slid out from under the truck when he heard us pull up. He stood and slapped his hands against his jeans, leaving greasy finger swipes. Mr. Wellington stayed in the cab of his own truck while I got out and went to meet Hal.

"What you doin' here?" he said.

"I'm property of the state for a few more days."

"Then you goin' to Mobile?"

"That's right."

"Your lawyer told me about your uncle."

"Yeah. I've got one, all right. A little one that climbs trees."

Hal smiled. "You gonna whip up on him?"

I shook my head. "I'm not gonna whip up on him."

"I gave the lawyer that rifle. He said it might help. I don't guess you want the crappy wheelbarrow back."

"No, I won't need it anymore."

"That's good."

"You didn't have to come out there with the dogs like that."

"I know."

"You still got 'em?"

"Sanders's momma come and got the wiener dog. Daddy said he'll keep the bloodhounds for company if nobody comes for 'em. They're prob'ly lyin' in the shade down at the shop."

"Sanders won't be comin'," I said.

"He in jail?"

"Yeah."

"Good. That's where he needs to be."

We walked over to the truck. Hal opened the door and got into the driver's seat. "I got me some holes drilled in the muffler. Listen to her." He cranked the engine, and it began popping and snapping small explosions from the rear. He grinned at me.

"I like it," I said.

"You wanna tell Daddy bye?"

"Yeah."

"Get in."

"We're gonna go see Mr. Mitchell," I called out to Mr. Wellington. He waved at me that it was okay and I climbed into the passenger side of Hal's truck. I held on to the dashboard when Hal straightened out his leg. We fishtailed out of his yard and down the hill towards the clay pit. When we passed the shop, the bloodhounds bolted out of the shade and fell in beside us.

A dump truck pulled away from the front-end loader just as we skidded to a stop. When the dust cleared, Mr. Mitchell was squinting at us from his driver's chair. He finally recognized me sitting beside Hal and shook his head. He shut off the loader and climbed down while Hal and I got out and walked to meet him.

"I shoulda known it was you had him wound-out, Moon."

"He's goin' to Mobile, Daddy."

Mr. Mitchell put his arm around Hal's shoulder and pulled him close. Hal didn't complain this time. "I heard about your uncle," Mr. Mitchell said.

"He's gonna let me live with him."

Mr. Mitchell smiled. "You gonna get fancy on us with a real house and grass and cars with all the windows?"

"I don't know anything about that."

"Well, we're gonna miss you." He squeezed Hal against

him. “Especially this fellow.” Hal glanced away and didn’t say anything.

“I had the most fun ever here,” I said. “I wanna come back sometime. Maybe we can work some more on the truck.”

“Daddy says he’ll keep it waitin’ for me till I get out,” Hal said.

“You’ll have to come get me in Mobile and take me ridin’. I might have my own truck by then. We can race.”

“Jesus!” Mr. Mitchell said.

“What?”

“You with a truck. Racin’.”

I smiled and looked at the ground. “Thanks for lettin’ me stay with you.”

Mr. Mitchell patted me on the shoulder. “Any time, son. You get in touch with me if you ever need anything.”

Hal and I drove out of the clay pit. He went slow this time and I realized how much I’d miss the place. I figured Hal would miss it more.

“It ain’t gonna be so much fun without you around anyway,” Hal said, like he knew what I was thinking. “I might as well let ’em take me off for a few more years.”

“It won’t be so bad.”

“Daddy’s pretty pissed off about it.”

“Let him come visit you in this truck. That’ll make you feel better.”

“Yeah.”

“You’ll be all right, Hal.”

Hal started to say something, but didn’t. “I know,” he said.

We pulled up next to Mr. Wellington’s truck and stopped. He was still waiting patiently. Hal got out and I met him by the tailgate. I lifted my hand in a wave. "I guess I better go."

"I guess you better. You gonna see Kit?"

"Goin' there now."

"Tell him I said 'hey.' And tell him I'm gonna whip his little ass if he doesn't take his medicine."

I smiled. "Okay. I will."

Mr. Wellington let me out at the entrance to the hospital, and I walked into the lobby holding Kit's deerskin hat. This time, I waved to the woman at the front desk and she lowered her head and looked at me over her glasses.

I rode the elevator to the fourth floor and walked down the hall to Kit's room. I knocked on the door and waited. After there was no answer, I opened the door. The room was clean, the bed was made, and Kit was gone. I walked back to the nurses' station and stopped in front of the attendant. "Did Kit leave?"

She eyed me for a few seconds like she was trying to remember who I was. Finally, she asked me if I was related to him.

"I'm his best friend," I said. I held up the hat. "I brought him this."

She didn't look at the hat. "Are your parents with you?"

"No. I don't have any parents."

"Who are you here with?"

"Mr. Wellington. Where's Kit?"

"He's in the intensive care unit. Only immediate family members are allowed in there."

"What's an intensive care unit?"

"It's where people who are really sick go."

My ears began to buzz with panic. "But he's better. I just saw him a few days ago."

The nurse looked around and then back down at me. "He's had a relapse. He's become very sick again."

"Where's his room?"

"No visitors are allowed in the intensive care unit."

"I can't see him?"

The nurse shook her head. "I'm sorry."

"But he doesn't like to be alone!" I yelled.

The nurse stood and leaned over the counter at me. "I think you need to go find the person who brought you here."

I sat on the floor and crossed my arms. "I'm not leavin' until I see him."

The nurse picked up the phone and watched me while she dialed. "Security," she said, "I've got a young boy up here without a guardian and he's giving me trouble . . . Yes . . . I don't know . . . Okay." She hung up the phone and sat down again.

"I'll whip anybody that tries to take me out of here before I see Kit."

When the security officer arrived, he bent down to grab me. I sprang to action and rolled over and clamped onto a metal pole. He followed and began to pry my arms loose. I was just about to punch him between the legs when I heard Mr. Wellington behind us. "Hey!" he said. "That's enough. I can handle him."

The security officer stood, stepped away, and took a deep breath.

"Thank you," Mr. Wellington said. "I can take it from here. Moon?"

I hugged the pole tighter and didn't answer. Mr. Wellington knelt down and put his hand on my shoulder. As soon as he touched me I began to cry. "I just saw him a few days ago!"

"There's nothing more we can do here, Moon. The doctors will take care of Kit."

"I don't trust anybody. Leave me alone!"

"Sir," the nurse said, "may I speak with you privately?"

I saw Mr. Wellington step away with the nurse. I hugged the pole and fought off my tears, still keeping the shoes of the security officer where I could see them.

After a few minutes Mr. Wellington and the nurse returned. "Moon," he said. "Kit's in very serious condition. There's a chance you might not see him again."

I didn't answer him.

"He—"

"I'm not leavin' him. He doesn't wanna be alone."

Mr. Wellington stared down at me without speaking for several seconds. Finally, he turned to the nurse and said, "I can tell you that it's going to take more than one security officer to get him out of here. Can he stay for the night?"

"Not right there."

"He'll stay in the waiting area."

"Fine with me," the nurse said. "Just as long as he doesn't cause trouble."

There were no windows or clocks in the waiting room down the hall, so there was no way for me to tell how long I was there. I didn't sleep but just stared at a picture of a flower garden that hung on the wall over a telephone. People moved in and out of the room, some crying and some without any expression, all talking in whispers. But none of them talked to me. Mr. Wellington had said that he would come back, but I didn't care.

At some point a nurse came into the room and asked me if I needed anything, and I shook my head.

"Mr. Wellington's been calling to check on you. He said to tell us if you need anything to eat or want him to come pick you up."

I nodded and she watched me for a minute before walking away. I continued to stare at the picture and after a while began to count the flowers. Many more people came and went from the waiting room before Mr. Wellington came through the door and sat down beside me.

"Moon, you've been here for twelve hours. The nurse says you haven't slept or eaten."

"I don't need anything."

"I can get you something to eat."

"I just wanna see Kit."

"I checked with the doctor and they don't have anything to tell me yet. He's still in intensive care."

"Why won't they let me see him? I just wanna give him his hat."

"Even if they did let you in, he wouldn't know you were there. He's unconscious."

"He'd know."

Mr. Wellington sighed. "So you want to stay here?"

I nodded.

"Very well. I'm leaving money at the nurses' station in case you want to buy something to eat."

---

I counted the flowers in the picture over and over until my eyes were stinging. More visitors moved in and out of the room and sat on either side of the chair I was in. Eventually, I fell asleep.

I dreamed of the shelter again, and the stage-two box. This time Bigfoots were not trying to get in, but I could hear them howling like wolves in every direction. It seemed that they had taken over the world, and I was the last human alive, hidden from them in the safest part of our shelter. Then I heard Kit yelling for me from somewhere outside.

"Moon!" he screamed. "Let me in!"

The howling of the Bigfoots suddenly quit like they, too, had heard Kit's cries for help. I imagined them running towards him with their long, silent strides. I began wrestling with the door of the box, trying to open it. Kit screamed for me again.

A man beside me nudged me awake, and I lunged for him and grabbed his arm. I opened my eyes and he stared at me. "Are you okay?" he asked me.

I didn't answer him. I leaped from my chair and ran into the hall. I looked both ways, hearing my breathing and my heartbeat as the only noise in the hospital. The women at the nurses' station stopped what they were doing and watched me. I began to run down the hall, looking for any sign of where Kit was. "Kit!" I yelled. "Kit, I'm right here!" I heard the nurses calling after me. A set of swinging doors stood in my way, and I shoved them open and kept running.

"Stop that kid!" a nurse behind me yelled.

Suddenly I felt someone grab me. A doctor in a white uniform lifted me from the ground and hugged me to his chest. "Kit!" I cried. He began walking with me back towards the nurses' station, and I relaxed in his arms and didn't try to escape. "I'm not whippin' up on anybody," I mumbled. "I just want my friend back."

When I opened my eyes, Mr. Wellington was sitting beside me. I could tell he was tired by the dark circles under his eyes and his messed-up hair. He reached over and picked a cup of water off the table beside him and handed it to me. I took it and drank, the water soothing my dry throat.

"It's time to go, Moon."

I looked up at him and his eyes were red.

"I tried to find him," I said. "He's alone."

Mr. Wellington put his hand on my shoulder. "Kit's gone. I'm sorry."

It was three in the afternoon when I left the hospital with Mr. Wellington. I leaned back against the truck door and watched the countryside pass outside the window.

"Do you want anything to eat, Moon?"

I shook my head no.

"It's tough to lose a friend, Moon. I've lost friends myself. But I promise you things get better again. You just have to try and look to the future. Try not to dwell on it for too long." Mr. Wellington reached across the seat and started to take the hat from me. "Why don't you let me take that—"

"Don't you touch it!" I yelled.

# 48

When we got back to the lodge, the sun had just set. I told Mr. Wellington that I wanted to sleep outside that night, and he nodded that he understood. I took a yellow pad of paper and a pencil from inside the lodge and walked to the edge of the clearing. I scraped the leaves from the base of a juniper tree and sat against it and began building a small fire from its bark. Once I had the fire going, I took the pad and pencil and began writing to Kit.

At first I told him how much I missed him and reminded him that we were best friends. Afterwards I began to tell him about when I was little. I started with the first memories of my mother, like a yellow finch, beside me in the bed at night. My first clear memory was of Pap carrying me on his shoulders up the trunk of a leaning gum tree. We sat in its branches and waited for deer in the dawn hours of a cold winter day. He hugged me into the warmth of his lap, and I could see his breath clouding over my head and dissolving in front of us.

The first time I killed a deer I was six. Pap cut open the doe's stomach and cupped his hands to bring out the warm and steaming blood. He brought it up to my face and smeared it so that it streaked past my ears and into my hair that became sticky and matted. I was proud of this time, and I told Kit all about it.

It seemed that I was always watching Pap's hands. They

were careful, powerful hands, and they taught me what I knew of survival in the forest. I told Kit about these hands and then about what they had taught me. I described the process of building a snare, stick by stick. I described a deadfall for him, complete with pictures. I made a list of everything that went into skinning and curing hides. I listed the vegetables that we grew, the best times of year to plant them, and how deep to place their seeds in the soil. I knew that Kit would want to know all of these things.

Finally I told Kit exactly what had happened to my pap and what I'd felt when he died. I remembered the daylight creeping into the forest that cold morning. Pap was already stiff by the time I could see his face in the light. My hand had rested on his cheek and felt it grow cold. I remembered how cloudy it was and how much wind passed through the trees that day. I told Kit about struggling to get Pap into the wheelbarrow as the fog hung between the giant trunks of the loblolly pines and squirrels fussed at the struggle from above.

I wrote and burned my pages of memories well into the night. It was late when Mr. Wellington came to check on me.

"I just wanted to make sure you weren't planning on settling into your old ways again."

I shook my head.

"Do you have enough paper to keep that fire going?"

"It's not to keep the fire goin'. I can keep a fire goin' without paper."

"Of course," Mr. Wellington said, and held out a blanket. "I'm going to leave this in case you need it."

I shrugged.

"I've got just about everything worked out with your uncle. He'll be here the day after tomorrow."

I nodded.

"I'll be in the house if you need me."

I lay on my side in the leaves and watched the last of the smoke curl away over the juniper fire. I listened to the wind in the trees and the needling of the insects and the settling of birds in the brush. I trained my ears to filter all of these for some sign that Kit had gotten my message. I searched the dark shapes and patterns of the forest, hoping that they would turn into Kit's ghost. I was so tired that my eyes stung, and the last thing I remember of that night was trying to keep them open.

I saw Mr. Wellington leave in his truck the next morning. He returned in an hour and he had Hal with him. The two of them walked over to me and stood looking down at my head.

"He's just been burning paper in this fire," Mr. Wellington said.

"He thinks he can talk to dead people that way," Hal said. "Moon, we're gettin' worried about you. You gotta get straight again."

"Nobody else liked him," I said.

"I liked him," Hal said. "Sometimes I gave him a hard time, and I shouldn't have. I liked him, though."

"I don't think it works, Hal."

"What?"

"This smoke stuff."

"I told you that."

I felt my throat swelling and tears sliding down my cheeks. "He's by himself, Hal."

"Moon, he had the best time of his life out in the forest with you. He knew he was sick. He wasn't alone because of you."

I looked up at Hal. "Did he tell you that?"

"That mornin' I left y'all in the forest, I tried to get him to come with me. I told him you might be crazy. I said you might get us all killed. You know what he told me?"

I shook my head and wiped my face.

"He said he'd never been happier in his life. He said he wanted to stay out there in the forest with you no matter what happened. He knew he was takin' a big chance."

I wiped my eyes with the back of my hand again. "But I miss him, Hal."

"I know you do. Nothin' wrong with that."

Around noon Mr. Wellington took Hal home again. When he returned to the lodge, I got up and went back inside. He made a sandwich for me, and I forced it down. I still didn't feel like talking and Mr. Wellington said he understood. I lay on the sofa and watched the television and everything it showed me of a world I knew so little about.

Gradually I began to think of my new uncle. I began to picture him climbing trees and trimming their branches. I thought of my new aunt and pictured her like Mrs. Crutcher, the teacher back at Pinson. I tried to imagine what my cousins would look like, but images of Kit kept appearing, and I had to draw up my knees and roll over and blank my thoughts.

# 49

The morning my uncle was to come get me, I rose from the guest bed before daylight and left Mr. Wellington's lodge with Pap's rifle and the deerskin hats. I walked into the forest and made my way down a trail that was familiar only to my feet. It had long since grown over with honeysuckle vines and cane stems, holly branches, and gallberry. I could tell where I was by looking up into the trees. The outlines that the branches made against the sky were burned into my memory like thousands of lightning strikes. The forest was alive with the sounds of crickets and katydids. The creeks I crossed gurgled in their dark cuts through the bottom.

I stopped just beyond the shelter clearing. I closed my eyes and listened to the forest, waiting for something. There was nothing. I opened my eyes and continued. Daylight was starting to leak into the sky, and what was left of the shelter was a dark mound before me. I looked around and listened, but still there was nothing. I approached the shelter and stepped down into its hollows, which were not so dark anymore with parts of the roof missing. I shoved Pap's rifle into its old hiding place and hung the two deerskin hats on the wall. Finding a couple of the scattered animal hides, I stacked them in their old spot and lay down on them. I listened and stared at the roots over my head. Still there was nothing. The forest told me nothing. It gave me nothing.

After the sun rose and the ugliness of the old shelter appeared around me, I stood and left the dead thing. I put my back to it and set out again.

The Noxubee River seemed unchanged when I looked down at it from the cedar grove. I thought of Pap telling me that catfish the size of beavers swam the bottom of it. I wanted to dive into its muddy water once and spear one until he told me that dead animals also floated along the bottom.

Pap's and Momma's graves were undisturbed. Pap's was already rain-smoothed, with pokeweed and a pine sapling beginning to take hold. I didn't have anything to say to either one of them. I just stood there and felt like all my insides had been scraped out. I knew that I would never come there again.

I didn't go inside once I reached the lodge. I sat beneath a magnolia tree where I watched the driveway. Eventually Mr. Wellington came out and stood over me.

"It might be a little while," he said.

"I wanna stay right here by this tree."

He sat down beside me. "Are you worried?"

I shook my head. "No, I'm just ready to get on to wherever I'm goin'."

"Well, I've got the paperwork done. Your uncle is now your legal guardian."

"He's my new pap?"

"That's right."

I nodded and stared at the ground. I began plucking blades of grass and folding them between my fingers.

"Moon?"

I didn't look up. "Yessir?"

"I think you'll be happy where you're going."

"Yessir."

"Are you sure you don't want to come inside?"

I shook my head. "I'll just stay out here."

His truck looked dusty and used. It came slowly up the drive, and I saw only one person in it. Before long, the face in the picture rolled to a stop beside me where I sat against the magnolia tree. He stared at me out of the rolled-down window for a moment, then stepped out and stared at me some more like I should say something.

"How come I've never seen you?" I said.

He shrugged his shoulders. "I didn't know where you were."

I stood up. "You're not mad about all this, are you?"

He smiled at me. "Shoot, no! I'm not mad about it. Moon, you've got all kinds of people down in Mobile ready to see you."

I walked over to him and looked up at him. "How many?"

"You've got two cousins, or maybe I should say a brother and a sister. You've got my wife and your grandparents and some more aunts and uncles and cousins. There's a bunch of people that you're hooked into in Mobile."

I smiled and felt myself beginning to choke up. I started to cough but ended up crying. I hadn't meant to do it, but I didn't seem to have any control over myself. I could tell he was a nice man.

"I just wanna leave here," I said.

He pulled me to his stomach and pressed my head into him and rubbed my hair. I tried to talk, but I couldn't. We stood there for what seemed like a long time, and I cried on his shirt, which smelled of pine sap.

## 50

After loading my things and saying goodbye to Mr. Wellington, we followed the rivers south on a two-lane highway, leaving behind the limestone hills and cedar groves of Sumter County. We moved through a land of hard, dusty clay and broom sedge and pines that I had never seen. Uncle Mike's truck was worn and comfortable, and he sat back and drove with his wrist flopped over the top of the steering wheel like nothing worried him. The cool spring air swept across our faces, and I sensed I was being drawn to a place I had been stolen from long ago.

"I guess you're my pap now?"

He smiled. "I'd like for you to think of me that way."

"Then I'd like to ask you some things."

"Go ahead," he said.

"What about Mr. Wellington and Hal? Will I get to see them again?"

"Sure. I'll drive you up sometime if you want. It only takes about four hours. And you can always write letters."

"I'm good at writin' letters."

"Mr. Wellington said he was gonna come check on you in a couple of weeks. He said he'd try to bring your rifle when he came."

It made me feel better to think that I'd see Mr. Wellington again in so short a time. I watched out the window and saw a school and students standing out front waiting to be picked up. Station wagons and parents and buses clustered and moved about. A boy was taking a flag down from the flagpole.

I turned to Uncle Mike. "Do you remember me?"

"We all remember you when you were little. Your daddy and momma didn't disappear until about a year after you were born."

"Why didn't you come lookin' for us?"

"As a matter of fact, I did. At first we were worried that somethin' had happened to you all. It didn't take long to find out that Oliver had shut down his bank accounts in Birmingham and sold his house and car. He didn't leave a note or anything. I drove up several times after that and asked around about you. You never had grandparents on your mother's side, so there wasn't anyone to talk to there."

"Why didn't he want you to find us?"

Uncle Mike was quiet for a few seconds. Finally, he looked over at me. "No one really knows why he did what he did. I can tell you that I remember him as a boy no different from any other boy. He was my best friend growin' up. Some people change when they get older. Sometimes things happen that make them change a lot. In your father's case, he saw somethin' in Vietnam that caused him to lose trust in everybody around him."

"But you were his best friend."

"He saw a lot of his friends die over there. Maybe he didn't want any more friends."

"My friend died, too," I said.

"Mr. Wellington told me about Kit. I'm sorry that happened."

I looked out the window again.

"Moon?"

"Yessir?"

"The important thing is that you don't have to feel the way your father did. Most people don't."

I leaned my head against the door and slept with the wind licking through my bangs. I woke when Uncle Mike pulled the truck over at a Spur station for gas. He smiled at me in the rearview mirror as the pump numbers clicked over. Afterwards he strolled inside, and I watched him pay through the store glass. He came out with two bags of potato chips and threw one into my window as he passed.

Back on the road, Uncle Mike dialed the radio to a country station and played it low. I sat with my back against the door frame and ate my potato chips and watched his face while he chewed. He looked at me once and smiled and then stared ahead at the blacktop. "You like 'em?"

"Yessir."

After a second, I turned and sank in the seat and watched the countryside. We were passing fields of rich, black dirt, plowed up nearly to the road. The pine trees were taller and greener and stood in the yards of white farmhouses. The land was mostly flat and the air was thick and humid like nothing I'd ever felt.

"Uncle Mike?"

"Yeah?"

"Thanks again for comin' to get me. I'm glad I've got a

place to go. I don't wanna be locked up anymore. I'm done bein' alone."

He put his hand on my head and brushed my hair back and a warm feeling passed through me.

## 51

"How much farther?" I asked.

"About a mile."

I sat up in my seat and stared ahead. The sun was setting outside my window, and the smell of soybeans and corn was strong in the cool dusk. We had skirted the outside of the city and were moving into the countryside again. To the east I could see the tall buildings of downtown Mobile standing against the horizon.

"How much farther now?"

Uncle Mike pointed ahead of us. "That house up there."

The first thing I noticed about Uncle Mike's house was that it was a one-story brick home backed up to a pecan orchard.

"I like pecan trees."

"Well, we've got a bunch."

They had put up a small banner on the fence that read WELCOME HOME, MOON, and my new family came out of the house and stood in the yard as we drove up. I felt my hands growing fidgety, and I looked at Uncle Mike. "What do I do?"

He laughed. "You'll be okay. Just get out of the truck and meet everybody."

I felt my face burning red as Aunt Sara knelt down and hugged me. My new brother, David, was only a year older than me, and my new sister, Alice, a year younger. They said hello and I nodded at them while my face was pressed into Aunt Sara's bosom. She finally pushed me back by the shoulders and stared at me. "He looks just like his mother."

"They say he doesn't eat like her," Uncle Mike said.

Aunt Sara stood and sniffled and wiped her eyes. "We'll just have to see about that," she said. "Are you hungry, Moon?"

"Yes, ma'am."

"I can't imagine all you've been through. I'm gonna have to feed you four times a day to get some meat on your bones."

"I feel pretty good now, but I'd like four times a day."

She laughed and turned around. "My Lord," she said. "Let's all go inside."

David and Alice crowded beside me while we walked. David kept glancing over at me. "I heard you beat up grown men," he finally said.

"I had to whip up on a couple. People were chasin' me all over."

"They said you had your own rifle."

I nodded. "Me and Pap both."

"I've got some climbin' spikes Daddy gave me."

"Climbin' spikes!"

"Yeah! You can strap 'em to your legs and climb up a tree straight as a pole."

"Man! I wanna see those. What else you got?"

Uncle Mike laughed and put his hand on my back. "You

two'll have time for all that later. Let's go inside and get Moon cleaned up and fed."

The house had three bedrooms. Uncle Mike and Aunt Sara slept in one and Alice had another. I was to share the last room with David. My bed hadn't arrived yet, but Aunt Sara assured me that it would look just like David's. She showed me the place where my bed would go and a closet where I could put my things.

"I don't have much," I told her. "Just some old traps and some clothes I made. Got Pap's personal box."

"We'll take care of that," she said. "You'll have the same things that every other boy has."

I looked at David and he smiled and nodded like they'd been talking about it.

We seated ourselves around the dinner table, and Aunt Sara served pork roast and creamed spinach and buttered sourdough bread. It was better than any food I'd had in the forest or in jail or at Pinson or even at Hal's. At first nobody said much, but I could feel them watching me. I was uncomfortable at the table and did my best to hold my silverware the right way. Eventually, Uncle Mike reached over and took my bread and pinched my pork with it and held it out to me like a sandwich. I set my fork and knife down and smiled and took it from him. Everyone began to laugh, and before long we were all eating our pork in a sandwich.

"So show us somethin', Moon," Uncle Mike said.

"Like what?"

"Make an animal sound," David said.

"What do you wanna hear?"

"Your best one."

"It's a loud one," I warned them.

"Do it anyway."

Aunt Sara set her glass down. "I don't know if—"

"It's okay, Sara," Uncle Mike said.

I set my sandwich down and got out of my chair. I bent over so that my hands rested on my knees and sucked in my breath and twisted my face in the right way. I made the sound of a bobcat scream.

"*Reeeowww!*"

When I looked up, everybody was staring at me with wide eyes. After a second, Uncle Mike began to clap.

Aunt Sara scooted her chair back and wiped the corners of her mouth with her napkin. "My Lord," she said.

"That's a bobcat. Supposed to sound like a screamin' woman," I told her.

"A wolf!" David yelled.

Aunt Sara shifted in her chair and straightened her back. "Now, I don't know about a wolf."

"Me neither," I said. "There's no wolves in Alabama. I know a coyote, though."

"Coyote, then," said Alice.

I looked up at the ceiling, pursed my lips, and began barking like a coyote.

"*Yip yip yip! Yi yi!*"

When I looked down, David was sitting on top of his chair back and leaning forward towards me. "What else?" he stammered.

"Deer?"

David and Alice nodded. I tossed my head from side to side and snorted like a flagged deer.

"That's enough for now," Aunt Sara said. "Moon, you're very talented."

"They're gonna love you at school," David said.

I smiled and got back into my chair. "You think so?"

"Yeah. Nobody can do all those sounds."

After we finished our meal, I told them about living in the forest. I described how Pap and I had built the shelter and the types of books that we studied. They wanted to know about the strangest things that we'd eaten, and I told them about armadillo stew and snake rolls. I told about the time that it rained real hard and a rattlesnake family tried to move into the shelter with us. They listened to me late into the night until Alice fell asleep against Uncle Mike's shoulder.

"I think it's time for all of us to go to bed," he said. "It's been a big day."

After saying good night to David and Alice, Aunt Sara got a blanket from the closet and spread it over the sofa for me. When she was done, she put her hand on my back and asked me if I was okay sleeping in the living room my first night with them.

"It's better than pine straw and ticks," I said. "I like it just fine."

She smiled and yawned. "I'm glad you're so easy to please, Moon. Good night, you two."

"Good night," I said.

I lay on the sofa and pulled the blanket up to my chin. Uncle Mike sat across from me in a chair.

"You still okay?" he finally said.

I nodded.

"I know you've been through some tough times. I don't expect you to just slide into things around here. There's a lot to get used to."

"I'm feelin' better already."

"It takes time to start a new life, especially when you've come from a background as different as yours."

I felt the soft pillow under my head and listened to the ticking of the mantel clock. "I like everything about this place."

Uncle Mike smiled. His eyes told me what I needed to know about the type of father he would be. They were Pap's own eyes, but there was something more gentle and calm about them. I could tell that he wanted to say something that would make me feel better about all I'd been through in the last few months. But he didn't need to say anything.

"I'm gonna be fine," I told him. "You don't need to worry about me."

# GOFISH

questions for the author

**WATT KEY**

**When did you realize you wanted to be a writer?**

I wrote my first story when I was ten. It was about a collie surviving a tornado. I was into Jim Kjelgaard, a writer of dog books, then, and I wanted to try and make stories like his. I kept writing short stories for fun throughout the rest of my prep school days. My high school creative writing teacher convinced me that I had talent as an author and this gave me the idea that maybe I was meant to be a writer. It wasn't until my sophomore year in college that I knew this for certain. I was running the outdoor skills department at a boys' camp in Texas. I was alone and far away from home, with lots of free time in a little cabin by the Guadalupe River. I wrote my first novel there. Although it was a terrible book that will never be published, it was the most satisfying thing I'd ever done. After that summer, I continued to write a novel a year without regard to whether it would be published or not. I'd written ten novels by the time *Alabama Moon* sold.

**What was your worst subject in school?**

I remember making an 88 out of 100 on just about every test I took in high school, regardless of the subject. So I wasn't an outstanding student, but neither was I a poor one. At my school, 88 was about average. Before I went to college, my parents took me to see a psychologist in New Orleans. I went through a series of aptitude tests that were supposed to help us decide what profession I was best suited for. Basically, I scored an 88 on everything. The conclusion was that I would always have a hard time deciding what I wanted to be because none of my abilities seemed to stand out above the rest. This didn't help me directly, but ever since then, I've been conscious of the fact that I need to specialize in one thing to be outstanding at anything. For example, as much as I would like to play a musical instrument, I don't. I shun it like a bad vice. I know I would enjoy it too much and it would take away from my focus on being the best writer I can be.

**What was your first job?**

My brothers and sisters and I always had chores assigned to us that we didn't get paid for. My first duties were emptying the wastebaskets around the house, feeding various pets (we had lots of animals), and raking and mowing the lawn. I landed my first paying job when I was about eight years old. I was the fly killer for the snack bar at a resort not far from my home. I killed them with a washcloth, stored them in a paper cup, and received ten cents per fly. As soon as I would get enough dimes, I would cash in my pay for a drink to quench my thirst.

**How did you celebrate publishing your first book?**

My wife and I went to the Mexican restaurant up the street. It was a fairly low-key celebration. It took a while for me to accept that I'd gotten a legitimate book deal. You may have seen the episode of *The Waltons* when John Boy gets scammed by the vanity publisher. He told all of his friends and family that he'd gotten a book deal and they had a big celebration for him. Then he got a letter from the publisher asking him how many of his books he wanted to pay them to print. It was a scam. This exact thing happened to me years before I sold *Alabama Moon* and it was very embarrassing and eye-opening.

**Where do you write your books?**

After college, I built a small camp several miles into the swamp that you can only get to by boat. I made it from lumber that washed up on the beach after a hurricane. It took me nearly every weekend for a year to complete it. I develop and outline most of my ideas up there. The bulk of my actual writing is done at home in a spare bedroom that doubles as my study.

**Where do you find inspiration for your writing?**

I'm not always inspired to write. Fortunately, I have a backlog of stories in my head that I feel have to be written whether I'm in the mood for it or not. I often tell people that writing is like an addiction to me. I liken this addiction to people who jog every day. I don't feel good about myself unless I'm doing it. Most of the time, it's a very enjoyable process. Sometimes, it's not. But I decided long ago that I was supposed to be a writer, so that's what I do.

**When you finish a book, who reads it first?**

My wife, Katie, reads my first drafts most of the time. I've learned that if I don't want her to read it, it's probably not ready. Then my agent reads it, and finally my editor.

**Are you a morning person or a night owl?**

I'm a night owl. But to feel good and productive, I have to have eight hours of sleep, no more, no less. I usually write from about eight until eleven at night and get up at seven in the morning.

**What's your idea of the best meal ever?**
Rib eye steak. Egg noodles with real butter and garlic. Real mashed potatoes without gravy. Cream cheese spinach. Brewed iced tea with lemon, real sugar, and mint. Lemon pie without the meringue for dessert.

**Where do you go for peace and quiet?**
My swamp camp.

**What makes you laugh out loud?**
Mark Twain.

**What do you value most in your friends?**
Honesty. Originality.

**What is your favorite TV show?**
I don't recommend television. One day I was driving through Mississippi and came across a folk artist with a yard full of his scrap iron creations. Out front was a sign that read "Look what I did while you were watching TV." I like his attitude.

**What's the best advice you have ever received about writing?**
Continue to write even when you don't feel like it. If you're a real writer, that's what you have to do. I knew this on an instinctive level for many years, but never heard it described as well as what a painter friend of mine told me. I was watching him create an oil painting of an outdoor scene. He was doing his work in a small, rocking boat, crouched beneath an umbrella in the pouring rain. I remarked that he was the most dedicated artist I'd ever met. He responded by telling me that he wasn't an artist, he was a professional painter.

PRAISE FOR

# ALABAMA MOON | by watt key

---

*Parents' Choice* Gold Award Winner

Winner of the 2007 E.B. White Read Aloud Award for Older Readers

2007 SIBA Children's Novel of the Year

Bank Street Best Children's Book of the Year

*VOYA* Top Shelf Fiction for Middle School Readers

Book Sense Autumn 2006 Children's Pick

---

★ **"[An] excellent novel...populated with memorable characters...and studded with utterly authentic details about rural Alabama and survivalism."** —*Booklist*, Starred Review

★ **"This book is reminiscent of *Huck Finn*, *Hatchet* or *Far North*, perhaps even *The Curious Incident of the Dog in the Night-Time*, but it's also completely original."**—*Kliatt*, Starred Review

**"An unusual coming-of-age story."**—*The New York Times Book Review*

**"For boys who dream of unfettered life in the great outdoors...Moon's a bona fide hero."**—*The Bulletin of the Center for Children's Books*

**"A wonderful villain and touches of distinctive humor...absolutely first-rate."** —*Parents' Choice*

**"Moon is young, but his wise yet naïve voice is compelling...an excellent addition to any public or school library."**—*Voice of Youth Advocates*

**"It's a winningly fresh and sympathetic look at a life and culture almost never seen in children's books."**—*The Horn Book Magazine*

**"Absorbing."**—*Publishers Weekly*

**"The book is well written with a flowing style, plenty of dialogue, and lots of action."**—*School Library Journal*

---